I0612708

Cole's Reckoning

by

Gabbi Grey

Bonded in Love, Book Two

Copyright Notice
This is a work of fiction. Names, characters, places, and incidents are either the product of the author's imagination or are used fictitiously, and any resemblance to actual persons living or dead, business establishments, events, or locales, is entirely coincidental.

Cole's Reckoning

COPYRIGHT © 2024 by Gabbi Grey

All rights reserved. No part of this book may be used or reproduced in any manner whatsoever without written permission of the author or The Wild Rose Press, Inc. except in the case of brief quotations embodied in critical articles or reviews.
Contact Information: info@thewildrosepress.com

Cover Art by *Diana Carlile*

The Wild Rose Press, Inc.
PO Box 708
Adams Basin, NY 14410-0708
Visit us at www.thewildrosepress.com

Publishing History
First Edition, 2024
Trade Paperback ISBN 978-1-5092-5589-4
Digital ISBN 978-1-5092-5590-0

Bonded in Love, Book Two
Published in the United States of America

Dedication

Catherine
Judith
Rota

Chapter One

Cole

As I endured what was probably the most awkward dinner of my life, sitting at my dining room table with my two best friends, that life flashed before me in snatches. Michael, Caressa, and me when we were five years old and realizing for the first time we had only ourselves to count on. We'd been inseparable from the age of five until twenty-seven when Caressa left for Africa. Some slight daylight might have streamed through the fissures of the bond we'd had for twenty-two years—but they had been minor.

Caressa spun the deliciously aromatic spaghetti she'd made onto her fork. Michael gingerly ripped off a bit of the crispy garlic bread and shoved it in his mouth. Then he winced at the crunch it made when he chewed. I glanced down at the truly amazing food, and my stomach churned.

Still, none of us spoke.

Meanwhile, a pair of handcuffs, a whip, and a flogger sat on the far end of the dining room table.

Mocking me.

Just a couple of days ago, Caressa and Michael had agreed to move into my mansion in one of Vancouver's priciest neighborhoods. Ostensibly to help me with my rehabilitation over an IT band injury. Being bright people, though, they had figured out my underlying motive.

In other words, they had seen right through my bullshit.

I placed my fork on my plate in the five o'clock position. Caressa glanced over and glared. I chanced a glance at Michael. He merely raised both eyebrows. Poor guy. Unlike Caressa and myself, he couldn't manage the one eyebrow arch.

We'd all just been friends until the moment, five years ago, when Caressa left for Africa to do a stint as a nurse with Médecins Sans Frontières. Only she'd stayed and done twelve rotations in five years.

And I'd pined away because, as soon as she told me she was going, I realized I was in love with her. Not the easygoing friendship we'd shared for almost twenty years. No, the deep, abiding, soul-crushing love where I wanted to yank her back and demand she stay in Vancouver.

I didn't, of course. I supported Caressa in every way I possibly could from halfway around the globe—all the while fretting, worrying, and generally wanting to stomp over to Africa, grab her by the hair, and drag her back to Vancouver, Canada.

Very uncouth. Very un-feminist. Very unlike me. Possibly even caveman and boorish. Still, I kept those urges in check. I sent care packages, money to the aid agency she worked for, and generally bided my time.

On the heels of her departure, I had another realization.

I loved Michael. Pretty much the same way.

Five. Fucking. Years.

"Is there something wrong with your spaghetti?"

Caressa asked.

Her words pulled me from my intense reverie with a jolt. I should have been focused on this moment instead of wallowing in the past. "Nothing."

This time, she arched an eyebrow. So much said in just that one little action.

Somehow, becoming a television superstar with a promising career in the movies and working my ass off every goddamn day hadn't increased my articulateness around either of them. "I was just thinking, since it's Christmas Eve, perhaps we should put on some music."

Caressa'd been sent home from work by the psychologist she started seeing because of her distress over a child who died on her watch. Not my lover's fault—but she blamed herself, nonetheless.

Michael, the engineer, had been sent home from work early because his bosses decided his crew had earned an early Christmas treat. Believing Caressa would be at work for another six hours, he and I had headed for one of the most exclusive jewelry stores in Vancouver. And the bag with our treasures from the store sat farther down the table.

Still unopened.

Mocking me.

Michael ate a mouthful of spaghetti, and I watched, mesmerized, as he chewed. He caught me staring and cocked his head. I pointed to his chin. He blushed, then dabbed at the offending spot of sauce with a cloth napkin.

Caressa snickered.

We both looked at her where she sat—at the head of *my* dining room table. Somehow, I really didn't feel like I was in charge of anything around here anymore.

Gabbi Grey

Even as I had the thought, I sighed inwardly. Caressa shouldn't have been snooping. She'd had no reason—that I could discern—for going down to the basement. And the door to the dungeon *should* have been locked. I honestly believed I'd left it locked after the last time I was down there.

I hadn't quite found the courage to ask her if it actually had been.

Did she find the key? And why the fuck are you so chickenshit about asking?

"Snap out of it, Cole." Caressa barked the words.

I straightened, then cast my glance her way.

"You're moping."

"I'm not—"

She held up her hand.

At the same moment, Michael muttered, "Yeah, you are."

"Are you two ganging up on me?"

They turned their gazes to each other, and the moment spun out.

Fuck a duck.

They had come here as a solid couple. And I didn't want to disturb what they had found—but I also didn't want to be excluded from it.

Finally, Michael nodded ever so slightly.

Caressa turned her pale-blue eyes back to me. "Why didn't you tell us?"

I fiddled with the fork on my plate. "It didn't seem important."

She snorted. "I saw the photo album, Cole."

My stomach dropped. *Jesus fucking Christ.* How long had she been down there? What else might she have discovered? Nothing incriminating, I didn't think, because I didn't do anything illegal. But I got up to some pretty kinky shit down in that room.

And you thought you could keep it a secret? From your new live-in lovers?

Well, frankly, I had. I'd gone as far as considering disassembling the room. I had everything I'd ever wanted sitting at the table with me. The rest of it felt less important. Like I was disconnected from it. Like it was my past and the two lovely creatures before me were my future. I didn't know how to process this. What words they wanted to hear.

"Donovan knows, though, right?" Michael's lips twitched.

His question caught me unawares. *What does my friend have to do with this?* "Uh, yeah, he does."

"He's been down there with you. Done things…with you…"

Jealousy?

But that didn't make any sense. Yes, Donovan was a good friend—only slightly behind in my devotion to these two. But why was Michael bringing him up?

He cleared his throat. "He made some comments the other night—when he and I were alone. Just briefly." He toyed with his spaghetti. "But something tweaked in me. I meant to ask you, but we went to bed and…"

And he'd given me a blow job. His first blow job with another man. Then he'd fucked Caressa into the mattress while I jerked myself off.

Yeah, we'd been a little busy.

I would need to have strong words with Donovan. And maybe see if he had any advice. "Look, um, I'm not sure what the big deal is—"

Caressa smacked the table.

Michael and I both jumped.

"It's a fucking big deal, and you know it." She dropped her fork, and it clattered to the plate. "You think I'm naïve. That I've lived a sheltered life."

I almost spoke up to refute the assertions—I knew she wasn't naïve, and I, of all people, knew she hadn't lived a sheltered life. She'd been exposed to more shit by the time she turned five than many people dealt with their entire lives.

Except she was right. I did do everything in my power to shield her. Always had, and always would. But that wasn't healthy either. She needed to see she could stand on her own two feet. Surely, her five years of living among the deprivation and starvation in Africa had shown her she was capable.

And should have shown me as well.

But I hesitated. Looking at her now, I saw more fragility than I remembered ever seeing before. Not just physically—although the dark circles under her eyes didn't help. No, she carried herself differently.

How have I missed this?

"Okay, you're not naïve, and you haven't lived a sheltered life." I ventured the words, holding in the wince.

She glared. Michael snickered. She took her glare off me for a moment to move her attention to him. He held up his hands in surrender. She pivoted back to me.

"I'm not being sarcastic or trying to appease you. But I'm trying to figure out how this fits with…" I gestured toward the end of the table. I would have happily put away the equipment, but one look from Caressa assured me the discussion was far from over. "What's the big deal?"

6

"The big deal is that you should have told us." She pressed her cloth napkin to the table. "We had a right to know."

"But it doesn't concern you." *Try to make her understand.* "What came before? That's over. You're all that matters to me." I made sure to encompass Michael in my royal *we* of sorts.

"But it's part of you, Cole. You can't just shut it off."

"Of course I can. I'll get rid of everything. I'm sure there are people who'll be happy to take it. That's some expensive equipment—"

"You're making my point for me. You didn't buy a bit of rope, some handcuffs, a whip, a flogger, and a riding crop on a whim."

To my horror, my cock liked the way she sounded when she listed off the basic BDSM equipment that I'd started with. She couldn't have known how accurate her assertion was.

"The cost of the equipment doesn't matter. I have a friend who owns a kink club. He'll be happy to take everything off my hands. He'll either keep it for himself or find suitable homes for the stuff. It won't go to waste."

Her arched eyebrow assured me I'd made the wrong guess. I thought she was worried about adding garbage to the environment. She obviously was thinking of the ramifications of the disposal of equipment.

Or maybe the fact I had a friend who owned a kink club.

Could go either way.

"I think she's thinking in terms of lifestyle." Michael also laid his fork down—far from finishing his meal either.

7

"Right. Lifestyle. As in, I can choose whether or not to partake in it. I chose to before. Now I choose not to."

She sighed. "I saw the pictures, Cole."

"You had no right to snoop." *Shit.*

"*That's* what you're choosing to focus on?" Her light-blue eyes flashed. "You don't just walk away from something like that. That's inside you, Cole."

"God, you sound like a shrink. I'm fine, Caressa." I turned to Michael. "Honestly. I can lock it all up, and we never have to talk about it. It'll be like it never happened."

He ran his hand through his hair. "In the interest of fairness, I think I should at least get to—"

"No." My firm answer.

"Yes." Caressa's firm rebuke.

Michael looked uneasily between the two of us. Of late, he'd been calling the shots. At least in the bedroom. That had come as a shock to me, and I suspected Caressa'd been surprised as well.

She could be headstrong.

I could be stubborn.

Michael was usually the mediator.

Truthfully, I hadn't been entirely comfortable with him taking the dominant role in the bedroom. Two things precluded me from speaking up. First, my injury made it impossible for me to do many things physically that I normally enjoyed. The injury wasn't permanent, but it had sidelined me for more than a week, and I faced more recovery time before I could even walk without a cane— let alone fuck, and get fucked, the way I wanted.

Usually, in my relationships, I preferred doing the fucking.

But Michael'd expressed an interest in nailing me.

Since he was new to all this, I figured the least I could do was let him experiment. In the end, I was good either way—as long as I was the dominant one.

Aside from the injury, we were, as a throuple, still on shaky ground. Still feeling our way around things. We might have been three-way best friends, but Caressa and Michael'd hooked up a couple of weeks ago. Had planned a life.

Without me.

Well, at least in the romantic and sexual ways. They had assured me we'd always be best friends.

That wasn't good enough for me.

"So do I get to see this…" Michael's brow furrowed.

"Room," I supplied.

"Dungeon," Caressa corrected.

His eyes widened.

He hasn't figured this out yet? "I'll take him down. After we clean up from this delicious dinner you graciously made us."

I was grateful. And possibly a little leery. Something was up, and I couldn't tell if this was just because of the dungeon or if she was hiding more bad news.

"No, Cole, you won't." She pointed to my cane, propped against the dining room table.

"I can—"

"I said no."

Okay, well, then. Apparently, I'd been schooled. I'd known she could be defiant—but it wasn't a trait she brought out very often.

Michael rose. "I'll do the plates."

Caressa attempted to rise, but he waved her back down.

I didn't bother trying to get up. I was still next to

useless. Fuck, I was so hating this injury. One moment of inattention in a fight sequence and suddenly I was sidelined for almost a month. After the new year, the studio had plans for me to shoot some material where I didn't have to stand. At one point, the writers considered writing in my injury.

Fortunately, the director had put the kibosh on that. My character was fluid, graceful, powerful, athletic, and a physical badass. Having any kind of injury just didn't fit. The studio had hired me a kick-ass physiotherapist who promised to have my butt back to normal soon.

Couldn't happen soon enough. This afternoon's visit to the jewelry store had been my first foray out of my fucking house in more than a week.

A nice fucking house, to be sure, but somewhere that was starting to feel like a prison nonetheless.

While Michael removed the leftover food, Caressa continue to stare out the windows into the darkened night.

Wasn't that what Donovan had said would happen? That I'd feel trapped? Not because of the injury, but because Caressa, Michael, and I wouldn't be able to come out as a triad. Society hadn't reached a level of tolerance for people being more than two in a relationship. Since I was the last to the party, it stood to reason I should forgo the public displays of affection.

Except I was, by far, the highest profile of the three of us. My name hit the tabloids every few months with some rumor or other.

None accurate.

You're playing with fire.

You're going to get burned.

Even just having a dungeon was a risk. Few people

ever got invited over, and they all knew the score, but even that posed a danger. But to add a true ménage to the mix? A few of my fans would eat it up. Some would hesitate at the fact there were three. Others would have issues with me and Michael as a couple. A whole segment would walk away from me entirely.

Do you really care? You can have everything you've ever wanted.

I clung to that truth.

Michael did three trips into the kitchen with dishes, glassware, and cutlery. Still, Caressa fingered her cloth napkin.

When I could bear the silence no longer, I asked what had been bugging me the most. "Why?"

She flinched.

"Talk to me. What's going on?" I wanted to help—I really did. But I couldn't fix what was broken if I didn't know the root cause.

"It's complicated, Cole."

Ouch. "Okay, fair enough. But shutting me out isn't fair either."

She looked down her nose at me.

I held my ground.

Michael returned, hands empty. He held out one of those hands to Caressa.

She took it and rose. "We'll be back."

As she said the words, Michael put a hand to the small of her back and led her toward the stairs to take them down.

I'm fucked.

Chapter Two

Michael

"Is this an actual dungeon?"

As Caressa led me by the hand down the stairs to Cole's basement—our basement?—I wondered what the hell I'd signed up for.

You love her. You love him. Just cling tight to that.

Except this felt bigger than that. Bigger than all of us.

When we arrived at the bottom, we paused. The space was bifurcated. The wide, open space before us was a party room of sorts. A wet bar sat at one end, with plenty of seating areas clustered. The walls were plate glass and looked out over the water. The view here was almost as stunning as the one above. At one end of the room sat a door. Beyond that door sat the media room. Or the cinema room. Ten plush theater-style seats to watch movies on a big screen. This house was old enough that it used to have an old-fashioned projector. That was gone, although Cole kept it in storage, but it had been replaced by one of the fancy digital ones.

Beyond that room was a tiny mechanical room that held this entire house together.

When Cole had given me a tour after buying the house, what I'd noticed but not commented on was the room that ran half the length of the house, but that was on the street side. Below ground—so no windows. The space wasn't huge, but knowing the footprint of the upstairs, I'd figured a significant amount of the basement hadn't been accounted for. I'd spotted the door, assumed Cole had omitted the room for a reason, and hadn't given it much more thought. Storage or… Truthfully, I had barely given it a moment's consideration. The house was massive—some rooms wouldn't be important. Now, given the revelation, I kicked myself for having not questioned it more. The substantial space couldn't have been explained away by a storage area.

Caressa pulled a key from her jeans pocket.

"Did you steal that?"

She pursed her lips.

Bad question.

"I was looking for Cole. It never occurred to me that he might be out with you. So I came down here and figured out—as you likely had—there's a massive room here." She winced. "Okay, I was looking for Christmas decorations. The house only has the tree, and I just wanted something…more festive."

We'd never done festive as children. Aside from putting up any craft projects from school. And when we were in university, we hadn't had time for stuff like that. Then we'd gone our separate ways…

"Yeah." She touched my arm. "This is our first *real* Christmas." She let me go, then inserted the key in the lock. "I wasn't expecting this."

Hesitantly, I followed her into the room.

She flipped the lights on, but the room didn't illuminate fully, as I might have expected.

Strategically placed torches around the room flickered to life. They let out an eerie yellowish glow.

Now, I was pretty naïve when it came to all things BDSM, but I'd seen one or two mainstream movies—so I wasn't totally ignorant. Still, I was overwhelmed. Two of the corners held some sort of odd crosses, with manacles hanging down. The shorter was adorned with every implement imaginable—and a few I couldn't conceive of.

Perversely intrigued, I headed in that direction.

I recognized whips of various types, floggers, handcuffs, manacles, dildos, butt plugs…nipple clamps?

Ouch.

Paddles of various sizes, and several other things I truly was clueless about.

I cleared my throat. "You said there's an album?"

"Michael." Her voice was a whisper.

"What? If you saw it, why can't I?"

She winced. Then went over to the bed, which I'd somehow missed, and extracted a box from underneath.

"You were only alone for, like, an hour?"

"Almost two." She shrugged as she put the box on the bed, then removed the lid. "I came down in a hurry so I could get everything set up." She gazed around the room. "No Christmas decorations here." After a moment she shrugged. "I went back upstairs and found the key in the junk drawer. I thought this might be a storage room and I'd find what I was looking for. Felt logical, you know?"

She had a point.

I made my way over to the bed and sat. She placed the album before me, then pushed the box away and sat on the other side.

Part of me wanted her closer, but since I didn't know what my reaction might be, I left the space.

The album was supple black leather. The title page was blank, so I flipped to the first page.

And my breath caught.

A man. A beautiful man. Trussed up, strung from one of the crosses, completely naked. I looked closer, and yep, he had some kind of weird contraption about his cock.

Involuntarily, I winced. Caressa chuckled.

I glanced up. This was the first positive emotion I'd seen from her pretty much since we got home. And the burst of emotion was over the suffering of some random dude. *Not sure how I feel about that.*

"Keep going…there's plenty more."

I continued to look. None of the photos held dates, and no one wore clothes, so putting together a time frame proved impossible. The photos were black and white with a glossy finish. High quality—with an artsy vibe. These weren't taken off someone's cell phone.

The women and men depicted were, I assumed, in traditional BDSM poses. Some bore whip marks or bruises, while others simply appeared restrained in some definitely creative poses.

Cole wasn't in any of the photos. Neither, I noted, was Donovan. Yet, weirdly, I felt both their presences. I couldn't put my finger on the irrational thought, but I held it pretty tightly.

The intensity of the poses didn't increase as the album went on. Instead, the thing just a steady stream of a visual feast.

Am I supposed to be repulsed by this? Unsettled? Since I was neither of those things, what did that say about me?

I met Caressa's gaze as I tucked the album back into

the embossed cardboard box. "I'm not sure how I'm supposed to feel about this."

"Gut instinct, Michael. Don't think about it. What's your first reaction?"

"Fascination. Curiosity. And…" I swallowed hard. "A little turned on."

Her eyes widened.

Shit. "But…it's wrong, right? I mean…" I wiped my hand over my face. "I don't know what I mean."

"Do you want to know what my reaction was?"

I cracked an eye open. Of course, I wanted to know what she thought—but I'd been too chickenshit to ask. Her brow was knit in what I knew to be concentration. I pushed the book aside, slid to her, and took her hands in mine.

She met my gaze. And sighed. "Michael…"

"Yeah."

I couldn't get a read on her. In some ways, she'd always been closed off—protective of herself after her nightmarish childhood. In other ways, to me, I'd always been able to read her. That secret knowledge was the reason I'd brought her home after the pub. Why I'd taken her to my bed. Why I'd pushed for a relationship. Why I wanted to spend the rest of my life loving her. Cherishing her.

Protecting her.

She took a deep breath and met my gaze. In the low light, her pale eyes were almost completely eclipsed by her large pupils. "I'm…intrigued…"

I sat there, dumbfounded.

Is she…

Am I…

Could we…

I just didn't know. I cleared my throat. "So you think Cole does this"—I indicated the album—"to other people."

"Yeah. I guess." She twitched her nose. I released one of her hands, and she scratched it. One of her tells.

"You're thinking we should consider this. And approach Cole about…what, teaching us? Do you want to be…whipped? Flogged—"

"Dominated."

This time, my eyes widened. Caressa was such a feminist. A take-charge kind of person. Someone who held her own at all times. This…felt wrong.

And yet it also felt right.

"You and Cole." *This isn't about you. This is about what she wants. What will make her happy.*

"And you." She squeezed my hand. "This relationship doesn't work without you."

"Which is why you wanted us to come down here alone." I glanced over my shoulder at the door. I wouldn't have been surprised to see Cole there. He'd risked his health by pushing me up against a door earlier today and frotting against me. I'd borne the bulk of his weight—but that kind of wasn't the point. If he thought he might lose Caressa, that he might lose me, I didn't doubt he'd take those stairs two at a time, heedless of injury, and barge in here. That he hadn't spoke, I believed, to his faith in us.

Or he thinks he's already lost you. "We should be heading back upstairs."

She gripped tighter. "You haven't told me what you think. I won't do this without you. I sound like a broken record, but it's the truth. If you tell me to lock that door and we never talk about this again, I'm okay with that."

I examined her face. She wasn't lying—but she wasn't being truthful, either. She wanted this. She really wanted this. And what that meant for our relationship, I wasn't sure. Hell, I wasn't sure about anything anymore. But I knew I loved her, and my feelings for Cole, the romantic ones, were deepening by the day.

"We need a really long conversation with Cole. He might not want to…do those things to you. He might equate romantic love with protection." I squinted. "I'm struggling to see a world where he thinks hurting you is okay."

Hell, I struggled to think of a world where *me* hurting her was okay. And for that matter, what if Cole wanted to hurt me? The album contained roughly the same number of men as women. To the casual observer, there mightn't have been a distinction. Except perhaps Donovan had a hand with the men.

If Donovan is even involved.

So many questions—and so few answers. I knew I needed more information—beyond that, I didn't have a clue. "Was this the only album?"

She nodded. "Or the only album I could locate. You think there might be more? Hidden away somewhere?"

"I honestly have no idea. I'm surprised you located this one."

"Well, the thing was hidden."

"Oh, really."

She had the decency to look a little sheepish.

"Surely, you'd known we'd be back."

"I didn't care. Once I found this space…I needed to know everything."

No arguing with that logic—I'd have done the same thing. "I take it you didn't find any Christmas

18

decorations."

"It occurred to me later that they might be in a closet somewhere or there might be another room entirely. This is a modern house, so I don't believe there's an attic or crawl space."

"Can't argue with that. Maybe in the electrical room?"

She shook her head. "Nope. Seems Cole doesn't like Christmas."

I wasn't sure any of us were big fans. When we were growing up, Christmas had just been another day.

No, that wasn't true. It'd been a day when most kids received gifts from their parents. Our gift would be if they ignored us. We just wanted to be left alone and in peace—and we'd spent every Christmas Eve together, huddled in my bed. None of us ever believed in the mythical Santa Claus—that was for sure. We'd make appearances at our families during Christmas Day, and then we'd congregate back in my room for the next night. When we were older, we bought little gifts. And little they were. I hesitated to use the word cheap, because that took away from the heart involved, but we were pretty proficient dumpster divers in some of the ritzier neighborhoods. Boxing Day was always great because people threw away their old stuff—replaced by the new received at Christmas.

I'm getting maudlin. "Maybe this year we can pick up some stuff in the after-Christmas sales. So we've got plenty for next year."

Caressa'd started to rise, but she eased back down. "You see us being here next year?"

Her question startled me. "Don't you? I thought this was a forever thing. Was I wrong about that?"

"No. I just…" She bit her lower lip. "Next year feels so far away, Michael. So much can happen between now and then, you know?"

"I do know." All too well. On December fifteenth, her contract with St. Paul's would officially be over. Would she head back to Africa?

I was too terrified at the prospect to ask—as if I believed asking the question would somehow put the idea in her mind. Which was ridiculous. If she was determined to go, nothing Cole or I could do would stop her.

Unless you got her pregnant.

Holy shit.

I pressed that thought right out of my mind. That was barbaric. I would never put Caressa in that predicament. *If* she chose to have a child, that was up to her. *When* she chose to have a child, was also up to her. And finally, *with whom* she chose to have a child would be her decision. And frankly, her selecting Cole as the father only made sense—better financial stability to provide a safe home. Better looks. Better…everything. Any woman would be nuts to select me over him.

Pick me. If you decide to have babies, please pick me.

I thrust aside the notion. Tying her to me—to us— in that way was just plain wrong.

Finally, she rose, gently tugging me with her.

"Should we put the album away?"

She considered for a moment before nodding.

I tucked it under the bed.

"You know they must clean in here."

"Huh?"

"Cole's cleaning crew. They must come down here,

because I didn't find a speck of dust. Somehow I don't think he's been in here cleaning in the past few days."

"You're probably right." I snagged her hand. "So do we speak to him tonight? It'd be a little mean to make him wait."

"A little sadistic, you mean?"

"Oh God, tell me you didn't just make a BDSM joke." I paused. "Bondage, uh, and sadism and masochism."

"The *uh* would be discipline." She shut off the light as we passed the switch. "Or dominance—which might make it submission instead of sadism."

"This sounds super complicated." I stood by her side as she relocked the room.

"Or super easy." She gazed up at me. "It's as hard as you want to make it."

My cock, not for the first time in the past few minutes, sat up and took notice. "And you're interested in…submission?"

We held hands as we walked back up the stairs. Just before she reached the landing, she stopped.

She made one step up so our eyes were level. "I don't know what I want." She tilted her head. "Well, I don't want to ignore that room."

After pressing a kiss to my lips, she stepped onto the landing. I was just a fraction of a second behind her. The muted sound of the television filtered through. Proof, if we needed it, that Cole was being respectful of Caressa's request for privacy. We rounded the corner to the living room.

Cole glanced up from his seat on the sectional with his phone in his hand. "I have to go. Have a Merry Christmas and all that shit."

"You too."

The phone disconnected with two beeps. Then he turned off the television with the remote.

Oh, he'd had the caller on speakerphone. "Donovan?"

He nodded.

"You tell him what's going on?" Caressa still clung to my hand.

Cole winced. "I might've called for advice."

"And?" I prompted.

"He laughed his ass off." He ran his hands through his overlong mane of black hair. "He might've warned me to be honest with you two from the start, and I might've ignored that advice." Another wince. "To my own peril."

Caressa indicated I should sit in the large chair, which I'd always thought of as perfect to curl up and read a book in. To my surprise, she sat on my lap.

Immediately, my arms went around her waist. Ah, so she wasn't completely over her anger with Cole.

Don't ever keep secrets from her.

Good thing I had none to keep.

Or so you tell yourself.

The longing in Cole's expression almost brought me to my knees. The man hurt. Badly. Caressa could alleviate his mind. Yet she chose not to. Touch of sadism? I just didn't know what her game plan was.

"We have a proposal." Caressa put her hands on her hips.

Cole perked up at her words.

"But we have conditions."

He kept his face neutral.

Buckle up—this is going to be a bumpy ride.

Chapter Three

Caressa

Michael tensed beneath me when I suggested we had a proposal and also conditions. In retrospect, we probably should have talked some more about this.

Except, despite his assertion, I wasn't into sadism. As much as I wanted to make Cole suffer, I also couldn't bear to see him looking so miserable.

I'd told Michael I couldn't do this without him. Chances were, he understood. Not just because I sat on his lap—although that was a pretty big clue. But because we'd been a unit for more than two weeks now. Which, to some people, meant nothing. In my world, though, it meant everything. Time had a weird relativistic quality. My five years in Africa had passed by in a blur.

The past two weeks felt like a lifetime—in a good way.

Or maybe it felt like that because I foresaw this relationship as lasting a lifetime.

With just Michael, or with Cole and Michael?

Yeah, I didn't have a good answer for that.

"What proposal?" Cole shifted his gaze away for a moment, then back.

Why's he looking guilty all of a sudden? The dungeon or something else? I cocked an eyebrow.

"We might've…gotten a little carried away." Cole

winced.

Turning, I glanced down at Michael.

Who, in turn, looked a little sheepish.

"You assholes."

"My fault." Cole said the word tersely.

I pivoted my gaze back to him.

"I might've…gotten a little carried away. We went shopping, and when we came home, I just…" He rubbed his hands over his face. "I needed him, okay? Badly. And I understood the risk, but in that moment, I didn't care. About any of it."

Michael tightened his grasp around me.

Begging me to understand?

"Are you worse?" I jutted my chin. *Stubborn man. Men. Ugh.*

Cole shook his head. "No. Sometimes I'm a little achy in the evening. Nothing for you to worry about."

"I worry about you all the time, dumbass."

Michael stifled a snort.

Pivoting back, I shot him a glare. "I worry about you too."

He grinned. "Even while in Africa?"

"Especially while on another continent. You two shits might get into all kinds of mischief while I've got my back turned."

"So you'll just have to never turn your back again." Cole's gravelly voice echoed in the room.

His words hit me. Michael and I both gazed over at him.

I expected cheekiness, but he was dead serious.

"Cole, I…"

"We won't survive without you, Caressa."

His words echoed Michael's from just a couple of

weeks ago.

An echo that resonated through me.

And yet I had to acknowledge the pull to go back. To finish what I'd started was a visceral, living thing. I needed to do this. But leaving my men? The need to stay and protect felt like a pull just as strong.

As always, I was torn.

But I had a year to sort out my shit.

"My proposal." I glanced back at Michael, who nodded. "Our proposal," I corrected. I turned my gaze to Cole. "We're…intrigued."

He visibly perked up. But an odd wariness flashed in his eyes.

What's he thinking?

I quietly smiled inside—all the while maintaining my outward façade of implacability.

"You have questions." Cole's deep-blue eyes shone.

"Well, frankly, yes. Neither Michael nor I have any experience with this." I glanced back at Michael, just to make sure I hadn't missed something along the way.

He shook his head. "We're…interested in knowing more." He stroked my arm.

"Ask. About anything." Cole's eagerness couldn't be overstated.

But I still had my doubts. "You make it seem so easy."

Cole scratched his jaw. "BDSM is complicated— you're right about that. But answering your questions can be easy. I have no secrets—"

I arched my eyebrow.

"Anymore," he quickly corrected.

Still, I held his gaze. "Who does what to whom?"

Cole's eyes flashed fire. "I do it to other people. It's

all consensual—"

"That was a given." I injected dryness into my tone. "Because if it wasn't, we wouldn't be here at all. We'd be long gone."

His nod of acknowledgment assured me he understood.

"How long?"

He shifted again. I held my ground.

"Since I was nineteen…maybe twenty?"

Michael's grasp around me tightened.

"We were living together." This made no sense to me.

Cole chuckled. "Donovan's been a player since the day he turned nineteen and could go to the clubs. You think he didn't drag me with him every chance he got? And soon, my interest was piqued. Donovan had his own place, and we'd…bring people home."

"Men?" Michael's question. He gently stroked my hair, sending tingles down my spine.

"Mostly. Donovan's preferences really run to men or male-expressing. I…" Cole met my gaze. "Am open to everyone."

Michael shifted beneath me, loosening his grip.

"Am I too heavy?" I met his gaze.

He shook his head and gave me an odd look I couldn't interpret.

"Anyway…" Cole cleared his throat. "We'd go back to Donovan's place. Or one of several private spaces around town. We…played. Experimented. Figured out what we liked."

"Have you…"

"I've been whipped, flogged, and paddled." Cole said the words casually. "I won't do something to

26

someone that I haven't gone through myself." His grin was a little crooked. "Donovan loves me for that reason."

I cocked my head.

"He's the only person I'll let touch me in *that* way."

"So if Michael or I asked…"

Cole swallowed. Hard. "I'd obviously have to consider it seriously. Is that what you want?"

Reading him was proving more difficult than I'd anticipated. *You thought this would be easy? What are you, five?*

Even at five, I'd been pretty street smart.

"We don't know what we want." I almost turned to question Michael again, but he renewed his tight grip.

"I recommend trying anything that interests you." Cole tried to keep his expression neutral—but I spotted the longing. He took a deep breath. "I don't know what your level of knowledge is."

"Assume beginner." Michael snickered. "I've seen a couple of movies and some videos…"

"What?" I turned to gape at him.

He shrugged sheepishly. "Look, five days ago, I'd never considered having sex with a man. Now I share a bed every night with a sexy one who's made it very clear what he wants to do with me when he's healed."

"Gay porn?" I tried to wrap my head around straight-and-narrow Michael watching porn of any kind, let alone the gay stuff.

"I've watched straight porn too, you know." His hazel eyes twinkled gold in the low lighting of the room.

"Really."

"And you haven't?"

I shook my head. No, I never had. Too exploitative, as far as I was concerned.

"You need to get over your prudish notions." Cole again cleared his throat. "This is not our parents' porn."

"Ew." I didn't want to think of my coke-high mother, Michael's abusive parents, or Cole's alcoholic father watching porn.

He held up his hands. "I'm saying it's all consensual these days. Or most of it. You pick your sites carefully."

I gazed back and forth between Michael and Cole.

"We didn't always have a partner," Michael explained.

I expected Cole to argue, but he merely nodded. "Yeah, Caressa, a lot of cold, lonely nights."

"The album would make a liar out of you."

He held my gaze. "That's ten years' worth of photos. And admittedly, we didn't photograph everyone—not by a long shot."

"Again, consensual?"

"Always. And I've signed contracts the pictures will never be used for anything other than personal enjoyment."

"Your own spank bank," Michael commented on a chuckle.

Cole attempted a scowl—but it failed miserably. "Uh, yeah."

I waved my hand. "Did you plan to simply give up that part of your life? Walk away from it? Or were you going to resume it in secret?" I twitched my nose. "Or were you planning to invite us in?"

"Yes, no, and no." He ran a hand through his hair. "I can give it up. Done. I'd never resume it in secret. Ever." He did a half-hearted shrug. "But you've said you're intrigued." He scratched his chin.

I'd shaved him with a straight razor a couple of days

ago, and I wasn't sure if he planned to let it grow over the holidays so he'd have scruff, or if he wanted another close shave. He was always close shaven on his show, *Vigilante Justice*, but was laxer on hiatuses. Injuring himself wasn't a hiatus—just a forced rest that wasn't sitting well with him.

"What are you thinking?" Michael stroked my arm where he gripped me.

Was he referring to me or—

"That's up to you two." With annoyance, Cole indicated his leg. "Like Caressa said, I really shouldn't be doing stairs. But…"

"But," I prompted.

"Well, BDSM encompasses a wide range of things. Plenty we can do in our bedroom without needing much equipment."

I liked the way he said *our* bedroom. He meant all three of us. Thank God he had a big bed. A really big bed. Because with Cole and Michael both being six-foot-two, and with my own five-foot-eight, we took up space.

I was pretty slender these days. Cole was pretty muscular—had to be seeing as he did most of his own stunts. Michael was lither. He was all sinew and tight muscles. He had a runner's body.

"Shouldn't we, you know, talk about things?" My mind still whirled.

Cole's eyes flashed fire. "Of course. We'd need a negotiated contract."

Michael shifted under me.

"Are you okay?" I met his gaze. "Am I too heavy?"

He tugged my head down so he could press a kiss to my temple. "Never, sweetheart. I'm just trying to figure out what's involved. Like are we talking lawyers or

29

something less formal? And how will this impact our relationship? This is all so new, and to add another layer so quickly? I'm just worried."

Which was normally Cole's role. Oh, he tried to play things off like they were no big deal, but he'd always been the driving force toward Michael and me finding stability. Ironic because, as an actor, Cole had the least security of all of us.

Or it had been like that before he landed the lead role on *VJ* and started squirreling away money for a rainy day. I had some idea of his finances—and they were pretty damn sweet. Even after everyone took their cut—agent, lawyer, accountant, etc.—Cole did very well. All that was in jeopardy because of his injury. The film crew were working on other scenes for the season, but they were only a few weeks in. Cole needed to heal. He needed to do it quickly.

So no hanky-panky.

I hadn't liked hearing that he'd done something with Michael in the garage. Not because they weren't allowed to fool around without me, they totally were as long as they told me later. No, I didn't like the fact Cole'd taken a risk—even if he'd only been showing Michael how he felt about him. I liked that this relationship went three ways very solidly. I wanted them to enjoy each other's company, physically and emotionally, while I worked long hours.

"We need to have a discussion about limits." Cole scratched his chin again. "Which sounds simple until you realize how little you actually know about what might happen."

"I'm not a total innocent." I shot back the words, even as the heat rushing to my cheeks belied the argument.

"True enough."

At least he didn't have the gall to gloat. He'd always thought me more innocent than I was—and I'd never disabused him of the notion.

Michael cleared his throat. "Did you and Franklin…"

Cole made an inarticulate noise low in his throat.

Jesus, I so did not want to talk about my ex-boyfriend right now. "Not so much." I winced. "But he liked to show me videos…"

"Fuck, Caressa, that should've been your first clue." Cole's blue eyes flashed.

I glared back. "So you've never watched a video? Never looked for inspiration?"

His flushed cheeks assured me I'd nailed it.

"Look, BDSM was becoming more mainstream while we dated. He had things he wanted to try—"

"Tell me you didn't." This time, Michael's tone commanded.

"I didn't." I tucked my hair behind my ear. "As you know, things didn't work out."

"His wife." Cole's contribution.

I scowled back at him. "I don't want to talk about Franklin."

"If him showing you videos is your only exposure to BDSM, then we kind of have to."

"Bullshit. I'm telling you he showed me videos, and I'm assuring you we never did anything. That's it. End of story."

Michael offered a smile. "As titillating as this conversation promises to be, I'm flagging."

I eyed him.

Cole sighed. "I agree it's been a long day. We still have some pie, right? Maybe à la mode? Sitting in front of the Christmas tree? It's Christmas Eve. We could, I don't know, sing carols—"

"No." Michael and I said the word at the same time with almost the same ferocity. I met his gaze. His smile came across as forced.

Cole clapped his hands. "Then pie in front of the Yule log and we can call it an early night." He cleared his throat. "Sleeping arrangements haven't changed, have they?"

Ah, he worried I might grab Michael and make a beeline for a bedroom upstairs and cut him out entirely. I would admit a small part of me was tempted. He'd kept a big-ass secret from us. One that could destroy everything we were working toward—everything we might eventually achieve as a triad.

Michael'd expressed the same intrigue as myself. But what if he was simply going along with my keen interest? What if he didn't really want these things?

And while on introspective questions, why was I so sure I did?

"We're still sharing a bed, Cole." I didn't need to check with Michael. Not just because I knew he'd go along with me on this, but because he'd have spoken up while we were alone if he wanted something to change. He was very much about not rocking the boat or causing a scene. Or fighting. He'd endured too much of that as a child—issues I still wasn't convinced he'd dealt with.

I placed a kiss on Michael's lips before levering myself off his lap.

He expelled a little *oof*.

Cole chuckled.

I headed to the kitchen and sliced the pie while Michael organized the ice cream. Cole had Neapolitan, which sort of surprised me. He loved the chocolate, I enjoyed vanilla, and Michael always devoured the strawberry. This selection had made a great choice when we were growing up as we each could pick our favorite. As an adult, though, Cole'd be stuck with all three. Maybe he'd developed a taste for the other selections. Or maybe he tossed out the container with ice cream still left.

Nah, couldn't see it.

Life had drilled frugality into us. Even before I spent time in Africa, I'd never wasted anything. Deprivation had been the norm in my house, with my mother often spending our food budget on drugs. Cole's father had had a good job, but he'd drunk and smoked much of that money away. Michael's parents hadn't been much better off, but at least they'd kept food in the fridge. Had their booze-fueled haze prevented them from seeing how much of their food disappeared? I'd lived in fear of them discovering how much Michael fed Cole and myself. But they never did. Or at least, they never beat Michael because of it.

Small mercies.

"Caressa." Michael encircled my waist and pulled me against him, nuzzling my temple.

I was only a few inches shorter, but these days that difference felt substantial. Like I couldn't quite stand up straight and proud. Like things looked bleaker.

It shouldn't be that way. I had my two best friends, and we were embarking upon a glorious new adventure.

He nipped my ear. "Is this—"

"No."

"You didn't know what I was going to say." The admonishment held no heat.

"True." I leaned against him. "But you couldn't possibly know what I was thinking."

"About our childhood." He released me to pick up two plates.

I gazed up at him. He offered a warm smile, pressed a light kiss to my lips, then headed back into the living room. After an unsettled moment, I grabbed the forks, my plate, and headed out as well.

Cole had, as promised, turned on the Yule log on the television.

"Your gas fireplace doesn't work?" I pointed as I plopped down.

Michael'd conveniently left the middle spot on the sectional for me—undoubtedly so Cole and I could begin to heal the mini-rift.

"Gas fireplace works, but it's bad for the environment." Cole forked a piece of pie, ensuring just the right amount of chocolate ice cream. "I mean, we can do it for one night, but I don't like—"

I held up my hand. "I like that you're concerned about the environment."

"Well, I was peripherally aware." He held the piece aloft. "I mean, I bought the house that has geothermal heating and cooling as well as the electric docking stations…but I didn't give it much thought until I starred in that movie with Peter Erickson. He's a staunch champion for the environment—and has a much bigger platform than I do."

Peter Erickson had been in the movie business for twenty or more years, and he was a giant in the business. One of the biggest action-hero stars out there. I might have been living in a remote village in Africa, but news of Peter coming out as gay had hit my news feed when I'd snagged a moment of downtime. At the time, Peter had been shooting a movie with Cole. Where they played gay lovers. "I've never seen that film."

Cole'd just put the food in his mouth, so he scowled.

"Which film?" Lovely Michael, always willing to help out.

"The one Cole made with Peter."

"Really?" Michael's face showed pure shock. Then just as quickly, it morphed into something more neutral. "Well, yes, I guess they didn't show many movies in the places where you worked."

"Africa has movie theaters." I tried for annoyed.

"Showing little queer art films?" Cole'd finished chewing and swallowing his food.

"They might have." I swirled my fork in the vanilla ice cream. "I was pretty busy." Truth was I'd kept my nose down and worked my ass off. I'd heard of Peter's Academy Award for the film—and that Cole'd been nominated for a Golden Globe for *Vigilante Justice*. Again, everything had been a distraction I couldn't afford. I was running from my guilt, and anything that reminded me of the life I'd left behind in Canada just intensified that guilt.

"We should watch the film." Michael nudged my shoulder. "Truly, Caressa, it's a brilliant film. I cried." He pointedly looked over me to meet Cole's gaze. "You should've been nominated as well. I mean, Peter deserved the win, but you were fucking brilliant." He scowled. "And those Golden Globe people need to get a clue."

"I've been nominated for an Emmy."

"Well, they should figure out things as well."

I smiled at Michael's obvious displeasure and upset on Cole's behalf. We certainly hadn't followed award shows as children, so clearly this new avid interest came as a result of Cole's career success.

"Being nominated is an honor." Because that's what we'd been taught, I thought.

Cole nodded at my comment. But I caught the transitory moment of sadness.

I got it. We'd grown up in such dire circumstances. If he could win, then it would be proof that if one worked hard enough—and had talent, looks, and the right break—then they stood a real chance at success. I suspected Cole didn't covet, but he certainly wouldn't turn down, any accolades.

"And yeah, we can watch the film."

"Oh, we need to do a *Vigilante Justice* marathon as well." Michael took all the empty plates and piled them. He tisked. "You're working this insane schedule— almost every day between Christmas and New Year's Day."

"I am."

"But you're off on the second, right? I've got work, but you and Cole could watch all the episodes." He headed off to the kitchen.

After rising, I offered a hand to Cole. Clearly disgruntled, he took it. I helped him, and soon he was steady with his cane.

"You don't have to watch the marathon." He held my gaze.

I tilted my head. "Four seasons? What, twenty episodes a season?"

He nodded.

"Well, we can make a dent in it. But I want to see your *little gay film* first. Maybe tomorrow night after I get home from work?"

"You're going to be exhausted, and we still have to do presents."

I glanced over to the Christmas tree, which had a surprising number of wrapped gifts below it. "You and Michael go ahead—"

"Fuck no."

His sharp tone had me looking up. "I get that presents make you uncomfortable. Hell, they make me uncomfortable as well. But this is our first Christmas together in years. Michael and I will happily wait for you."

He nudged me toward the master bedroom. "I'd like to get into bed."

No doubt he'd had a long day. He and Michael had gone out to the high-end jeweler. Huh. Was I supposed to recognize the turquoise-colored bag, or was I to remain in ignorance?

Tough call with these two.

"Yeah, let's go to bed." I yanked my phone from my back pocket. As I strolled behind him, I set the alarm. I dreaded getting up that early, but I'd need to shower.

At the threshold to the bedroom, he stopped. "Why don't you take my car tomorrow?"

"Parking is expensive." I headed over to the nightstand where Michael and I had set up our charging cables.

"Caressa." Cole's voice was quiet.

I turned.

"I'll pay the fee for parking. Do you want cash or just to take my credit card?"

Gabbi Grey

Jesus. "First, I can pay. Second, I'm not taking your credit card."

"Why not? In January, I plan to set you and Michael—"

I held up my hand. "Do you want to fight before bed?"

He cocked his head. "Of course not."

"Then don't get me started on finances."

Michael breezed into the room, already undoing the button on his jeans. "Finances?" He stopped. Then he looked between Cole and myself.

"Not tonight." Cole maneuvered himself over to the chaise lounge and started to remove his clothing. "But soon."

Michael and I exchanged glances. He and I'd fought over finances—and we both had a shit-ton less money than Cole.

Yeah, this is about to get interesting.

Chapter Four

Cole

Well, it didn't take long for things to go south again.
Undressing while keeping weight off my left leg wasn't impossible—but damn nearly. Within a fraction of a second, Michael was by my side. Caressa huffed. Then marched into the bathroom.

Oh, I'd not heard the last from her.

Michael helped me pull my jeans and underwear off. Then I sat so he could yank my sweater over my head.

"How'd you get dressed earlier?"

"I can be creative."

He scowled.

"I didn't do anything against Zoey's rules." My physiotherapist had paid me a visit today and was pleased with my progress. Hence being allowed to move from crutches to the cane.

"See that you don't."

While I made my way over to the bed, Michael stripped out of his jeans, work shirt, and socks. He moved to plug in his phone.

"Those can come off as well." I pointed to the boxers.

He offered a wicked smile. "Yeah, but I still need to piss, and until then, I don't need shrinkage."

I scooted under the covers. "It's not that cold." I

pointed to the thermostat. "Feel free—"

He waved me off. "It'll be plenty warm once we're all in bed." He headed into the bathroom.

The warm glow settled in my chest every time he used the word *we*.

Caressa reentered the room wearing the robe I'd given her and, hopefully, nothing else. I pulled back the covers and patted the bed beside me. She pursed her lips.

Inwardly, I sighed. "What's up?" I tried for light and casual.

"It just feels like today's been a big day, you know? And I'm wired when I most need to be sleepy."

"Well, I always find a good orgasm knocks me on my ass and puts me right to sleep. In fact, sometimes it's a struggle to stay awake."

"In order to escort your guests out the door?" She placed a hand on her hip.

Michael wandered back into the room—still wearing his boxers. "What guests?"

"All the people Cole shared orgasms with."

His eyes widened in confusion. "I was only gone a minute…"

"Jealous?" I wasn't sure I wanted her to be, because I so disliked the emotion, but I was curious where she was going with this.

"Of those people? Of course not." Finally, at length, she removed her robe.

Naked, thank God.

"Michael, you get in first." Caressa being bossy in that endearing way she had.

He looked back and forth between Caressa and myself, obviously contemplating her command. "Uh, sure." He shucked his boxers, tossed them onto the chaise, and climbed into bed. He lay beside me and immediately turned back to Caressa. She eased herself in and yanked the covers up to her chin. He leaned over her to turn off the bedside light. I turned off mine. Again, the low light from the nightlight illuminated the space. Taking a deep breath, I hit the base of the lamp, which shut the thing off.

The darkness immediately felt oppressive.

Total darkness was foreign to me. Because of childhood trauma, I didn't like not having a light at all times. Sure, the power had gone off twice since I bought the house, but I'd slept through both outages, and things had been restored before I even realized. I had hurricane lamps strategically placed around the house so I'd always have a light if we lost power again.

Michael snagged my hand and held it tight.

"Are you going to be okay?" Caressa's voice carried across the space.

"I'll be fine." *Please believe me*.

"Phobias are real, Cole."

I slashed my hand through the air—although no one could see it. "I don't have a phobia. It's just…we live in the city. Light pollution is a thing. I'm used to it, that's all. I'm never somewhere that's completely dark."

"Not even your dungeon?" Caressa's tone was…interested.

"Especially not the dungeon."

The room hadn't been a dungeon when I bought the place, obviously. The previous owner had just thrown a bunch of junk in there and clearly hadn't given it much thought. When I'd seen the space, though, the possibilities coalesced in my mind. I'd told my realtor to get me the house—no matter the cost. Luckily, it had been the offseason, so I hadn't been involved in a bidding war. I'd paid the asking price and walked away with a sweet place I could call my own.

I'd consulted with the owner of a local BDSM club who knew about private party spaces. In fact, the dungeon had been set up before much of the house.

But I doubted Caressa needed to know that.

"There's a light in there attached to the emergency generator. If the power goes off, that light goes on automatically."

"Emergency generator, eh? Sounds…eminently practical."

"That's me." I tried to inject some enthusiasm.

"Turn the nightlight on, Cole." Caressa's tone brooked no opposition.

I could tell her I was fine—but I wasn't. And she knew it. I tapped the base of the lamp, and the faint white light illuminated the space.

"Just because the monsters are people doesn't make them any less real." Michael whispered the thought.

His quiet words caught me off guard. His parents were still, after all these years, some of the monsters I most feared. And hell, they were dead. My own father came a close second, but I'd sort of reconciled with him at the end. He'd honestly regretted most of his life choices—the drinking, the smoking—and felt a small amount of remorse for how he'd treated me. I could have ignored him when he reached out—as I think Caressa would have preferred—but I was starting to make a name for myself. I didn't need him going to some tabloid and talking about how his son wouldn't give him the time of day.

The feature article that came out about me around

the same time simply said I'd grown up in near poverty and had a rough start in life. No one needed to know my shit.

Except Michael and Caressa already did. Michael released his grasp of my hand, and at first, I missed the contact. Then I realized, as he shifted, that he intended to kiss me. I was totally fine with that. The way he turned, though, meant his back was to Caressa. As he pressed his lips to mine, I made a futile gesture over his head toward Caressa.

"I'm fine." She said the words on a yawn. "You guys do whatever you need to do. I'm tired." With that, she turned her back, huddled under the covers, and appeared to go to sleep.

I met Michael's gaze. In the low light, his pupils were dark orbs.

"She'll be okay." He angled his head to press his lips to mine.

Immediately, I opened for him. I wanted this as much as he did, apparently. Or even more. I needed him like I needed oxygen.

He grasped my cheek in his fingers as he thrust his tongue in my mouth. His fingernails raked down, sending little tingles through me. His tongue was unrelenting in its exploration of me.

I felt like he wanted to know me down to the depths of my soul. To the parts no one ever saw—no one ever touched. For as much as I'd savored each connection with those people in my dungeon, and even more, my time with Donovan, I'd never given myself over completely to someone. I'd always held a part of me back. Even when balls deep inside someone, be that a man or woman, I never connected the way I did in this moment.

Gripping his back, I urged him closer.

"Your leg." His breath was hot against my skin.

"Fuck my leg." In this moment I didn't care. Not about *Vigilante Justice*, not about my career, not about anything except for the driving need to connect with Michael on an elemental level.

"Cole Hamilton." Caressa snapped the words.

Oh shit.

When she used *that* tone with me, she reminded me way too much of Lisette Grenier, our director. Any thought of the five-foot-nothing dynamo who could tank my career was the equivalent of dumping ice water on my previously interested cock.

Michael eased back so Caressa could stick her head between the two of us.

She glared. "Now, I know I did not just hear you say to *fuck my leg*. Which, aside from being anatomically impossible—"

I started to speak. She smacked my chest. I desisted.

"You've come this far, and I get that you're horny. You seem to be horny a lot, in fact."

A long pause ensued, and I chose not to fill the silence.

"But I'm pretty sure Zoey'll lose her shit if you suddenly slide backward. She'll want to know why."

I didn't have to tell my physiotherapist, but I decided pointing that out in this moment was liable to get me in serious trouble.

Apparently, not answering wasn't the right choice either. Caressa got right in my face. "I will not let you slide back, Cole. You'll hate yourself, and I won't stand for that. You know what you need to do—no fucking."

"But blow jobs and hand jobs are fine…" I echoed the words of the professional tasked with whipping me back into shape.

"Take your pick." Her unearthly pale-blue eyes flashed nearly white in the light.

My cock, previously deflating, sat up and took notice. "You're tired."

Her grin nearly undid me. "Never too tired for you."

"I may hold you to that."

"Do." She nuzzled my neck. "Do you want me or Michael?"

Since both of them had given me blow jobs in the past few days, her question made sense.

"I want to see Michael eat you out. Then while you drift to sleep, I want him to use that same mouth to blow me." I inclined my head. "If that's okay with you."

He grinned. "I get a twofer? Awesome."

At some point we'd need to get him off as well, but those logistics would sort themselves out in time. I patted my chest.

Caressa arched an eyebrow.

"Lie against me."

She nodded. After snagging a pillow, she laid it so she could lean against me without straining her neck. She settled as Michael crawled between her thighs.

He gently parted her knees, opening her up to him.

"Do you need…" Me, always being prepared.

"Nah. She's ready to go." Michael said the words with supreme confidence as he exposed her labia.

She squirmed, and the scent of her arousal reached me. Little minx. She hadn't nearly been close to sleep. Had she planned to pounce or just quietly let Michael and me get on with things?

45

As Michael laved her, she bucked. I stroked down her arm, then settled my hand on her belly. She pushed it up so I cupped her breast.

Fair enough.

As Michael continued his diligent endeavor, and as Caressa made little moans of approval, I tweaked her nipple.

She sucked in a breath through her teeth and arched up into my touch.

The angle was wrong for me to grasp the other nipple, but I gently stroked her hair back from her face. Sweat coated her brow as she tried to buck up against Michael's persistent mouth.

"Come, baby. Show Michael how much you love him."

Within moments, she arched her neck and let out a guttural groan. Her body stiffened as the orgasm ripped through her, and she continued to let out little whimpers and sighs.

Michael rocked back on his heels, a huge grin on his face.

God, how I envied him.

Your turn will come. Be patient.

Caressa was right, damn it. I couldn't do anything to jeopardize my recovery. That being said, the moment I got the all clear from Zoey, I had a lot of pleasure to wring from both my companions.

Michael crawled up Caressa's body and gave her a long, lingering kiss. After several very long beats, he pulled back. "You tired, sweetheart?"

She nodded.

He coaxed her back to the far side of the bed, tucked her pillow under her head, and encouraged her to pull into the fetal position. "I'm going to rock Cole's world, and then we'll all sleep."

Ineffectually, she batted him away. Turning to me, he chuckled. I pulled the covers back to show my impressive erection.

He licked his lips.

Where I expected him to get to work, though, he pressed his hands to my chest and levered in for another kiss.

Remnants of Caressa's arousal tinged his lips, and my libido kicked into high gear. He thrust his tongue into my mouth—demanding, overwhelming, overpowering.

Will he always take the lead? Will he ever yield to me?

Does it matter?

Those thoughts swirled in my head as Michael trailed his hand down my neck along my sternum, past my belly button, and on to my very interested cock.

The first touch had me bucking up, seeking friction. He tisked his disapproval. I held myself in check.

"You said you wanted my mouth." He pulled back to meet my gaze.

"I'll take you however I can fucking get you."

Desperate much?

Honestly, I didn't care. I just wanted to come— needed to come. However that happened was just fine with me.

Michael squeezed.

Stars danced before my eyes.

Then, slowly, he shifted until he knelt by my waist. He winked, then he bent so he could lick my crown.

Mindful of Caressa sleeping, I moaned softly.

Michael chuckled as he took me in. He tongued my

slit, then nibbled at my head.

The sensation overloaded me as my balls grew heavy.

Still, he sucked me nonstop. His cheeks hollowed as he continued his diligent work to bring me to climax.

I reached out to touch his short hair—so different from my own. I raked my hands down his scalp, using my fingernails.

He hummed his approval.

Then he took me to the root, and things devolved quickly from there.

Because he held my hips in place, I couldn't buck up. Instead, I rode the sensation of warmth all the way through to my climax. I didn't warn him I was coming because he likely would have known, and just as importantly, he hadn't pulled off the last time.

How many more times will there be?

Would I really be lucky to have these two in my bed for the rest of my life? I wanted this—of that, I had no doubt. I just didn't know if I could grasp something as ethereal as love and hold on without it slipping through my fingers.

I spurted, and Michael valiantly continued to suck me. I tipped my head back to rest against the headboard, riding the orgasm for all I was worth.

Eventually, when I swore he couldn't extract another drop from me, he climbed over me to give me another toe-curling, soul-searing kiss.

Immediately, I acquiesced to his demanding tongue. For tonight, I'd give him control. At some point in the future, though, I needed to take control of this situation. No one topped me.

Except Donovan.

Well, my good friend was the exception to many of my rules, but even saying that much, I reflected a long time had passed since I'd given him that kind of access to my body. Now we mostly co-topped.

Leaving us breathless, Michael finally pulled back.

"Jack yourself. I want you to come on me."

He quirked his eyebrows, and a lazy smile crossed his lips.

From this angle, I couldn't see his cock. From personal experience, I suspected he was hard—or damn close. For me, giving pleasure was a potent aphrodisiac. If I could make someone else come, I usually teetered on the edge—ready to go over myself.

Michael rocked back on his heels. I caught sight of his cock in the pale, weak light. Oh yeah, he was ready to go. To my surprise, he moved closer to my torso. Suddenly, he wasn't out of reach.

The angle wasn't great, but I was able to hold his velvety smooth yet unyieldingly hard length in my hand. He pulsed when I gave him an experimental tug.

"We need lube."

I started to pull back, but he secured his hand over mine as I held him.

"Like this." Said through gritted teeth.

Who was I to argue? A bit of precum leaked, but I didn't worry about trying to use it to ease my way. If he wanted rough and demanding, then that's what I'd give him.

Our gazes met. He released his grasp on my hand. I began to work him in earnest. He leaned back, offering me maximum access.

If we had company, I would have asked Caressa to stroke his hair. Maybe even tweak a nipple. If hers were

49

sensitive, why not his?

"Tweak your nipples." What the hell, why not try?

His eyes widened in surprise, but he quickly obeyed. He pinched them, and in response, he thickened in my hand.

I renewed my vigorous jerks, and within moments, he erupted. I tried to control the cum as I milked it out of his body. It spurted over my hands even as I gentled my strokes.

He whined almost silently. Our gazes locked. I grinned. Then after one final stroke, I let go of his cock. And brought my cum-covered hand to my mouth and sucked.

"Jesus," he whispered.

"Indeed."

"I should wash us off." Which would have involved him climbing over either Caressa or myself since the bed had a footboard.

I reached for the strategically placed box of tissues. He chuckled. We cleaned ourselves up as best we could. Then we got under the blankets. Michael reached for Caressa and gently coaxed her to roll over. He pressed his back against my side. I stroked his hair. Caressa sighed. Before long, I was out as well.

Chapter Five

Michael

I lay awake a long time after Cole drifted off.

Caressa was already far gone, and she snuffled in her sleep when I drew her closer.

Who'd have thought giving blow jobs could be so much fun?

I'd never contemplated it. Well, not seriously. In the abstract, I'd wondered what it would be like to take a guy in my mouth. Whether I'd be able to do it without gagging. Whether I could bring him as much pleasure as my partners over the years had brought me. I never asked for blow jobs. If they were offered freely, I'd happily say yes. But I never asked.

Caressa seemed to enjoy giving them, and I had the distinct impression Cole enjoyed giving as well as receiving.

Which did and did not fit my image of him.

The photographs in the album confirmed, to me, at least, that Cole preferred to be the one inflicting…whatever he did. I might have been wrong, though. Maybe he enjoyed receiving. Maybe he just hadn't memorialized that in those artsy photographs.

Something told me that wasn't the case.

Where does he see me?

Remembering those trussed up people, I squirmed. I

didn't have any hang-ups or anything, but I wasn't sure I liked the idea of being tied up. Tied down.

And Cole implied these acts involved more than just the infliction of pain. Which was what I'd sort of gleaned from the little research I'd dabbled in, accidentally, while researching gay sex.

Isn't that enough for now?

Part of me said yeah, if I managed to have actual penetrative anal sex with Cole, going either way, then that was a pretty fucking big deal. The other part of me was beginning to understand how fundamental BDSM was to Cole—and how much of a big fucking deal his offer to give it up really was.

I didn't want him to have to give up part of himself just to satisfy Caressa and myself.

But you'd do it for them.

Damn, I hated when I was right. I didn't have much to give up. But for example, if they wanted me to stop going up towers under construction, I'd have to seriously consider it. Just like, although she put up a good show, I was certain Caressa had at least listened to us when we expressed concerns over her job.

The job she was headed back to in the morning.

That thought broke a part of me inside.

A toddler had died on her watch. Not her fault, but something she needed to deal with. I was relieved she was seeing a psychologist…but that psychologist had sent her home early from work. Obviously, the session had been more impactful than Caressa'd let on.

I needed to reach her. I just didn't know how.

Cole and I'd have the day to talk about it while she worked tomorrow.

On that thought, I pressed a kiss to her cheek,

reached back to stroke Cole's hip, then slipped into slumber.

Only to be rudely awakened by Caressa's blaring alarm at five thirty.

The three of us simultaneously groaned as she escaped my grasp and snagged her phone to turn off the obnoxious sound. Something told me she'd selected it because the thing was just so annoying that trying to sleep through it was impossible.

"Sorry, guys." She scooted out of bed, nabbed her bathrobe, and headed out of the room. Obviously planning to use her private bathroom.

"I'm going to get up and make her a quick breakfast and some coffee." I sat up.

Cole groaned. "I'd offer to help…"

I patted his good thigh. "She'll understand. I'm planning to come back to bed."

"I look forward to it." His eyes drifted shut, as if keeping them open just took too much effort.

Grinning, I rolled out of bed. I stretched as I made my way to the bathroom and scratched my belly as I took a piss. I needed a shower, but that could wait. I cleaned my cock and pubes, then threw on pajama bottoms and a T-shirt I'd tucked away in Cole's room.

Our room?

His walk-in closet had space for both Caressa and me to add a few things of our own. We'd also each selected a bedroom upstairs we could call our own. Cole predicted we might all need our own space. What wasn't lost on me was he hadn't staked out his own territory. Maybe his office? Right now, between the desk and the workout equipment, there wasn't much space.

Funny how he hadn't set up the equipment before.

That being said, Cole wasn't a gym rat. He preferred martial arts. Kept him lean, keen, and in tip-top shape for his stunts.

As I rummaged in the kitchen for the ingredients to make an egg sandwich, I winced.

Cole needed to heal, and he needed to get back to *VJ*. He needed his life back on track. Having Caressa and me here threatened to derail him.

Fuck my leg.

Careless words. Enough to get Caressa up and actively participating in our sexual escapades, but she wouldn't always be around to scold Cole and put him in his place.

Do you have the strength to do it?

Funny how Caressa had no problem standing up to Cole, but I hesitated. When it came to sex, I had no problems being the bossy one. But in other things I…faltered.

The toast popped as Caressa breezed into the kitchen, her hair still damp. She had an elastic in her hand, and efficiently, she had her hair up in a ponytail. "You didn't have to do this."

I indicated the coffee machine. "Should be done in a minute. You still prefer coffee early on workdays, right? And tea the rest of the time?" We hadn't lived together for nearly eight years, and some things might have changed for her. I was much the same, however, and I'd taken a chance she hadn't changed.

She kissed my cheek. "This is perfect." She grabbed a travel mug and poured milk and a bit of sugar inside.

After ensuring the eggs were properly cooked, I spooned the egg onto the bread. I added a tomato slice, put it together with the other piece of toast, and then cut it into four triangular slices.

Caressa giggled.

I raised my eyebrows.

"You remembered."

I remember everything. I didn't say the words, however. Even to my ear—and knowing the context— they sounded creepy.

After putting the sandwich in a container, I nabbed the spaghetti.

As Caressa sipped, I prepared a container for her lunch. I even found a mini-container to put parmesan cheese in. I lamented we hadn't done a baguette last night when she grabbed a lunch bag and shoved the containers inside.

"This is perfect."

"It's okay if you don't eat it and…"

She shook her head. "I don't want to waste money on takeout if I don't have to." She met my gaze.

"I get it. Knowing he's got all this money is weird because it's not our money and we're so accustomed to being frugal."

"You know I have a car."

I'd tried very hard not to think about the piece of junk sitting in my garage at the condo. I'd moved it to my spot and had seriously considered selling it. "Caressa, that thing is a piece of junk."

She winced.

"And you don't need it now you're living in the city. If you were commuting from Mission City every day, then yeah, it made sense." Even the thought of her making that long commute in that death trap twisted my gut. When I first saw it, I'd tried to devise a plan to replace it. I'd hoped Cole could help me. Like maybe he'd upgrade his ride and give Caressa his car. Far-fetched, but I'd hoped.

Maybe I could still convince him.

"We can get your car." Inwardly, I winced. "But it's not going to fit the aesthetic of the neighborhood."

She glared. "I'm going to pretend you didn't say that. I'm going to go after work tonight." She held out her hand. "I need the garage remote."

"I'll pick you up after work, and we'll go together." That way she wouldn't be driving it without me following closely behind.

The glare morphed into a scowl, but after a bit, she relented. "Fine. Whatever. The bus leaves in ten minutes."

"And it'll take me three minutes to get dressed. Wait, and I'll run you."

"Not needed."

Yet she didn't head out the door.

I hotfooted upstairs to my room. Deodorant wasn't optional, but socks were, and I was back downstairs in about four minutes.

Caressa eyed my bare feet and pointed back up the stairs.

Fine.

Lesson learned.

I came back downstairs wearing socks.

She'd donned her winter coat, boots, gloves, and had her lunch bag in one hand and her knapsack slung over her shoulder.

I needed mere moments to don my own winter gear, and soon we were in the garage and loading into my car. Silently, I pulled out and headed up to West Fourth.

"What kinds of mischief are you two going to get up

to today?"

"While the cat's away, the mice come out to play?"

She guffawed. "Oh, I'm a cat, am I?"

"All lithe, sleek, and lethal? Yeah, you're definitely a cat. Like a lioness or a panther."

"Well, that's a new one."

I smiled at her wry tone. "I'll be waiting for you at seven. If there's a change of plans, just text me. Or call. Or, you know, whatever."

This time, a snicker. "There are other options? Like a bat signal?"

"I was thinking email, but I didn't plan to check it. If you tell me, you might—"

"I'm not emailing you on Christmas Day, Michael."

"And we'll wait to do presents tonight."

I stopped at the red light at Burrard Street and waited for the dedicated arrow so I could turn left.

Caressa fiddled with her knapsack strap.

"What is it?"

"What did you buy at the jewelry store?"

Ah. I'd wondered if she noticed—and if she did, how long it would take her to comment.

Apparently not long.

"I can't answer that."

She snickered.

"Well, I suppose I could. I mean, I saw what Cole selected."

"You were his wingman."

"Well, I certainly couldn't afford a single thing in that store."

Not quite the truth—they had some lovely pieces that would have cost me a pretty penny but that I probably could have fit in the budget.

Except I didn't see Caressa as a jewelry person. And she certainly couldn't wear anything to work. Except maybe a necklace under her scrubs.

Something to consider.

"It's up to Cole to share. I think he meant them as a Christmas present."

"Them?"

The light changed, and I maneuvered the turn. I waved her off as I started up Burrard Street and over the bridge.

"You think because of what happened yesterday that he might change his mind."

I noted that she didn't phrase it as a question. Here, I could at least allay her fears. "Yes, our dynamic changed yesterday. This whole BDSM thing, at least. But Cole's feelings toward you—toward both of us—hasn't changed."

"That must've been some blow job."

No missing the sarcasm. "I think he enjoyed himself."

"And you got off?"

"Hand job."

"Yours or his?"

"His."

"Nice."

"Yeah, I have to agree." Remembrances of the night before flooded me, and heat rose to my cheeks.

"Michael Dubois, are you blushing?"

"Maybe. Is there a right way to answer that question?" I turned left and headed for the back of the hospital.

"Honesty." She sighed. "All I ever want from you is honesty. Same with Cole."

58

"Then I'll let you know what we get up to today while you're at work." I pulled up to the door and put the car in park. I looked over at her.

She looked back. "This is a lot to take in."

"We can slow things down." I flashed to the rings in the bag. They were, basically, the opposite of slowing down.

"I don't know." She bit her lip.

I cupped her cheek. "Sweetheart, you haven't even been back in the country for a month. You should've taken more time before landing such a stressful job."

"And before jumping into your bed."

God, please let her not regret me. Or us.

Her shy smile returned. "I have no regrets, Michael. About any of it. I'm just okay with taking baby steps."

"I'll let Cole know."

She leaned over, clearly meaning to give me a peck on the cheek.

I turned so our mouths collided. Then turned her surprise into a full-on tongues-clashing deep kiss.

She moaned.

I reciprocated with a rumble deep in my chest.

After a moment, she pulled back. "We're going to be okay." She hopped out of the car and disappeared within moments into the building.

God, I hope she's right.

And I didn't just mean *us*. Cole and I were hearty and strong. We could manage just about anything.

Except losing Caressa.

Decision made, I headed to my condo. I parked in visitor parking and headed up. I'd done a pretty good job cleaning before we left to temporarily move in with Cole, but I needed to bring more stuff, and Caressa had a few

Gabbi Grey

belongings she hadn't thought she needed.

I cursed not having brought the empty suitcases but snagged a few boxes from the recycling bin in the garage. Fortunately, I had some packing tape, and within an hour, I had four boxes of stuff loaded into my SUV.

Renting this place out made the most sense. Real estate was at a premium in Vancouver, and similar units in our building brought in thousands of dollars a month. I could put the extra toward the mortgage and try to get it paid down sooner.

And if I secured a tenant on a month-to-month lease, if things went to shit, I could easily move back.

I hated that I was thinking like this, but things still felt too tenuous and new with Cole. Like we were still walking on eggshells. Like he could change his mind at any moment and turf us.

Of course, he'd never do that.

Ever.

If things didn't pan out, he'd give us time. We could move into the upstairs bedrooms and have time to figure things out. And I even hated that was my consideration. But I needed to protect myself. Protect Caressa. Even protect Cole. That was my nature. The nurturer. The protector. And I did best when I didn't fight my instincts.

Returning to Cole's, I found him in the den, doing his exercises.

"That took a while. Is Caressa okay?"

"Yeah." I leaned against the doorframe. "She thinks we're moving too fast."

He stopped his reps. "Does she want out?"

I shook my head. "No. She worried things yesterday might've changed things for you."

He tilted his head.

"The dungeon."

He winced. "Not my proudest moment."

"Well, she's intrigued."

"There's that word again."

"If we take things at her pace, I think we'll be okay. Just…" I scratched my stubble. "I think we need to put away the rings for now. You bought her the brooch as well, right?"

"I was going to give her that to wear at the gala. I still need to convince her to let me buy her a dress. Or at least rent one."

"Maybe find a place she can afford. She might be more amenable if she can do it herself." I didn't have a problem with Cole buying her a dress—but she likely would.

He sighed. "Okay, so we put the rings away for now. But promise me you'll tell me when the time is right. Because my instinct will be every day."

"I promise I'll tell you." I still wasn't certain of the ramifications of us all donning matching rings, but we would cross that bridge when we came to it. "Oh, I was later than expected because I stopped by the condo to pack some more stuff."

"You should consider renting it out." Cole resumed his reps.

Exactly what I'd thought, but somehow him saying it felt like pressure. "Maybe next year sometime."

He met my gaze—those blue eyes penetrating. "I'd ask you to sell it, but I know that would induce panic. I'm a forever kind of guy, Michael, and so are you."

After a long moment, he turned back toward his spectacular view and resumed his workout.

After a long moment, I turned tail and ran.

Chapter Six

Cole

After I finished my workout, I took a shower and then headed off in search of Michael, hopeful I'd find him on the first floor. I located him at the dining room table with his laptop open and several drawings surrounding him.

I tapped the back of the chair. "There are plenty of ergonomic chairs around."

He glanced up, his eyes a little glazed. "I'm not comfortable in your office, and the rest are upstairs. I figured you might try to come find me." He eyed my leg. "How are you?"

"Doing amazingly well, all things considered."

"Still, you shouldn't be standing. Do you want me to come join you in the living room?"

I eyed the work spread out.

He waved me off. "It'll keep. I have a week. I probably shouldn't be working on Christmas Day anyway, but I wanted to get the jump on things."

"You work harder than I gave you credit for." Which was saying something, since I assumed he worked his ass off.

"This is my biggest project to date. The first time I'm in at the ground floor, so to speak. Everything needs to be perfect."

I grasped his cheek and ran my thumb across his cheekbone. "That's a hell of a lot of pressure you put on yourself."

"My work isn't quite as life-and-death as Caressa's…but critical mistakes can cost millions of dollars. Getting this right, the first time, is critical."

Of that, I had no doubt. Soaring structures of concrete, steel, and glass required a precision I found mind-blowing. "Donovan's going to be over in a few minutes—why don't we crash in the living room?"

He held my gaze for a long moment. "This visit wasn't planned, was it?"

"Well…" I couldn't lie to him. "No. Not planned. After last night, he figured I could use a boost in support."

Michael scowled, visibly bristling. "Cole, I thought we worked this out."

He might feel that way, but I most certainly did not. "Maybe." I hedged. "But I'll be brutally honest and say I'm too close to this to be objective."

"Caressa and I know Donovan."

"True. But he can put on the *safety-first, everyone follows my rules* Dom hat much better than I can."

He snickered. "Oh, something tells me you'd do just fine at bossing us around. That, in fact, you'd like it very much."

I would…but that wasn't the point. And while we were on the subject— "Does me bossing you around bother you?"

Yet another snicker. "Cole, that's a dumbass question. Of course I don't mind. I'm here, aren't I?"

Point Michael.

"But I also like to be in charge sometimes, and that

chafes you. I think, in the end, that's a bigger issue."

Shit. I thought I'd hidden that…discomfort…pretty well. "Let's go sit." I indicated my leg, even though I probably could have stood for another couple of minutes.

He clicked a few keys on the laptop and shut it down. He started to tidy the papers.

I waylaid him. "It'll keep."

"Uh, yeah." He rose. "Are you hungry?"

After he'd dropped Caressa off this morning, he'd come home and made me breakfast. He'd presented me with an egg sandwich, and I'd eaten it while we sat at the kitchen table before I'd headed off to do my workout. A meal in silent contemplation. He wasn't a chatty guy, none of us were known to run off at the mouth, but he was the most reflective of all of us. Occasionally, his silences made me uncomfortable. Something I'd have to learn to live with again. "Not particularly hungry. I figure we can make a pizza when Donovan comes."

"We still have leftover pasta, and I think there's turkey as well."

I shook my head. "I ate it in a sandwich before you picked me up yesterday. Sorry."

"Don't apologize." He rose, then pushed in his chair. "I'm just glad the leftovers got eaten."

I wanted to point out that a bit of food waste wasn't the end of the world, but that went contrary to Michael's philosophy. To Caressa's. And, mostly, to mine. "How about a drink?"

"Alcohol?" He checked his watch. "It's not even eleven."

"I was thinking coffee."

His features relaxed.

"I don't drink, Michael. Nothing's changed." I

might have an occasional beer or a shot, but no more than one a night and never while playing.

"Just…I spotted the wet bar downstairs."

"A place I spend very little time in." I indicated the way to the kitchen. "We're all children of alcoholics and drug addicts. Frankly, none of us are good bets in that regard." And we'd had the discussion early on and made a pact to never drink to excess. Actually, if memory served, we'd sworn to never drink at all.

We'd been seven.

Even when we'd moved out on our own, none of us imbibed with any frequency or quantity.

"Caressa still doesn't drink." Michael rinsed out the coffeepot and put on a fresh pot.

I leaned against the high-top kitchen table. "And I don't either. I might have one at the gala—"

He shot me a look.

"Okay…or none…"

He waved me off. "I'm sure it'll be fine."

"But you think Caressa'll notice."

"Well, I haven't had a drink around her, so I can't say. Do you want me to broach the subject with her?"

This time, I waved him off. "I'm a big boy, Michael. If I need to talk to Caressa about something, then I'll do it."

He raised both eyebrows.

Heat rose up my chest. "Yes, well…"

The sound of a key in the lock carried through to the kitchen. The front door opened. Then shut. Two thunks, undoubtedly of boots being dropped, resonated. Finally, the front closet door opened and closed.

"He's not quiet." Michael said the words with amusement.

"He's giving me a chance to let him know it's a bad time."

"He could always call first."

"*He* did." Donovan bounded into the room. He eyed first Michael, then me. He grinned when he spotted the cane. "Progress." Then he narrowed his eyes. "How long have you been standing?"

"We just got here. Michael put the coffee on. I presume you'd like a—"

Donovan threw his arm around Michael's shoulders. "My new best friend."

Michael grinned goofily. "You're an easy guy to please."

"Oh, you have no idea."

"Donovan," I growled.

His gaze snapped up at my warning tone. His grin turned wicked. "Oh, this is going to be so much fun."

"Why don't you guys go sit in the living room?" Michael pointed to the coffee. "I can bring it in when it's done."

"Cole's going to go put his leg up." Donovan continued to hold his arm around Michael's shoulders. "We're going to talk."

Jesus fucking Christ.

Michael's grin slipped as he eyed Donovan.

You're right to be wary.

Yet Donovan was closer to me than anyone else in the world—except Michael and Caressa.

Well, since he knew all my secrets, maybe even closer. But if someone asked me who my *best* friend was, I always answered Caressa and Michael.

Donovan winked.

My cue to leave.

66

I hobbled out, using my cane, and into the living room.

My floor-to-ceiling windows showed me the darkening gray skies outside. Snow in the forecast. I didn't like the idea of Caressa trudging around in the stuff.

You're going soft.

Because I didn't want her to suffer or because I wouldn't go out in the stuff myself? Well, unless I was skiing or shooting a scene. My director asked me to go out in the white shit, and I was all over that. A snowy night when I didn't have commitments? Sign me up for a streaming service and a nice quiet night in.

I positioned myself on the sectional and adjusted with a small pillow in my lower back. God, I felt so fucking old. Thirty-two wasn't old, but a weariness enveloped me. I wanted the injury healed. I wanted back on set. I wanted everything between Caressa, Michael, and myself settled.

Straining to hear noises from the kitchen proved futile, so I had to just sit back and stew in my own juices.

By the time the men emerged, the snow was starting to fall and my nerves were taut with tension.

Donovan handed me a coffee, then patted my knee. And winked. Again. He made his way over to his favorite chair.

Michael stood beside the sectional. I patted the seat beside me. He hesitated. My heart plummeted. He nodded and sat gingerly beside me. My equilibrium righted itself, and I draped my arm casually around him, trying to tuck him into my side. Several moments passed before he relaxed into the embrace.

"Michael and I were just chatting—"

I held my breath.

"—about your recovery. He says you're doing all your exercises and behaving yourself."

"In my presence, at least," Michael clarified.

"All the time," I interjected. No way was I leaving any room for equivocation.

Donovan sipped his coffee, eyeing me over the rim.

My gut churned.

"Relax." Michael pressed a hand to my chest. "We really did just talk about how you're doing."

I met his gaze. His hazel eyes were more green in the muted light of the late morning.

He held his stare. "And I also put a frozen pizza in the oven. Caressa'll pitch a fit, but there's enough pasta left over for the three of us for dinner."

"What, you're not inviting me?"

Both Michael and I turned to Donovan.

Michael sniggered. "Uh, we're still reeling from your last visit."

Donovan cocked his head in question.

"You know, when you suggested I should be your date for the gala while Caressa and Cole attend together?"

"Or suggesting that Michael and I go together and that you'd accompany Caressa."

Donovan grinned widely. "Glad to see my suggestions prompted a discussion. What did you all decide?"

Michael and I exchanged looks. He turned to Donovan. "Cole and Caressa are going together. I'm fine to stay home on my own. I'm sure I'll have work."

"It's a charity benefit. Surely Cole can spring for a ticket for you—"

"I can buy my own ticket." Michael's voice was a low warning growl.

Given the cost of the tickets, I wasn't certain that was the case. Even if he did have that kind of cash sitting around, I was pretty sure we could find better uses for it.

I squeezed his thigh. "I'll get you a ticket, if you want to come." *Please, don't be jealous.*

He gave me a curt nod—whether in acknowledgment for my offer, acceptance of the offer, or merely the reassurance I needed—I wasn't sure.

"Cole tells me you found the dungeon."

Michael's hand, which had been resting gently on my chest, tightened. Again, he looked back and forth between Donovan and myself.

After a beat, I gave him a nod.

He turned to face Donovan. "Yeah. Well, not me. Caressa did while she was looking for Christmas decorations yesterday."

"They're in the garage." Something I should have said a long time ago.

He cocked his head toward me, and his eyes rolled up toward the ceiling. "Those large plastic bins on the upper shelves?"

"Yeah, one of them is decorations."

"You might want to label them, although maybe it's a good thing Caressa didn't figure it out."

I nodded. "Yeah, she's pretty strong, but those bins are heavy. Next year I'll hire someone to put everything out. I was so busy that I didn't even get around to hanging Christmas lights."

Donovan snickered.

Michael and I tore our gazes away from each other to look over at him.

He held up his hands in surrender. "I'm just thinking what you've been up to."

I did some quick mental calculations. "Oh."

Michael's hand tightened on my chest.

"No, nothing bad. We just…had a couple of parties in late November and early December. Before I found out Caressa was coming home." Which had come completely out of the blue. We'd finished a night of harrowing shooting on a building in the downtown core, and when I checked my phone on the way home, I discovered she was not only back in the country but wanted to meet me with Michael at the pub. Had that really only been two weeks ago?

"Parties?"

Donovan laughed.

Fucking laughed.

Michael shot him a glare.

"Oh, my young friend, I have much to teach you."

"We're the same age, for fuck's sake." Michael's tone clearly held the note of irritation I'd learned precipitated him either blowing up or, more likely, walking away.

The oven timer beeped. Michael rose to his feet. He pointed to my half-empty mug. I handed it over. He inclined his head toward Donovan. My friend shook his head. Michael headed to the kitchen.

"Will you knock it the fuck off?" I spat the words low, even though Michael likely couldn't hear.

"Cole."

Donovan's tone had me straightening.

"You called me last night in a panic. You worried you were going to lose everything. I'm here to make sure you don't. But that means riling your man up a bit."

I wasn't sure I saw the logic, but I knew better than to speak up.

"Has he said anything else?"

Even knowing we were alone, I glanced over my shoulder. "They said they're intrigued. I just…we haven't had any substantive discussions."

"You get a sense if either's a Top?"

"Jesus, Donovan."

His grin was unrepentant. "It's a fair question to ask."

And one I'd only asked myself a million times since they used the word *intrigued* last night.

I adjusted slightly, wincing.

He started to get up.

I waved him back. "Just a muscle cramp. Too much sitting around doing nothing."

"Well, aside from doing your exercises, you shouldn't be doing anything else. Seriously, Cole."

"No question, buddy. I'm doing everything Zoey tells me to. I want back on set as soon as possible. I'll do anything to make that happen."

"Even forgo pleasure with your *best* friends?"

No missing the emphasis.

Michael snickered as he entered the room. He caught my gaze as he handed me the steaming pizza. "He might've had a momentary lapse last night."

Fuck.

"But Caressa put him in his place, and he's stayed there ever since." He raised both eyebrows before turning to hand Donovan his plate. "He gets it. And we don't want him to risk his recovery. He's a bear with a thorn in his paw, and we're willing to be patient."

I kind of resented the implication I was not better

than a pissed-off wildlife creature—but he wasn't wrong.

Michael vanished. Donovan eyed me. I took a huge bite of piping-hot pie. Within moments, Michael was back with two glasses of ice water. This time, he snagged Donovan's coffee mug.

"I can—"

He waved Donovan off. "My pleasure." Then he was gone again.

"And here I worried you might be suffering."

I glared.

Michael returned with his own pizza and water. He plopped down right next to me, then put his drink on the coffee table. "I'm curious." He took a bite.

Donovan nodded slowly as he chewed. Finally, he ventured, "About BDSM?"

"Yes." He dipped his crust in a small pile of salad dressing—one of his odd quirks. "And Caressa is as well. But we're ignorant—and we know it. I mean, Google's great and all—"

"No way." Donovan sat up straighter. Then relented. "Okay, some first-person blogs talking about the lifestyle are good. But everything needs to be curated. Carefully reviewed. There's a shit ton of misinformation out there and plenty of people who'll be happy to exploit your ignorance."

"Fair enough." Michael glanced between the two of us. "So how am I supposed to know what to do?"

"We'll teach you—"

"I'll teach you," I said over Donovan's offer.

Michael chuckled. "You afraid you're going to lose me to him?"

Until that moment, I hadn't.

And maybe I should have.

Donovan was a damn attractive man with his dark skin, dark-brown eyes, toned body, and quick wit. Any guy would be lucky to have him.

"Cole." Michael's tone expressed his exasperation. He turned to Donovan. "No offense."

Donovan held up his hands. "None taken. I can see where your heart lies, and I think that's awesome. I don't poach. Ever."

Which was the absolute truth and did ease my stress—a bit.

"I'm also someone who's been in the lifestyle for almost fifteen years, and although this guy's good"—he indicated me—"he's not a teacher."

His words struck me. No, I wasn't a teacher. Never had been. I was a practitioner. A Top. A Dominant. I could do, but I certainly couldn't teach.

"You're proposing you…teach me?" Michael tilted his head. "How does that work?"

"Depends what you want to learn."

Michael made a sound of frustration at Donovan's comment. "How am I supposed to know what I want if I've never done anything?"

Donovan steepled his fingers. "I always recommend starting with receiving. If you don't know how something feels, then you'll have a tough time satisfying your partner."

"So you mean getting whipped."

"Whipped, flogged, paddled. I wield a riding crop with ease, am amazing with ropes, and love CBT."

"Donovan." I injected as much warning as I could. "CBT?"

I faced Michael. "Cock and ball torture."

His hand went protectively to his cock.

Donovan laughed.

Yet again, I shot a warning glare at my friend. Then I turned back to my lover. "It's not all about the pain. I can elicit a lot of pleasure as well."

"Orgasm denial is one of his favorite tricks." Donovan crossed his legs casually. "And he's a master at delivering multiple orgasms."

Michael's eyebrows nearly rose to his hairline.

"I'm all about the pleasure." I reached out to scrape my hands through his hair. "And yeah, if you want, there can be pain. But we start slow, take it at your pace, and stop when you've had enough."

"How will I know when I've had enough?" He cleared his throat. "And what do you get out of it?"

The eternal question asked of Dominants.

"I get pleasure from knowing I've given someone else pleasure—given them what they want. And you might not know at first. That's totally fine. We experiment together. We learn together. It's possible we won't find anything that works for you."

His face actually fell, and his eyes grew wide with distress.

"Or we might find a smorgasbord of things that get you off and leave you begging for more."

"Where does Donovan come in? If you can do all those things…"

"I can help if you or Caressa decides you want to Top." Donovan grinned wickedly.

"Oh." A slow blush stole across Michael's face at his words. "That sounds…interesting."

"You have no idea." Donovan uncrossed his legs and leaned forward. "So when do you want to get started?"

Chapter Seven

Caressa

Working Christmas Day generally sucked. Knowing Miles, and other co-workers, were home with their families helped. A bit.

Losing a patient on Christmas took away any possible joy from the world.

Especially when that patient hadn't needed to die. Okay, she probably would have anyway, but there had been a window when we might have saved her. When Franklin might have saved her. But he'd ignored my suggestion of aortic aneurism with an atypical presentation and had posited the woman had an upset stomach from too many pancakes. By the time she felt the tear in her chest, the time for early intervention had passed. We rushed her to surgery, but she died on the table.

Word filtered back to the ER how the distraught husband lost his shit on the surgeon and had to be restrained. I expected the guy to come down here and go after Franklin and myself.

He hadn't.

I was eternally grateful. Not so much concerned about myself—I could hold my own—but worried Franklin would open his big mouth. I had no doubt he'd throw me under the bus. He'd told the surgeon that he'd had no idea she might have the aneurism and that because of the asymptomatic presentation, he couldn't possibly have known.

Whether or not he knew I'd overheard his conversation, I couldn't be sure. But I tucked myself into a stairwell and carefully documented the entire incident. I was going to have to learn to cover my ass when working with him.

I need a new job.

Except I didn't. I'd helped a pile of people today. Some in little ways. Some in bigger ways. Of course, some people complained about the long wait times—others were just grateful to see a nurse at all. I believed in our universal healthcare system, but things felt even more broken than the last time I'd worked within the confines of the program. Sometimes I felt my job was to man the life raft and to make sure no one went overboard unnoticed.

Michael sat patiently in his SUV, waiting for me.

After I was in and secure, I pecked him on the cheek. "We need to get my car."

He grunted as he pulled into traffic.

"What does that mean?"

"It means Cole's upgrading to a new SUV, and he wants to give you his little electric."

"And when did this discussion take place?"

As we went up the Burrard Street Bridge, he waffled.

"When?"

"As we, uh, sat around."

I crossed my arms. "And what did you do today?"

"Well, frankly, not a whole lot." He veered to the right as we disembarked the bridge. "Cole did his exercises. We ate frozen pizza for lunch—"

I growled.

"Well, we have just enough pasta for three for tonight. I promise we'll do better tomorrow." He stopped at a red light.

It being Christmas night, the heavy traffic surprised me.

"And Donovan might've come over." He studiously looked anywhere but at me.

Interesting.

"And…" I was just about at my wit's end and not interested in playing around tonight. I needed a shower, food, and bed. In that order.

"We might've discussed BDSM." He drove through the intersection on a green light.

Well, shit. "And how did that discussion go?"

"Uh, something like I'm an excellent teacher. Oh, why would I need a teacher? Well, do you want to do or be done to? Uh, I don't know. Well, I'm here to help you figure that out."

He didn't differentiate the voices, but from context, I sorted out who said what. "And Cole?"

"Well, he's a doer but not a teacher. He feels if I— or you—wants to do something, we're best learning from Donovan."

"Holy shit."

"Yeah, my thought exactly. I mean, I never actually thought about doing it to other people. And yet I'm also having trouble picturing Cole doing it to me. Or you, for that matter."

I shot out my hands. "I'm not doing anything to anyone." Even as I said the words, I felt the truth of my conviction. "The thought of inflicting pain…"

"Donovan and Cole maintain it's about pleasure as well. I just… We need to talk about this."

"Not tonight, okay? I'm exhausted."

He shot me a glance.

Ten years ago, I'd come home from a twelve-hour shift with energy to spare. As a newly minted RN, I'd had enthusiasm in spades.

Those days were a long-distant memory.

"I'll heat up dinner while you shower. After you eat, we can all go to bed."

"You guys don't have to."

"Maybe not. But we'll want to. He and I can…do other things."

I snickered. "You're really getting into this. Like I said, that must've been some hand job."

"You have no idea." He sighed as he pulled into the driveway and raised the garage door. "Over dinner, will you tell us what happened today?"

I shot him a glance as he drove in. He shut off the engine and hit the remote.

"If Cole buys another electric car, that'll make three. How are we going to charge all three at the same time?" I was grasping at straws. Being obstinate.

He grasped my hand. "We'll make it work."

"There's nothing wrong with my car."

"Caressa, you know I love you. And it's out of that deep and abiding love that I tell you it's amazing that piece of junk is still on the road. You can donate it or something. Or scrap it and give away the cash. Just…don't drive it again, okay?"

"Cole doesn't need a new car." Now I sounded churlish.

"Come inside, and we can discuss it together."

We exited the car and headed into the house.

I let my backpack fall to the floor, then I removed my gloves, coat, and boots. "I sure won't miss winter."

Michael snickered. "Uh, winter's barely four days old."

"Whatever." I might have grumbled that.

When I went to snag my backpack, however, he took it away. "I'll sort out your lunch stuff while I heat dinner."

"Where's Cole?"

"Ordered to stay on the couch by Donovan."

"Is he okay?"

He nodded. "Just stubbornly wanting to do more. So, nothing new."

"Fair enough." I held his gaze. "Thank you for coming to get me. Thank you for heating up dinner."

"Least I can do. I just…" He cleared his throat. "I can't imagine you barely having started your journey to Mission City, knowing you'd be turning around in less than eight hours. That's not a life."

"Not being able to afford rent in Vancouver is a thing, Michael." But yeah, driving out to the Valley, barely getting any sleep, and then having to come back would have sucked shit.

"You never have to worry about it again." He pressed a kiss to my temple and watched as I dragged my sorry ass up the stairs.

I supposed I could have gone to Cole's bathroom—our bathroom—but my pajamas were up here along with my toiletries. I should grab spare toothbrushes for Michael and myself to put in Cole's bathroom.

Jesus, this is my life.

I stripped out of my scrubs, tossed them in the

laundry hamper, and pulled out a pair for tomorrow. I laid them on the bed, then headed into the bathroom for a shower.

Since I wasn't a dawdler and because my hair didn't need to be washed—thank God no one had puked on it—I was done pretty quickly. I donned my pajamas, a warm, fluffy robe, and my thickest socks.

Wearily, I sighed. We still had presents to do. I'd be happy to watch Cole and Michael open their symbolic gifts from me, but pasting on a smile while opening gifts I didn't need? That didn't appeal. At all.

I trudged down the stairs, trying to put on a cheerful face and not feel like I carried the weight of the world on my shoulders.

Michael stood at the microwave. He spotted me, grabbed a plate and fork, and handed them to me. "I put a glass of water in the dining room for you. Cole's waiting. Can I steep a tea for you? Chamomile?"

He was in such earnest. He gave me puppy-dog eyes. The ones I could never say no to.

"That'd be lovely, thank you."

"Great. I just gave Cole his plate, and I'll be in momentarily."

Seeing he had everything in hand, I headed to the dining room. Cole indicated I should sit at the head of the table.

I considered for a long moment before doing as bade. This wasn't a comfortable place for me. "Michael should get the spot."

"Why?" Cole cocked his head.

"Well, he did food prep."

"We can take turns, you know. Or flip a coin."

"A coin only has two sides."

He laughed. "Okay, you've got me there."

Michael breezed in. "Please, eat." He made his way to my right and sat.

I also didn't like this angle because I had to move my head back and forth to see each guy. I was so tired that even such a simple movement caused a wave of fatigue to wash over me.

"We'll get you right into bed." Cole's eyes shone bright with concern.

"I'm fine. We have, you know, presents."

"We can do presents in bed." Michael offered a grin as he spun spaghetti around his fork. "We're adults. We can do whatever we want in bed."

Cole snickered.

I tried for a smile but couldn't manage.

Cole dropped his fork and snagged my left hand. "What is it?"

"Lost another patient." I bit my lip.

"Which I imagine happens." Michael snagged my other hand. "Another child?"

I shook my head. "No. And probably not preventable. But I'll always wonder."

In response to Cole's raised eyebrow, I took a deep breath and began my recitation of the afternoon's events.

Twenty minutes later, Michael was reheating our food, and Cole continued to grip my hand. "The man's a menace."

"Franklin? Yeah, just a bit. He used to be a really good doctor…"

"Was he, Caressa? Was he really? Or were you only seeing what you wanted to see?"

He had a good point. My gut reaction was that no, he had been a good doctor. I'd never had rose-colored glasses about him—or anyone else.

So you tell yourself.

I met Cole's gaze as Michael returned with our food. "I'm sorry, Michael."

He patted my shoulder. "All good. I'll be right back."

Cole finally released my hand, and he dug into his food. As promised, Michael returned within a few moments, and he sat down to begin eating as well. My appetite had waned.

"You have to eat, Caressa." Cole's quiet words startled me.

My gaze shot to him.

"I know you're emotionally upset—and I'm worried that if bad things keep happening on shifts you share with Franklin, things will get dicey for you—but for now, you need to keep up your strength."

Again, he wasn't wrong.

Still, I struggled to swallow the great food down. Well, decent food. Michael would have done a much better job, but I'd managed okay.

"How about I heat up some soup for you?" Michael started to rise.

I waved him off. "I'll be okay. If I finish half, then drink the tea, I think that'll do me in."

He nodded.

When we finished our food, I snagged the plates. Michael and Cole's easily fit beneath mine since they had cleared theirs. That brought me a modicum of pleasure—at least I hadn't poisoned us.

Michael followed with the glasses, and we silently filled the dishwasher. While I turned it on, he heated my tea.

After he handed it to me, he cocked his hip on the counter. "We can do presents in bed, or I can waylay Cole, and we can do them another day. You've been through hell today, and you have to be back there in ten hours."

And despite everything, I was someone who needed a good night's sleep to function optimally. I could survive on less, but I knew, from long experience, that tomorrow would be a struggle and I'd be more prone to make a mistake.

Still, Christmas did come around only once a year. I should at least try to make it special.

"Presents in bed sounds delightful." I nodded and carried my tea out to the living room.

Cole stood next to the tree. Michael stepped forward and started to gather the few boxes. I tried to help, but he waved me off. Cole snagged my hand, and we headed to the bedroom together. We parted ways at the threshold of the bathroom.

Damn.

I also needed to pee, so I put the mug of tea on one of the nightstands in Cole's room. I plugged in my phone, then headed for the guest bathroom on the other side of the house. Even the thought of stairs was enough to fell me. Once I completed my tasks, I splashed cold water on my face. The woman staring at me in the mirror looked…haggard. I was only two days into a five-day stretch, and I already wished it was over. Vanity had me pinching my cheeks to give them a bit of color.

By the time I returned to the bedroom, Cole sat in his place on the right side of the bed, naked and under the covers.

Or at least I assumed he was naked.

Michael stood on the other side of the bed, arranging the presents. He indicated I should get in. "Caressa sandwich."

"Caressa has to get up early for work." Before he could interject, I held up my hand. "I don't need you to make me breakfast and to drive me."

"But I'm going to anyway, so just get in. I'll hand you the tea."

Uncertain of the value of arguing when exhaustion was already pulling me down, I acquiesced and sat in the center of the bed.

Michael handed me the mug of still-warm tea and then sat at the end of the bed with his legs crossed. He wore pajama pants and nothing else. His light dusting of chest hair shone in the low light, and his nipples pebbled in the cold.

"I'm sure we can turn up the temperature." Because *that* was the important thing I needed to bring up right now.

He waved me off. "We'll all be under the blankets soon, and we'll be plenty warm."

He wasn't wrong. Every night so far in our arrangement, I'd been toasty warm. But not too hot, thank God.

Michael handed me the first box with a glint in his eye.

I didn't want the attention to be on me, but his look of delight pushed me to smile back and unwrap the gift. "Oh, slippers."

"You can exchange them. If they're too big or too small or if you don't—"

"They're perfect, Michael, thank you." I pointed to the identical gifts—one for Cole and one for him.

Both men, simultaneously, opened their gifts. Michael gasped, and Cole cleared his throat. My gaze traveled between the two of them.

"This is…" Michael held the frame. "Perfect."

At my coaxing, that night two weeks ago in the pub on Commercial Drive, I'd insisted on a selfie. Then a server had leapt over and offered to take another shot for us. Truthfully, hers had been much better. So, not a true selfie, but a great photo of the three of us commemorating…being together again after five years? Memorializing our last night as platonic friends? There had certainly not been—to me, at least—any hint of the radical changes that would take place mere hours later.

"Seems kind of silly to give you both one—"

Michael shook his head. "I want this for my desk in the office."

"And I'm putting mine on the mantel in the living room." Cole pressed a kiss to my temple. "This is perfect."

Well, okay, then.

Michael handed me a wrapped box from the jewelry store. I held it in my hands for several long moments.

"From the two of us." Cole offered a sheepish smile. "And you can return it. No questions asked."

Finally, after receiving a nod from Michael, I opened the box.

The exquisite hummingbird brooch sat in a nest of satin cloth. The sapphire eye sparkled, and I assumed the gems sprinkled in the wings were diamonds. "It's…" Words failed me as I blinked several times.

"For the gala." Michael offered a smile. "You and Cole are going to make a handsome couple."

"But—"

He rescued my mug, which I almost turned over.

As he put it on the nightstand, Cole took my hands. "We've agreed to this. For now. I'm still trying to convince Michael to attend."

"As Donovan's date?"

Michael snorted. "Uh, probably not." He offered a sheepish grin. "We'll make it work." He handed me two envelopes.

I slid the first one open to find a gift certificate from him to a medical supply store.

"Nothing wrong with getting some new scrubs." Michael, being ever practical.

He wasn't wrong—mine were fraying at the seams.

I slid open the second. A gift certificate from Cole for a store I'd never heard of for an amount of money that had me almost dropping the paper.

"They do vintage and secondhand dresses. I thought you might want to do something unique." He patted my knee. "Or I can take you to the boutiques downtown, and you can find a gown. You're going to have to go all out for this."

Because Cole Hamilton's date would be a reflection of him. I needed to turn heads.

That thought terrified me.

"The brooch is lovely, guys." I held up the gift certificates. "You realize this involves shopping." One of my least favorite activities.

"Do you want me to hire you a private shopper? Oh, Elouise would love to go shopping with you."

"Elouise Hynes? *The* Elouise Hynes?" The woman was nominated for a Golden Globe and had Oscar buzz for her latest film. Someone had been talking about her in the break room. About her being Canadian, a *good* lesbian—whatever the fuck that meant—and how they had heard she now had a role on Cole's show. "Did I hear she's on *VJ*?"

Cole nodded. "Yeah, she plays my new executive assistant. She's badass. Not quite up there with Lyric mind, Julie's character, but they've got me surrounded by kick-ass women."

I yawned. "That's good."

Michael gently removed all the presents and laid them on the chaise lounge.

Cole coaxed me under the blankets. "I wish you were naked."

"You'd be up to funny business."

He pressed a hand to his chest. "You wound me. If you say we go to sleep, then we go to sleep."

I glanced over at Michael. He nodded. And removed his pajama pants. I huffed. And removed my pajamas. By the time Cole turned his light off, I was already drifting away.

Chapter Eight

Michael

After an amazing week, I sauntered into my office with renewed purpose.

Caressa'd worked six of the seven days since Christmas—leaving her worn out and spent at the end of each day.

Cole and I tried to rally her spirits, but it had been a challenge. Now she was heading into a more normalized routine of four days on and four days off. She'd finished her last shift this morning, and although I wanted to pick her up, she was insistent I head into the office on time. Which, for me, meant seven a.m. My actual work start time was eight thirty, but I liked to get in early when I was the only one around to get settled.

I booted up my laptop and let the memories from the last week wash over me.

Seeing as Cole and I were off work together, we'd spent a lot of time just hanging out. And making out. I worried it might feel awkward without Caressa, but she was thrilled to come home to hear I'd given Cole a blow job or he'd given me a hand job. I worried she might feel left out, but she never did. She just rolled with everything.

Or at least she appeared to.

I hadn't heard any more rumblings about Franklin—

which I took as a good sign.

And to top off what I hoped would be a spectacular New Year, Zoey was visiting again. Her third time since Christmas. Cole was ever so hopeful that some forms of sex might be back on the table.

Caressa would probably be happy about a pronouncement of Cole's gradual improvement.

I knew I would.

A knock sounded at my door.

With a jolt, I realized I'd been hazily wandering through reviewing my project for more than an hour—all the while reminiscing about the past week and looking forward to the future.

Pamela Strickland stood in my doorway. The woman stood ramrod straight. Her blonde hair was pulled up into a topknot, and her blue eyes were keen on me. For a shorter woman, she carried a lot of power in her compact form.

I rose. "Sorry, did we have a meeting scheduled? I thought—"

She waved me off. "I knew you'd start early this morning, and I wanted to come by to have a quick chat."

My ears perked. "Why don't you come in?" I was about to offer her coffee when I noticed she had a travel mug in her hand. "May I top up your cup?"

"No, but thank you."

My office was the smallest in the firm—but I was also the youngest engineer with his own space, so I didn't mind.

Pamela and I sat in the two chairs that were situated across from my desk.

I didn't like the dynamic of sitting behind the desk and lording over whomever came in. The senior partner of the firm did that, and it always came off as a bit arrogant.

"So what's up?" I suppressed my curiosity as to why Pamela was here.

"I read your email."

I wracked my brain. I had a pile in my drafts that I planned to send throughout the day—I didn't want people to know how much work I'd done during the holidays. Despite the firm's drive to be the best in British Columbia, they regularly admonished us about putting in too many hours outside of the workday. We all did it— we'd just learned to stay quiet about it. Work/life balance was a thing.

Or so they told us.

"The email from before Christmas?"

She nodded. "I don't believe your calculations are correct."

Calculations I'd triple checked. Then had a colleague review them. They were correct. "You disagree because it means you can't have the façade you want."

Her lips pursed.

Nailed it. "Look, I'm certain you can come up with another design—you're a brilliant architect. But I can't make your design work."

"The Markham Towers in Sydney have a similar design."

"Perhaps." *Damn, should've looked into this further.* "But Sydney's building codes are slightly different from Vancouver. We're prone to earthquakes in a way they're not." I wasn't actually familiar with the building codes for Australia—but I'd sure as shit be looking them up as soon as this huddle concluded. "I did everything to try to make it work, but your design wouldn't be up to code, and even if it was, the elements you want are too dangerous to risk. I could offer a few suggestions—"

She held up her hand. "You're an engineer, Michael, not an architect." She used as much disdain for *engineer* as she used reverence for *architect*. Finally, she rose. "I'm going to speak to Wells."

I rose as well. "She's going to give you the same response, Pamela. The design is beautiful—but not practical for Vancouver."

"Vancouver deserves grand architecture."

"Vancouver also deserves towers that don't fall over in earthquakes because of poor designs." I found this statement obvious, but today it bore repeating.

Pamela huffed. "We'll see." She gave me a quick nod and departed.

I stood, unmoving. Go see Wells? Send Wells an email? Wait for Wells to come to me?

Not having a suitable answer, I moved back to my desk.

Tyanna Wells was the senior partner and one of the smartest women I knew. She'd done her master's in engineering at the University of British Columbia twenty-five years ago and kept up on all the latest news.

I was due for a site visit on my current project this afternoon. *Should I go now?* If I did, I could be here when—

My phone buzzed with an incoming text.

—Have you heard from Caressa?—

I glanced at my watch. Not quite nine.

—Maybe she got hung up at the hospital.—

I kicked myself when I remembered Caressa was

stubbornly driving her old car. Cole had a new electric SUV on order for himself. He'd give it to her in a heartbeat if there existed a chance in hell she'd take it. No such chance existed, so he planned to gift his old car to her.

—*You're right. I'm panicking over nothing.*—

—*Not nothing. Call me in an hour if she doesn't turn up.*—

—*Okay.*—

The Cole I knew wasn't generally a worrier—except when it came to Caressa. I still marveled we'd survived five years with her halfway across the world.

A knock at my door had me looking up.

Then scrambling to my feet. "Hello Tyanna."

I would have called her Ms. Wells, but she was quite insistent she was *just one of us*. In one sense she was— we all worked here. In another, her name was on the door and letterhead.

Tyanna's contrast to Pamela couldn't have been clearer. My boss was striking, tall, and lithe. In her heels, she was almost level with me. Her skin wasn't quite as dark as Donovan's, but it came close and matched her dark-brown eyes. Insightful eyes. Eyes that always saw more than she let on. This woman's intelligence rivaled everyone else's, and as often as not, she was smarter.

Her scrutiny unnerved me.

"Am I interrupting?"

Did she see me looking at my phone? Personal cell phone use wasn't regulated, but the general consensus was private stayed private and we were to focus on work while here. "Uh, not at all. Would you like to come in?"

She nodded, entered, and closed the door.

Oh shit.

92

I moved around to meet her, and when she sat, I did the same. "You're here about Pamela."

Tyanna nodded. "We had an interesting meeting."

"I can explain—"

"Which I appreciate." Yet she continued. "I've reviewed your notes, Michael, and they're thorough. I also reviewed your calculations. They're precise—which doesn't surprise me."

I nodded, hoping my face didn't betray my stress.

"But they're also…conservative."

Okay, that I hadn't expected. "I'm following the building codes."

"True, but you've built in a substantial buffer."

Which I'd done for all my projects since starting here. No one had ever questioned it. "The façade Pamela is proposing is dangerous."

She met my gaze. "I don't see it that way."

My gut twisted. "Are you asking me to redo the calculations on her proposal?"

She shook her head. "I've had Walter go over them, and he's come up with new numbers that will work. This is…a courtesy visit."

Well, shit. This was a "get with the program" visit. Slowly, I nodded.

"Wonderful." Tyanna rose. "We need the documentation submitted to the city as soon as possible, and I'm looking forward to having you on board with the project."

I rose as well, although more slowly. My phone buzzed. *Damn*.

"Do you need to get that?"

"No. Not important."

The phone buzzed again.

Gabbi Grey

Her eyebrow arched.

"Just a friend concerned about a friend. It'll keep."

"Well, I'm glad to hear you have friends. You work too hard, Michael. I suspect you didn't relax over your vacation."

I flashed to the carnal pleasures Cole, Caressa, and I'd enjoyed. Or the massages I'd given Caressa. Oh, I'd relaxed... Unbidden, a heat raced up my cheeks.

She chuckled. "Wow, I had that wrong. Well, good for you. I look forward to connecting on the Jorgen project later in the week."

My phone buzzed again.

"Go check it, Michael. And I hope everything's all right. I'll see myself out."

As she departed, I rounded my desk and snatched my phone. Four texts from Cole. I opened the final one.

—She's home safe. We need to talk.—

I moved to my office door, and for only the fifth time or so in the seven years I'd been here, I closed it. I was big on transparency, and to me, closed doors meant something to hide. I hit call.

"Hey, sorry to bother you." Cole's voice sounded strained.

"You called Michael." Caressa. In the background. Clearly pissed. "I told you. I fell asleep."

"What?" I tried to understand.

"Caressa went to your old building because apparently you missed something of hers and she wanted to bring some of the food in the pantry..." No missing the exasperation in Cole's voice. "And she was tired and lay down on the bed for a quick nap."

My heart took a knock.

"Okay." I dropped into my chair. "So she's okay.

94

How are you?"

"Zoey's cleared me for…stuff…"

I dearly wanted to ask. But if I didn't miss my mark, Caressa was fuming. "Put her on the phone."

No missing the huff as she took the phone. "He shouldn't have called you."

"*He* was worried, Caressa. I would've wanted to know."

"You guys can't panic every time I'm ten minutes late."

I glanced at my wall clock. "Over two hours."

"Still." She huffed again. "I might've gone for breakfast with Miles."

"Who's Miles?"

"My co-worker."

Ouch. Yeah, I deserved that rebuke. I was out of line. "We're not saying you're not free to do whatever you want. But you've just worked an insane number of days—"

"I had one off."

"One in nine, Caressa. That's nuts. I hope you never do something so stupid again." I winced at my strident tone. This wasn't like me. I'd survived five years of never knowing where she was. A couple of hours shouldn't matter either way.

"And Cole's new SUV is arriving today. He wants me to donate my car."

"Donate? Oh, that program where the money goes to kids in need? That's a great idea. And you'll get a tax receipt."

Another huff. "I'll be beholden to Cole for *giving* me a very expensive car."

"It's six years old and I'm quite certain has

95

depreciated—"

"Watch it, Michael."

Her tone had me shutting up. I waited for her to speak, but she stayed silent.

"Why don't you take another nap? Or you and Cole could watch one of his movies…" *Or you can do whatever Zoey's approved Cole to do.*

Yeah, didn't want to think about that one.

"I don't want another nap. I want to be able to go out for a few hours without everyone panicking."

This time, I was the one who drew in a long breath, then blew it out. "If you'd texted one of us, we wouldn't have worried." Well, since she insisted on driving the death trap, we probably would have. But she'd get my point.

"Michael, I can't live like that." After a moment, she spoke again. "That goes the same for you."

I couldn't hear Cole's response. But I guessed a grunt. "Can we talk about this tonight?"

"There's nothing to talk about. I'm going out. I'll talk to you later."

I expected Caressa to cut the line, but Cole spoke before the line disconnected.

"That didn't go well."

"Is she leaving?"

"Well, she's in her scrubs, so she hasn't had a shower yet. I don't think she's mad enough to stomp out without showering first. Damn, she's got to be tired."

"She's got a point, Cole. We can't be cavemen, always insisting on knowing where our woman is." I let that sink in. "You wouldn't want to be accountable to me in that way either, I don't think. And if I go for drinks with the folks after work and forget to call, I don't want you calling out the calvary."

"I'd just track your phone."

His deadpan had me smiling. Obviously, if he could have, he would have done it with Caressa's. He likely didn't have the technology to do it to either of us.

Another conversation we needed to have.

"I have to get back to work."

"Yeah, of course. We'll talk when you get home."

"Not sure I like the sound of that."

"Oh, but we have things to discuss." He added just the right licentious tone to the ultimate word. Then he hung up.

I laid my phone back on my desk. Completely wrung out. And it wasn't even ten in the morning.

Chapter Nine

Caressa

Damn infuriating fucking idiots.

If I thought I could bash their heads together and knock some sense into them, I'd totally do it.

Alas, both their noggins were rock solid. As evidenced by the knock to the head that Cole had sustained during rehearsal of Macbeth with a broadsword. Or the time Michael'd gotten a kick to the head on the soccer field. He hadn't even had a moment of dizziness or headache. And I'd have known—given how close we'd been in high school.

We'd lived out of each other's pockets. Had been necessary, in order to survive.

But now?

I was thirty-two fucking years old. If I wanted to take some time, then I was allowed to take some time.

Apparently, my *lovers* didn't feel the same way.

The struggle's real.

Michael'd been right about one thing—working eight of nine days was nuts. I was young, healthy, and somewhat fit. It should have been a cakewalk.

By the morning of the ninth day, I was ready to drop.

And I'd only meant to rest for a moment on Michael's bed. No guys, no shuffling, no warm bodies— just the promise of a few minutes of blissful quiet. Not to say they hadn't left me alone to sleep when I worked nights. They had. But they had also hovered a lot—and that got really fucking irritating really fucking quickly. After having spent five years living on my own terms, I found their attention stifling.

Yet I knew they had the best intentions.

As I sat in a coffee shop on Broadway, nursing a cappuccino, I tried not to dwell. I didn't need the caffeine, but I wanted to stay awake until bedtime tonight.

Maybe tonight we'd finally be able to make a Cole sandwich.

Who knew sleeping three to a bed could be so complicated?

Not that I was complaining—just not sure how to figure out these dynamics.

I appreciated the guys had left me alone most of the last week. The mind had *almost* been willing, but the body had been completely incapable. The stress at work was getting to me. Several nasty bugs were ripping through Vancouver—including a deadly flu—and we'd been slammed every minute of all my shifts. Adding trauma cases, overdoses, heart attacks, strokes, and all the other ailments possible and it had been a rough go. The epidemiologists thought we were through the worst of the influenza wave, but people had gathered for New Year's just two days ago and had likely spread more germs.

All the more reason to hunker down and never go out in public again.

I glanced around the busy coffeeshop. Okay, so good in theory but hard to put into practice. Another sip of coffee had me wincing. *Going cold.* I snagged my phone. No new calls or texts. *Progress*.

Apparently, my request to be left alone was going to be honored. This time. I quickly reviewed my few outstanding texts and found nothing of import. Then I brought up my notes app. Slowly, I scrolled through everything I'd written up about Franklin. Nothing personal, thank God. After the aneurism incident, he hadn't made any more suggestions that we get together for coffee.

He wasn't wearing a ring—but he hadn't six years ago either.

Is he still married, or did she finally leave him? Is he still a distant and crappy father? Will he ever change?

Not that I cared. I didn't.

Or so you tell yourself.

I'd dated him for almost a year, having no idea about his wife and two daughters. Being a home-wrecker was inconceivable to me, and yet I'd done it. Unknowingly— or so I told myself. In hindsight, the signs had been there.

Cole and Michael had thought me leaving for Africa was a bit of an overreaction.

I hadn't.

Getting out of Vancouver had been an imperative.

That overwhelming feeling of grief engulfed me yet again for what I'd done. What I'd had to do. What I almost never let myself regret.

Deep in the recesses of my mind, I played the *what-if* game. What if I'd stayed? What if I'd told Michael and Cole the truth? What if I hadn't run?

I wouldn't be the same person today—that was for sure.

Would I be as strong? I'd done ten tours in a war-torn African country. I'd witnessed poverty and deprivation and inhumanity on a grand scale as well as the microcosm of my little camp where I worked. I'd also broken at the end.

A moment I certainly wasn't proud of.

A moment I still remembered with shame.

A moment that had changed the trajectory of my life. Again.

"Is this seat taken?"

I glanced up to find a handsome man pointing to the seat across from me. I quickly scanned the shop and found every other seat occupied. "No, it's not taken." I rose and tucked my cell phone into my back pocket.

He blinked his deep-brown eyes, and when he shook his hair, his short light-brown curls bobbed. "I didn't mean for you to leave."

Is he… God, I'm so out of practice… "It's okay. I need to be getting home soon. My boyfriend's expecting me."

Boyfriend. Boyfriends.

How awkward could that conversation wind up being?

"Well, he's a lucky man."

I narrowed my eyes.

He held up his hands. "I didn't mean anything by it. You just…seem contemplative. Like someone with depth." He scratched his scalp. "Sometimes, I think we're missing more of that in this insanely fast world we live in."

I couldn't argue. Blink and the world would entirely pass us by in a heartbeat.

"I'm Lawrence." He held out his hand.

After a moment, I shook it. "Caressa."

"You sure I can't buy you a coffee? You can tell me

about your boyfriend."

Again, I sensed no underlying intention. He apparently accepted I had a boyfriend and was just being friendly.

Which boyfriend will you tell him about?

And on that note… "Thank you, Lawrence. I really do need to be going." I snagged my ceramic coffee mug. "But I hope you have a good day."

He nodded as I headed off. I dropped the mug off with the barista and headed back into the cold air.

Except I didn't want to go home.

I snapped my fingers. That store… I dug through my backpack and found the two gift certificates. Not that I needed to justify my absence—but if I came home bearing packages, then I'd likely face less scrutiny.

First, I hopped on the 99 and headed toward the medical supply store, located near Vancouver General Hospital. Michael'd gone a little overboard, and between his generosity and the lingering Boxing Day prices, I wound up with five new pairs of scrubs.

I headed back toward Cambie Street and caught the Canada Line Skytrain to Waterfront Station and walked up Granville Street to the store listed on the gift certificate from Cole.

An hour later, I hailed a cab. No way was I going to carry the plastic-covered dress as well as the bag with the shoes plus the sack with the scrubs on the buses back to Cole's. Not to mention the excessively expensive clutch I'd tucked into my backpack.

The driver was only too happy to chat while he drove through downtown, wending his way over to the Burrard Street Bridge.

Part of me wanted silence, but the rest of me wasn't

bothered by the mindless chatter as it calmed the nerves of worrying about what I'd face when I got home.

Night came early, and dark had set in while I was in the vintage dress shop. The sales associate had been a little judgmental until I showed the gift certificate, and then the man had become absolutely obsequious. Clearly, he'd known who the giver was, as well as the likely occasion, because he'd presented me with some of the fanciest dresses I'd ever seen in my life. Certainly much gussier than I'd ever select.

We'd settled somewhere in the middle with a dress that I called understated. But still eye-catching. And heels that were tall but not skyscraper.

Practice was in order.

The driver pulled into the driveway.

I yanked my card out of my wallet. I selected a generous tip, tapped my card, and gathered my packages.

"Would you like a hand?" The cabbie gave me a smile.

Michael emerged from the door and headed my way.

"Thank you. I'll be okay."

I opened the cab door and thrust the dress bag and two others into Michael's waiting arms. He raised his eyebrows, nodded, and indicated the driver.

I waved him off. Jesus, he didn't think I could pay for a fucking cab? We needed to talk.

As I entered the house, though, all thoughts of confrontation fled. The most delicious aroma assaulted my senses. I glanced at Michael. He shrugged. I locked the door, hung up my coat, then bent down to unlace my boots.

"This looks promising." Cole appeared in the doorway—without his cane.

I cocked my head.

"Short periods of time while my leg gets used to bearing weight again. I don't even feel a twinge."

After searching his face for any signs of deception, I found none. "Well, that's great."

"Will you give us a show after dinner?" He indicated the bags Michael held.

I hesitated.

"Yes, please." Michael grinned.

His encouragement pushed me out of my complacency and hesitation. "All right. I trust you have a tuxedo." I eyed Cole. "Or are you wearing a suit?"

"Tux all the way—that night's all about the glamour." He grinned, his blue eyes alight. "And I've got one on order for Michael."

Michael's jaw dropped.

I grinned.

"Why don't we put these in the bedroom?" Michael held up the bag.

He headed for the stairs, but I waylaid him. "Our bedroom."

His grin matched Cole's.

Still, exhaustion set in after the adrenaline rush of shopping. "I'm going to run my knapsack upstairs and wash up."

"You can do that in our bathroom." Cole arched an eyebrow.

"I just need a moment."

He nodded but didn't look pleased.

Well, tough shit.

I headed upstairs while Michael veered off toward the master bedroom. Once I got into the bedroom, I snagged my pajamas and changed into them after a quick shower. I left my hair up in a messy bun because I just couldn't deal with the wild curls. All the trying on dresses had left it super staticky, and I didn't want to think about it.

Is tonight a formal dinner? Is Donovan coming over?

After staring at myself in the mirror for a good twenty seconds—longer than I had in a very long time—I decided *fuck it*. The guys had seen me in my sleepwear before, and they would survive. If Donovan arrived, he wasn't likely to be titillated by thermal underwear. And besides, he'd let slip he was way more into guys these days. And I might have caught him checking out Michael's ass, but he'd made a joke, and rather than obsessing about how men were looking at my man sexually, I'd opted to let it go.

Donovan's penchant for irreverent flirting was one day going to get him in trouble, and I only hoped I'd be around to see it.

After grabbing the clutch, I made my way downstairs. I tried to inject some enthusiasm into my steps. Truthfully, though, exhaustion had set in, and I wasn't long for the world of the conscious.

In the kitchen, I found Michael removing that amazing-smelling food from the oven.

"Chicken?"

He nodded. "Rosemary chicken with glazed carrots, mini-potatoes, and fresh rolls."

"How the hell did you cook all that?"

"I might've stopped in at the bakery on my way home."

I nudged his shoulder.

He grinned. "And Cole peeled the carrots—you'll

find tonight's fare was a group effort."

"Well, I can't wait to eat it."

He gazed sharply at me, his eyes narrowing.

Shit. I needed to up my enthusiasm and push through the exhaustion. "I'll set the table."

"We thought we'd eat in here." He pointed to the high-top table.

I grinned. "You got a third stool." It would make things a little crowded as the set was really only made for two, but I loved the gesture.

"Cole did."

Said gentleman headed into the kitchen. "Yeah…seemed like the right thing to do. And I love the view from the dining room, but sometimes a little cozy meal is in order."

"Caressa hasn't eaten today."

My hand stilled over the forks. *Fuck.* After a moment of silence, I resumed counting out everything we needed. Cole sat. Michael dished up three heaping plates of food. He knew very well I wouldn't be able to eat that much, but he didn't seem to care.

I hadn't eaten enormous meals in Africa—my appetite had never been great after the Franklin debacle. I was well aware I'd lost a few pounds. I wasn't skinny and certainly didn't have an eating disorder, but I wasn't the way I had been before. Not that I'd ever been big either…food had been a luxury growing up. How the three of us turned out healthy and tall was a testament to school lunches and Michael's determination to sneak food for Cole and me as much as possible.

Determinedly ignoring both men, I set the table and included ice water. By the time I slipped onto my bar stool, Michael also sat. He gave us a nod and dug into his food. Cole speared a couple of baby carrots, eyed me, and popped them in his mouth.

God, this is going to be awful.

Yet I *was* hungry. The brownie with my drink at the coffee shop felt like a million years ago, and I hadn't eaten breakfast after the whole clusterfuck of falling asleep and being *late* home. "We need to talk about today."

"When you've finished eating." At Cole's words, I glared at him.

He glared right back.

Michael, who sat between the two of us, sighed. He sipped his water. "Caressa's got a point—we don't need to know where each of us is every moment of the day."

"Speak for yourself."

"Cole." I let out a little sigh. "When you're working, you don't need to be thinking about us. You had your *moment* today because you didn't have anything else to occupy your mind. You go back to work next week, and I promise you won't have time to worry about whether Michael works an hour late or if I take a nap before remembering to check in." I scowled. "I shouldn't have to check in."

"She's got a point." Michael glanced at Cole briefly before spearing a potato. "My schedule's going to be nuts in the next few months. I've submitted permit requests for the new tower. We have preliminary approval, so this is more of a rubber stamp. It's going to be one of the tallest structures in Vancouver and is going to take more than a year to complete. I'm still working on the tower that's almost finished. My attention's going to be divided, and I can't be worried about whether or not I've remembered to check in."

We turned our gazes to Cole.

He prodded his chicken with his fork. "I finally have you two, and you expect me to be lackadaisical about holding on? It's not safe out there."

I snorted. "Cole, Vancouver is one of the safest big cities in the world. Yes, I work in an inner-city emergency room. We have guards and police. Yes, Michael works on tall structures. He follows all the safety protocols. Neither of us take unnecessary risks." I pointed to his leg. "Seems to me that we should be more worried about you."

He started to wave me off but then halted mid-movement. "It's not that simple."

"Yeah, it really is." Michael lightly tapped the tines of his fork against his plate. "Your need to control could doom this relationship."

Cole sat up straighter.

"For you, it's all about control. Have you ever considered for Caressa and myself that it might be the same thing?" He gazed between the two of us. "We none of us had control growing up. We fought fiercely to be independent—and we succeeded."

"Together."

"Together." Michael nodded at Cole's interjection. "But we also found our own wings and eventually went our own ways. And yes, we're here under your roof. And yes, we're trying this crazy ménage thing."

"Not trying." I placed my hand over his to still it. Then I met Cole's gaze. "We're committed to this—but you have to meet us halfway. We all need to feel control in our lives. That means not ceding it to other people. At least, not in the day-to-day running of things."

Cole placed his fork on his plate. "I'm a Dominant.

It's who I am. I go through life needing to control things."

"And although Michael and I had an inkling of that before we agreed to move in, obviously neither of us understood to what extent that part of you dominates your life." I also laid down my fork. "But, Cole, you can't control everything. Despite your immense power at work, you still answer to a director and a producer."

He scrunched his nose.

"Well, Michael and I have people we answer to as well—and those professional relationships are damn important for us to keep our jobs."

"Can we at least create a group chat?"

That caught me off guard. I knew about them, of course, but had never actually done one before. Hell, I had, like, six people in my contact list.

Michael and Cole both pulled their phones from their back pockets. I sighed and started to get down.

Cole snagged my hand. "We don't need yours. We'll send a group text, and it'll start things. I want you to get a new phone."

"Here we go with the pronouncements again. My phone is perfectly fine."

"It doesn't have the latest security features." He indicated his phone. "I need the latest everything, Caressa, so it's hard to hack. Nothing is infallible, but I have to do my best. I should've bought you a phone for Christmas."

I flashed to the brooch—about which price I might have checked out on the website and had a panic attack. "You were more than generous."

"Still, we can go tomorrow while Michael's at work."

"This is going to become a battle if I don't yield, isn't it?"

Cole pressed a hand to his sternum. "I just want you to be safe. We can have them scrub your old phone, and you can donate it if that makes you feel better."

Damn man. "Yeah, that sounds good." Better to give in on this one and acknowledge my respect for his privacy so I could stand firm on other issues.

Cole's look of triumph was short-lived when I pointed at him. "But this whole *I'm a Dominant.* What does that even mean? You're going to boss us around for the rest of our lives?"

He rocked back and sat straighter. "Uh, I like the sound of that."

Michael snickered.

I wasn't going to yield so quickly. "We fought like hell to get out from under our parents' thumbs." And all our parents had subsequently died, but I wasn't going to bring that up. "Michael and I've worked damn hard to achieve independence. Why would we give that up?"

"Because it can be liberating."

This time, I snickered. Yet in the same moment, he'd intrigued me. "So me letting you order me around, and letting you hit me, will give me freedom?"

Michael, who had been sipping water, sputtered. "Damn." He grabbed a cloth napkin and wiped his mouth.

Cole always insisted we use cloth napkins—for every meal. As if that somehow made us more refined.

Veneer.

We'd always be just a step above street rats. We used to dumpster dive to find things to make our lives better. That we now sat in a multi-million-dollar house eating fantastic food spoke to our dedication to improving our lives—but we owed most of it to Cole. If not for him, I'd be living in a questionable two-bedroom apartment in the valley. Or sharing a one-bedroom condo with Michael. Instead, we lived in this palatial home with sprawling million-dollar views and every convenience imaginable.

"Are you all right?" Cole was concerned for Michael.

That touched me.

Michael blew a raspberry. "Uh, fine."

"Hitting is a strong word." Now Cole's attention was refocused on me. "The word has a negative connotation."

"So…beating? Striking? Whipping? Flogging?" With each word, my voice became breathier.

Cole set down his knife and fork. He hadn't cleaned his plate, but clearly, he'd had enough. I was surprised to find my plate was mostly empty. Michael'd devoured his entire meal.

"I'll help Michael clean up while you put on the dress and give us a show. Then we'll talk. In bed."

"I'm capable of cleaning up by myself—"

"You cooked."

"And you should be off your leg." He shot Cole a pointed glare. "I promise you there'll be other nights when you can help." He indicated over his shoulder. "I cleaned as I went, so there isn't much. I made chocolate pudding for dessert." He glanced at me. "With whipped topping."

My stomach, previously complaining about being full, did a little happy dance. "How about after the fashion show? So at least dinner can settle."

"Perfect." Michael rose.

Cole and I followed. I noticed his movements were still a little slow—not back to fighting form.

"We'll meet in the bedroom?" I was just making sure we were all on the same page.

My two men nodded.

With butterflies in my belly, I stalked off to try on the most expensive piece of clothing I would ever own.

I planned to give my men quite a show.

Chapter Ten

Cole

So…beating? Striking? Whipping? Flogging?
Jesus.

As I pissed, I tried to keep the images from invading my mind. The last thing I needed was for Caressa to see me getting hard at the prospect of inflicting pain.

Even if that encapsulated my life in a single thought.

I flushed the toilet, then washed my hands and brushed my teeth.

Crap. Forgot about the pudding. Oh well, worse things than chocolate tinged with mint.

Caressa appeared to still be in the walk-in closet.

"Do you need help?"

She grunted. I moved that direction.

She spotted me in the mirror and ducked behind the door, only poking her head around. "I managed. I'm just…" She pointed to her hair.

"We don't care."

"Well, I do." She scowled. "Go lie down."

Ah, bossy mood tonight. I was never quite sure when that side of her personality would rise to the surface. She accused me of being controlling, and yet she frequently barked orders. Usually when it had to do with my health, though, so I tended to listen to her. She had the absolute ability to tank everything by ratting me out to my physiotherapist.

Knowing that, I headed to the bed. Gingerly, I sat and carefully positioned myself in the middle. Goddamnit, I wanted a Cole sandwich tonight. Whoever was on my left would have to be mindful, but I wasn't worried. Zoey, bless her heart, had approved sex. As long as I was on the bottom and pretty much just lay there. Fine by me. Not how I normally operated, but I'd do just about anything to get lucky tonight. Twice, if the stars aligned for me.

Michael entered carrying a tray of three mini bowls of chocolate pudding. He winked. "To help us recover our strength."

I might have, in my exuberance, mentioned the green light. His eyes might have lit with excitement.

He headed to the bathroom and a few minutes later emerged. Naked and with a wide grin. Then he faltered. "Where's Caressa?"

"I'm here." No missing her frustration.

"Honestly, baby, we don't care about your hair."

Michael cocked his head. I imitated Caressa's long, curly tresses. He nodded. Then he made his way over to the bed and crawled in beside me, placing himself to my left.

Observant man. And prudent. Caressa often kicked out during her nightmares.

The nightmares we never talked about.

Once she woke up, Michael would wrap her in an embrace and hold her tightly until the tremors passed. Until she eventually went back to sleep. I wasn't ever sure if she woke completely—and I hoped one day to be the man offering her comfort. Without being able to turn on my side, cradling her with my body proved impossible—and that rankled.

Damn, I wanted to be healed. Yesterday wouldn't be soon enough.

But pushing myself would only make things worse. And risk a relapse. Which would prove catastrophic. So until I was properly healed, Michael would be the one offering the comfort.

Finally, after what felt like forever, Caressa made her dramatic entrance.

My breath caught.

Michael gasped.

She was a vision of loveliness. The sequined gown matched her pale-blue eyes and hugged her every curve. The cleavage was just above what might have been scandalous, and as the fabric hugged her, her breasts were shown off to full advantage. She teetered a little on three-inch heels, and the side slit went a shocking way up her thigh. She'd managed to style her hair by piling it on top of her head, and little tendrils curled down around her ears. Finally, she wore the brooch on her left side— near her heart.

"Just…wow…" Michael gulped audibly. "You look stunning." He scooted out of bed and moved toward her.

For a moment, she looked like she was going to step back. Then she straightened her spine and held her head high. With Michael in bare feet, they almost were eye to eye.

He drew his hand along her cheekbone and down her jaw. "You don't even need makeup. You're just…" He grasped her hand and pressed it to his chest. "I keep thinking, how'd I get to be so lucky?" He glanced over his shoulder. "How'd we get to be so lucky? And now I'm not even worrying about going because my eyes, and everyone else's, are going to be glued to the two of you. You'll be the handsomest couple in the place."

"Oh, but Julie—"

He waved her off. "Is beautiful in her own way. Ethereal. An angel. You, though? You're a temptress. I'm glad you didn't pick red."

She cocked her head.

"Would've given men the idea you're wicked."

She giggled.

I cleared my throat. "You picked the perfect color."

After a moment, she swept her hand down her body. "Used, no less. Apparently, the previous owner used it for a private cocktail party, so unless I say something, no one'll know it wasn't made for me."

"Oh, it sure looks like it was. Truly, Caressa, you look amazing." She took my breath away.

Her cheeks pinkened. Yeah, she didn't like compliments. Michael and I had spent years trying to bolster her self-esteem. And we'd made tremendous progress—coming out of college, she'd been confident. Just a few years later, after Franklin, all that forward momentum had been lost.

Fucking Franklin.

I pushed his memory from my mind. Caressa hadn't mentioned him since Christmas, so I assumed he was no longer an issue.

"May I help you out of the dress?" Michael stepped forward, ready to assist.

Caressa glanced over his shoulder to meet my gaze.

I read indecision. "The dress is perfect. I couldn't have done better if I selected it myself." I noted the vintage silver clutch in her hand. The shiny beads sparkled in the low light of the room. "We should've put you in a spotlight."

She scowled. Michael laughed as he gently turned her so he could unzip the dress.

How'd she get into it?

Well, we'd have to help her the day of the gala. The charity, helping the homeless and underprivileged kids of the Downtown Eastside, was near to my heart, to all of us really, and when they had asked me to take over as benefactor not long after *Vigilante Justice* took off, I hadn't felt I could say no. I didn't regret elevating the charity and was aware my name brought in donations it might not have otherwise received.

I made no secret I came from the roughest part of town. Or that I'd lived a hardscrabble life until making it big as an actor. I told the story to inspire other kids—all the while knowing the odds stacked against them. This charity, with all its good works, at least gave some of them a fighting chance. If I could have, I would have sponsored all the kids. And maybe I should be giving more. I'd convinced the studio to offer a number of extra apprenticeships to young people from that area, but it wasn't enough.

It would never be enough.

But giving away all my money wouldn't fix the problem either. So I would don a tux, have a beautiful woman on my arm, and schmooze millions of dollars out of wealthy donors. And match a good portion of the money raised.

Michael helped Caressa from the dress. The dress that had a shelf bra so she wasn't required to wear one.

Oh, yeah, like that's not going to keep me hard all night.

Currently, she wore no undergarments. But I knew

her well enough to know she would never go out in public without some kind of underwear.

Have to buy her something special.

Because I'd bet a pile of money she hadn't worn satin or lace in Africa, and as much as she loved Michael, I doubted she'd acquired any in the month she was home.

She stepped out of the heels, bent to scoop them up, and took the dress from Michael with a grateful smile.

He watched her go until she disappeared behind the closet door. Then he turned to face me. "Uh, wow?"

"Yeah."

And his chub matched mine. Also, likely both of us had thought about peeling her out of that dress at the end of the night.

Caressa reappeared and, to my infinite relief, had her pajamas in hand. She tossed them onto the chaise, snagged Michael's hand, and pointed him to the far side of the bed. They released hands so he could crawl in on one side of me while she repeated the action on the other.

"A Cole sandwich," she remarked a little dryly.

I grinned.

She cocked an eyebrow as she pulled the covers up. "So what precisely did Zoey say you could do?"

"Well, both of you."

Michael sputtered.

I shot him a glance. We'd had this conversation. I turned back to Caressa. "I have to lie on my back still, but I can do you both."

Her grin was nothing short of devilish. "Me first."

"That was the plan. But I think Michael needs to get you ready."

We both turned to him, and he licked his lips.

Slowly, she lowered the blankets to reveal her

shapely form. Her beauty was inherent. And I saw most people as beautiful. Working in the entertainment industry, I spent time around plenty of objectively attractive people. But I sought, and found, something special in everyone I encountered. I truly tried to not judge people by their looks.

That being said, Caressa would fit right in with the actors I worked with. She could completely hold her own and would be lauded.

I still thought her a little on the slender side—but that was bias because I preferred her curvier. Healthy but with definite curves.

Instead of crawling over me, Michael rose, scooted around to Caressa's side of the bed, and then slowly crawled over her. He pressed her down into the mattress as she opened her thighs and welcomed him.

Their kiss was carnal, deep, and had my cock springing to life.

Jesus, I'm going to be inside her.

I'd waited five years for this moment, and part of me didn't believe it had finally arrived.

Michael drew his hand down her side and cupped under her ass, then he ground against her.

She arched up to meet the friction, letting out little moans of pleasure. Slowly, he pulled back from the kiss. She let out a little whimper.

"All in good time, sweetheart." He kissed his way down her body, taking time to suck on her pulse point, nip at her neck, and nibble on her nipple.

I palmed my cock. *In good time.*

He went lower still, kissing his way down her belly and eventually positioning himself between her thighs. She opened for him. After inhaling deeply, he used his fingers to pull back her labia. His first swipe with his tongue had her nearly bucking off the bed. He positioned his shoulders to hold her down while he went to town.

So to speak.

Her whimpers increased, and she moved her head restlessly back and forth, slowly dislodging the topknot she'd creatively created.

I stroked her temple and brow, wiping away the sheen of sweat.

"Michael?" She said his name breathlessly.

He hummed in response.

She whispered his name again. "I'm coming."

Let her come now or on my cock? Ah, she's multi-orgasmic. Likely, we can coax two out of her.

I snagged her nipple between my fingers and squeezed. She arched her back up, her body tightened, and then she held still. Michael continued to feast on her, making little noises of pleasure.

I am so fucking jealous.

Your turn will come.

A couple more weeks. Zoey said if I was careful and stayed on this trajectory of healing, I would be able to resume all normal activities by the night of the gala. If we weren't too tired after we came home, I planned a night of debauchery.

Caressa pressed her hands over mine where I held her nipple. I released my light hold. She met my gaze with glassy eyes.

"If you're too tired…" Would I ever stop worrying about her?

She shook her head. "Just finding my equilibrium." She glanced down at my cock. "I very much want to ride that thing."

120

Said thing thickened and hardened. It very much liked the thought of being buried deep inside her. "Whenever you're ready, baby."

Michael insinuated his way between the two of us and gave me a deep and long-lasting kiss. God, I loved tasting her on him. One day I'd flip the tables and do the same to him.

Caressa slipped her hand between us and pressed a hand to my chest. Finally, Michael pulled back.

"My turn." I was growing impatient.

He grinned. Then, with apparent tenderness, he helped her sit up.

She pushed the wild, flyaway curls from her face. The face that was still coated with sweat. "You like to make me work for it."

"Oh, you bet." Michael leaned over to give her a kiss. "You ready?"

She nodded, then he guided her so she straddled me. Slowly, she dragged her slick folds over my cock.

Her scent enveloped me. As did Michael's as he positioned himself right next to me so our shoulders touched. I glanced over at him.

He grinned back. "Best view."

Caressa snorted. Slowly, I dragged my fingers from her knees, up her thighs, and to her pussy. She bucked when I passed my finger over her clit.

"Too sensitive?" I didn't want her uncomfortable.

"Nope." She drew her lower lip through her teeth. "Just deciding when would be the right time for—"

I angled my cock and helped her sink down on me. I was so glad we'd been tested and had decided we didn't need condoms as we were monogamous within the relationship. And with Caressa's IUD, we had all the safety bases covered.

She met my gaze. Her blue eyes mesmerized.

Something deep in my soul shifted. I'd fucked a fair number of women and men over the years, but nothing had ever felt so tenuous. And precious. And fragile.

"Move, sweetheart." Michael drew his hand along her thigh to her hip, then gently ran his finger down to her ass.

After a moment, she pressed her hands to my stomach and lifted. She pressed down as I thrust up. We held still for a moment.

Understanding, I quickly reviewed how my thigh felt. "I'm okay."

She nodded.

Then she began to ride me in earnest. Her wet heat enveloped me as her frantic movements drove me closer and closer to the edge.

I grasped her breasts and squeezed her nipples as she continued her relentless assault on my senses. I didn't choose this position often, preferring to control the contact with other partners, but having her take control in this moment felt perilously close to perfect.

"Please, Cole." She gritted her teeth. "Need to come."

I slid a finger down her chest, through her pubic hair, and into her slick folds. With unerring precision, I flicked her clit.

She stilled for a moment and held my gaze. Then her inner walls battered my cock as the orgasm tore through her. Her eyes drifted shut as she leaned back, clearly letting the waves of pleasure surround her and eventually drag her under. She eased forward, and I slid out of her.

Still hard.

Still wanting.

Still needing.

But overcome, nonetheless, with a feeling of well-being that seeped deep into my soul. I pulled her into my arms and held on for dear life.

Michael snagged a blanket and wrapped it around her. Our gazes met.

You're next, I mouthed.

His hazel eyes glinted gold.

I can't wait, I assured him silently.

Chapter Eleven

Michael

You're next.
I can't wait.

Oh yeah, as I cuddled Caressa to my chest and tucked her into Cole's side, my cock leaked a drop or two of precum.

Around these two, I sported a hard-on a good portion of the time. Which sounded bad, given how much baggage we were working through. But it also spoke to the level of sensuality in our lives these days. Little touches here. Hugs there. Caresses everywhere. Anytime we were in close proximity, we took snatches of opportunities to connect.

I'd never been like this with anyone in my life before—and I really liked it.

Once I had Caressa settled, I turned my attention to Cole. And noticed the bottle of lube on the bedside table. Wow, this might really happen.

He held up his hand. "Only if you're ready."

I'd thought I was. Right up until this moment, I'd honestly believed I was. But looking at Cole's cock had me second-guessing this.

"Why don't we start with something simple?"

I met his gaze.

Soft, compassionate blue eyes raked over me.

"Well, prep is important."

Which I knew. I'd done tons of research over the past two weeks—since Cole'd made it clear he wanted a full relationship with me. And I'd done the investigation eagerly. And found myself way more turned on than I could have imagined. Funny, I'd never looked at men's bodies sexually before. Now, though? Like a light switch triggered in my mind. I wasn't obsessed with sex, that had never been a thing with me, but I was curious beyond all words. I wanted to know. Everything.

Cole snagged the bottle of lube and handed it to me. *My call.*

But hadn't it always been? As much as Cole blustered about wanting to fuck me, he would never come near me without my consent.

He sat, propped against the headboard, just gazing over my naked body.

My cock, with another drop of precum, sat curled against my belly. My balls, full and heavy, sat waiting for attention.

Slowly, I spread my legs.

Cole licked his lips.

The angle was all kinds of awkward. And I seriously considered just flipping over, presenting him my ass, and asking him to do this. Except I wanted to see him when I did this. Something told me I would need his encouragement—verbal and nonverbal.

I stroked my cock.

He nodded.

I uncapped the lube and drizzled some on my finger.

He nodded.

I leaned back on one elbow so I could be completely exposed to him. Then I slid my finger to my hole and started, ever so slowly, to work my way in.

I should've done this before.

Except when would I have had the time? Cole and I'd been here alone for a week while Caressa worked those brutal twelve-hour shifts. And sure, we could have done this without her, were essentially doing it without her now, but her presence in this bed was the encouragement I needed. I never could have snuck off to my bedroom and done this on my own. That truth was evident now as I pressed in farther.

My breath caught. This felt so foreign. Awkward. Uncomfortable. Not painful, though. At least not yet. So I kept at it. Eventually, I made it to the second knuckle.

"Wiggle it."

I giggled. Then obeyed. Okay, definitely an odd sensation.

"Add a second." Cole's lips quirked. "But only if you think you can take it."

Was that a smirk? *Fucking asshole.* Of course, I'd take it. For him, I'd do just about anything.

I slid a second finger in and started to wiggle my fingers again. This time, the sensation intensified. I grappled to find the right words to describe the intensity.

"Wiggle them."

Ah, to loosen me up. I wasn't convinced that was possible, given I'd never done this before, but I wanted to please him.

And was damn curious.

So I followed his instruction. I scissored my fingers. I sank in deeper. And after a few moments, I absorbed the burn. The feeling intensified as I sought relief from the intensity of fullness. Then I hit a spongy spot, and I jolted.

Cole mouthed *prostate*.

How he knew, I couldn't be sure, but I understood what he meant. Slowly, I touched it again.

Warmth cascaded through my body along with an electricity and a desire to come stronger than anything I ever remembered. "I need—"

"I know."

"I can't—"

"Yeah, you can."

Were we even talking about the same thing? "I want you, Cole."

"I know."

"But I'm not ready."

"I know."

Part of me mourned that knowledge. Most of me accepted it as the truth.

He snagged the bottle of lube. He squeezed some on his palm. Then he sat up and reached for my cock.

I knew it would be a matter of mere moments, but every time I came close, he'd back off and gentle his jerks.

"Cole, for fuck's sake." I tried to buck into his hand. Anything to find the friction I so desperately needed.

Caressa snaked her hand out to press to Cole's abdomen. "Let him come."

He chuckled. Then gave several frenetic tugs on my cock.

Finally, to my utter joy and relief, I came. I flopped back on the bed, narrowly missing hitting the footboard with my arm, which I flung out over my head.

Still, Cole nursed me through my aftershocks.

Little zaps of electricity still singed my body as I tried to take in the most intense orgasm of my life.

And given the things we'd done in this bed during the last two weeks, that was saying something.

Finally, Cole released me. He gently caressed my inner thigh. "You can't sleep like that, Michael." He snickered. "Not that I don't mind admiring that view all night, but even I'm starting to flag. All the stress of the day."

Caressa poked him in the ribs.

"Fine." He scowled down at her. "I promise I won't panic the next time you're late."

"You say that now." She yawned but didn't open her eyes. "But I know you, Cole Hamilton. Or at least, I think I'm starting to."

Her words struck me. How well did we know each other? At this point, intimately. As children, completely. But as adults? We'd spent eight years living apart. I'd believed we would remained close, but between Africa and our busy lives, we'd taken separate paths. I didn't know this overly protective Cole. It harkened back to our childhood—but I'd believed we had worked through the trauma.

Today proved that wasn't true.

For any of us.

Slowly, I rose, wincing at the soreness. I might've been a little too overexuberant for my first time. I snuck one last look at Cole's still-erect cock as I headed to the bathroom.

Need to take care of that.

Yet in the time it took me to wash myself down and head back to the bedroom, Cole was spurting.

Okay, so closer to the edge than I thought.

I turned around and headed back to the bathroom. Within a moment, I had a washcloth, and I returned to our bed.

Cole slumped back against the headboard with his eyes shut. Caressa remained tucked into his side and appeared asleep. I cleaned him off as best I could. Then I coaxed him to scoot down. He did, managed to offer me a dreamy smile, then his eyes drifted shut again.

My heart took a knock.

Loving this man was so fucking easy.

I tossed the washcloth into the dirty clothes hamper. I washed my hands again, then I headed back to bed. I kind of wished tonight was a Michael sandwich night, but Cole deserved to know how it felt to have the two people who loved him most in the world surrounding him. I'd selected his left side because I wasn't nearly as restless and therefore less likely to jostle his leg. I doubted Zoey knew we shared a bed.

Huh.

Actually, I couldn't make that assumption. The physiotherapist seemed pretty astute to me. She would also be able to see how seriously Cole took this recovery. He worked out every day, and even I noticed more definition in his arms and abs.

Will his fans notice?

He went shirtless quite a lot. Apparently, the viewers gobbled him up.

I didn't blame them. I also wasn't certain I wanted hordes of men and women drooling over my man. As I scooted into bed beside him, I took in his beauty.

Then I turned off the light, snuggled up beside him, and dropped into a deep sleep.

And stayed asleep until Caressa's nightmare woke all of us a few hours later.

She eventually calmed, but I remained vigilant

through the rest of the night, and when my alarm went off at six, I was mostly awake. I shut it off, slipped out of bed, and headed for the shower.

When I noticed Caressa struggling to get up, I moved to her side of the bed. "What're you doing?"

"Getting up to make you breakfast."

I tisked. "You most certainly are not. I'm going to grab something on my way into work. I need to be at my desk early."

Which wasn't the strict truth, but it would do in a pinch.

She cracked an eye open, barely visible in the low light of Cole's nightlight. "You made breakfast for me all those mornings. And drove me to work and—"

I touched my hand to her lips. "I was off work. And I wanted to."

"Well, I'm off work. And I want to."

Cole snagged an arm around her shoulders and tugged her back into his embrace. "Please, just sleep. You need sleep."

Caressa met my gaze.

I nodded.

She scowled but allowed herself to be pulled back. She curled into Cole's side again, closed her eyes, and was likely out cold. Her ability to fall asleep anywhere, at any time, was legendary in our group. I didn't doubt she'd needed that skill while working in Africa.

I showered and dressed in my jeans and plaid shirt, ensuring I had several layers. Today was forecast to be a wonky Vancouver day—frigid cold in the morning, warming up, with eventual clouds and rain. In the middle of the wet season, I longed for sun. At the height of summer, I prayed for rain and cool. I didn't do well with temperature extremes. I was a nice fifty-nine-degree guy. Not too hot and not too cold.

God, you sound like an old, whiny person.

Nope, no arguing with that voice. I didn't like it much, but sometimes I had to acknowledge I was stuck in my ways. Moving in with Caressa was way beyond my comfort zone. Yet even as I accepted that, I could also see how my horizons were expanding.

I did drive-thru and arrived at the site just as the first guys were headed up the tower. I scarfed down my food and headed up with them. Today was a simple "observe and ensure everything ran smoothly" day.

To my joy and delight, it did.

Things were great right up until I arrived in the office in the late afternoon. I hadn't needed to drop by, but I always felt putting in an appearance was important—even as I just wanted to go home and be with my lovers.

I sat at my desk, third cup of coffee in hand, when I opened my inbox. Scanning, I noted an email from the City of Vancouver. I opened it, read, and frowned.

Updated plans? I wracked my brains. When would I have sent updated plans? Everything had been signed off on yesterday, and I'd emailed everything myself. This didn't make any sense.

Still, I logged in to the secure area and checked the date on the file with the plans.

Today. The file had been updated at ten this morning.

While I'd been forty stories above the ground.

A knot formed in the pit of my stomach as I opened the plans and reviewed them yet again. I knew them by heart—and knew exactly what would need to be changed to accommodate Pamela's grand vision.

Jesus fucking Christ.

I ran over the calculations in my mind. Then I pulled up the regulations from the city's website. Our calculations fit. Perfectly. Without a single millimeter of cushion. Personally, I'd always felt the city's rules weren't stringent enough. The numbers assumed the big earthquake, if it ever hit, wouldn't be as big as the scientists predicted it might be. And sure, the consensus was the big one wasn't likely to hit for a bit. But one seismologist I followed calculated 250 to 800 years after the last big one. The last big one, in this region, was 1700. So by his calculations, we were within that time frame. And yeah, climate change didn't affect earthquakes that anyone had seen thus far, but wilder storms meant more stress on buildings.

To my mind, we needed to be more prudent—not less.

Am I being paranoid? I just didn't know. Tyanna would have signed off on this, and she was one of the best in the business. If she felt the design was okay, and if it met Vancouver's stringent code, that should be enough.

Right?

My gut twisted. Then I asked the question I'd learned in school—would I spend time in this building, knowing what I knew?

I added Caressa and Cole. Would I recommend they buy one of the luxury condo units and spend their lives there?

No. No, I wouldn't.

Which propelled me out of my chair and had me heading to Tyanna's office.

My boss's door was open, yet still I hesitated before knocking.

She glanced up from her laptop, offered me a wide smile, and indicated a chair across from her desk.

I willed myself to move forward with purpose, all the while feeling like I was slowly dying inside.

"How are you, Michael?"

"Great." *Don't wring your hands.* "I received an email from the City of Vancouver."

Her eyes flashed, but I couldn't figure out why. "Ah, Pamela didn't tell you that we submitted revised plans. Just a few modifications."

I wasn't convinced Pamela should've been responsible for telling me. She wouldn't have made the final alterations. I held Tyanna's gaze.

"Look, Michael, we did everything that was required of us. And we've incorporated the elements Pamela requested. The building's going to be stunning."

"Would you live there?"

A little V formed in her brow. "I'm sorry?"

"Would you buy a condo there?" I didn't need to preface the question with whether or not she could afford it. Our bonus on the last project alone would get her pretty close to in the door. Not that I was complaining—I'd taken home a nice tidy sum and had paid off my SUV and put a chunk down on the mortgage.

But that wasn't the point.

"Of course I would." Her dark-brown eyes flashed again. "Michael, the building's going to be perfectly safe."

I wanted to believe her. I really did. But my mind just couldn't make the leap, and my gut certainly wasn't going to do it either.

"You're entitled to your concerns." She tilted her head. "I've reviewed everything myself—it's going to be a safe building."

Is this the hill you want to die on?

I could walk away. I had a few months of savings in reserve. Cole would cover any shortfall—not that I should have taken that into consideration. But I did. We'd be okay.

But I'd also be leaving one of the most prestigious engineering firms in Vancouver. If Tyanna didn't give me a glowing reference, I could be stuck in some low-level job at a second-rate firm forever—assuming they would even hire me.

Eventually, I looked away. "Of course it'll be."

"Well, I planned to assign you the project. If you'd be more comfortable, I can give it to Carl—"

Who was a perfectly competent engineer. But...not as exacting as I was. No, better I be on this project to ensure not a single corner was cut. If everything was done precisely, then yes, theoretically the building should be safe.

I turned my gaze back to Tyanna. "No, I'll do it."

She offered a wide smile as she rose. "I knew you'd be the perfect person for the job. I've got my eye on you."

Is that a good thing or a bad thing?

I just wasn't certain anymore. I rose as well, nodded, and left her office. When I was back at my desk, I ensured all the plans were easily accessible. I planned to go over them one more time. The engineers over at the city were competent—hell, I'd gone to school with one of them—but I just wanted to be certain for myself. If I was to put my name on the project, I damn well better be able to sign off on every number.

Tired beyond belief, I packed up my laptop, touched the photo on my desk, and headed home.

Those three smiling people in that pub had felt invincible.

Reality was so much more complicated.

Chapter Twelve

Caressa

Cole'd wanted to take a limo to the gala, but Michael insisted on driving us in Cole's new electric SUV. As he pointed out, we'd make a statement about our environmental beliefs.

Donovan sat in the front seat, keeping Michael company. They were attending tonight as *friends*. We'd had no further talks about BDSM. Cole was back on set, Michael was neck-deep in work, and I'd just come off a four-day stretch of nights. At least I'd had a day to recover before putting on this glamorous gown and heading out to pretend like I belonged with these people.

If not for the charity, I wouldn't be doing this.

Or so I told myself.

Liar. You'd do anything Cole asked.

Yeah, I probably would.

He'd made tremendous strides with physio, and although he wasn't back to doing stunts on the show, he was able to move around without a cane. He still fatigued easily, so I intended to keep a close eye on him tonight.

Michael pulled up to the drop-off of the Queen Elizabeth Theatre.

Cole stilled my hand as I reached for the door handle. A moment later, a woman opened my door and held out her hand.

Mindful of the indecent slit in my dress, I took the proffered hand and let her guide me from the vehicle. As I gazed down at her, I was mindful of just how tall I was in these blasted heels.

After a moment, Cole rounded the SUV and was there to offer his arm. He looked so handsome in his tux—with his dark hair even longer than when I'd first come home. His blue eyes appeared stormy tonight. Turbulent with an emotion I couldn't identify.

And as much as I'd argued against it, his tie was a pale blue that matched my dress—and my eyes.

The mild January evening enabled us to go out without our standard winter coats. I wore a shawl while Cole was sans coat completely.

As we approached the small group of photographers, Donovan quietly slipped my shawl from my shoulders. Someone had set up heaters that blasted out warm air, and I worried the reporters and photographers might be too warm, but they appeared to have dressed for the conditions.

Cole laced an arm around my waist as he drew me over to a stunning woman. Her dark tanned skin appeared to sparkle, as if she'd dusted herself with a shimmering powder. Her black hair hung loose around her shoulders, and her dark-brown eyes shone with…warmth.

Oh shit, that's Geneva Alvarez. Recognizing her had taken me a moment, but I identified the reporter for our local station of the national broadcaster. Cole had shown me a few photos and videos to prepare me for the people we might encounter tonight. Along with organizers as well as cast and crew from *VJ*, he'd included some members of the media.

"Good evening, Geneva." Cole's voice oozed charm—but not in a slimy way.

She batted her eyelashes. "Good evening, Cole."

And just how well do they know each other?

Sheathe your claws—it doesn't become you.

So I did just that. Tried to take an objective step back and observe the interaction.

Except they'd barely exchanged pleasantries before Cole drew me in to his side. "This is my girlfriend, Caressa Klein."

Geneva's eyes sparkled. "That's lovely. How long?"

He glanced at me. "We've been friends since we were five years old, but the romance is new. Caressa's recently back from a tour in Africa. As a nurse." His eyes held nothing but pride. He turned back to Geneva. "We reconnected, and here we are—ready to celebrate this great charity."

"You donate a lot of money."

"And time, when I can."

I took in that information, which I hadn't known. Cole kept himself pretty fricking busy…and he found time to volunteer? Maybe he meant to the administration of the charity.

"Did I hear someone spotted you out on the streets a few weeks ago?"

Holding my gaze steady on Cole, I didn't miss the flicker.

"I've been out and about."

"You were giving out cash to people in the homeless encampment."

He shifted uncomfortably.

"Tonight's about raising money for the charity." I pointedly looked at Geneva. "That should be our focus."

Possibly because authorities weren't keen on people randomly giving out money.

But we all knew the charities and authorities couldn't handle the problem on their own. Still, for Cole to go down there alone… *Talk to him about it later.*

"Yes, of course." Geneva gave me a pointed look.

Ah, like that, is it? He's mine. You can't have him.

I tightened my grip on Cole's arm, nauseated by the overwhelming possessiveness. This wasn't like me. And I wasn't proud of the little green monster rearing its ugly head.

Cole and Geneva spoke a bit about the charity, but I became distracted as Michael attempted to slip in unnoticed.

A security guard stopped him, and he fumbled in his pocket for his invitation.

With everything being done electronically these days, I'd been surprised at the thick cream-colored invitation we received. Mine was tucked securely in my clutch, but Cole'd assured me we wouldn't need it.

Given how much attention he drew, his point became blatantly obvious.

Geneva lowered her mic, and her camerawoman turned in another direction. "Why don't we get a drink sometime? You can tell me more about your projects. Off the record, of course." Her eyes flicked to me and then back to Cole. As if I were no more than an annoying mosquito. "Oh, and we can discuss your co-workers. How is Julie doing these days?"

Cole stiffened. "If she isn't already here, she'll be arriving shortly. You can ask her yourself."

Those damn almost-black eyes flashed again. "Oh, I intend to."

Without another word, Cole guided me to the next reporter.

What the hell was that about?

As if reading my unspoken question, he whispered, "Geneva's had the hots for Julie for years."

I nearly snickered. Oh, so that piqued my curiosity. "And for you."

"She is unabashedly bi." He turned on the megawatt smile and greeted the next reporter.

In the end, he only did four quick interviews—and none were as unsettling as Geneva's. I made a mental note to check CNC's website in the morning. I didn't figure we'd make the evening news, but I couldn't be sure. Sometimes I forgot just how big of a deal Cole was—*hometown boy with a heart of gold does good*.

I just saw him as Cole. And now as *my* Cole.

And Michael's.

How would Geneva have reacted if she'd known we had another in our cozy new relationship? Something told me her antennae would be right up and honed in on our little domestic drama.

After bidding farewell to the last journalist, we headed into the theater. I'd been here once before as a teenager. We'd received free tickets to see *Aida*.

I'd been bewildered by both the theater and the show. Michael'd been intrigued by the set construction. Cole'd been enamored of the entire experience.

Little surprise he'd become an actor, Michael'd learned to construct things, and I'd wandered off to do something completely different.

With his arm firmly around my waist, Cole led me into the throng of people. I spotted a few people I vaguely recognized. On my last stretch off, we'd done a

VJ marathon as well as several of Cole's film roles in recent years.

I inclined my head. "That's…"

Even as I said the words, a man waved to Cole. He snagged another man's hand, and they headed our way.

When they arrived before us, the men shook hands. "Peter, Thomas…this is my girlfriend, Caressa Klein. Caressa, this is Peter Erickson and his husband, Thomas Walsh."

Peter Erickson, I recognized. One of the top action stars from the past twenty or so years. He'd been big long before I'd headed to Africa. The man was as gorgeous in person as on screen with his graying hair, distinguished beard, and piercing green eyes.

His husband, slightly taller with blond hair and stunning brown eyes, gave me a genuine smile. He leaned in and whispered, "It's all a little much. You'll be fine."

Although I appreciated his assurances, him seeing through my panic disconcerted me.

Our gazes met, and he winked. "I felt the same way the first few times. You're doing great."

Doing great as Cole's date or doing great at hiding it? Somehow I was pretty sure he meant the former.

I managed a smile before turning to Peter. "I was out of the country for a while, but I recently saw the film you starred in with Cole." I pressed a hand to my chest. "You guys were amazing. I can see why you won the Academy Award."

A slow blush crept across Peter's face, inching up over his beard line. "That's very kind of you." He blinked. "Damn, you're the friend who was in South Sudan."

Hiding my shock wasn't even possible. I turned to Cole.

But Peter continued. "He mentioned you during our shoot. I knew he had feelings for you, pretty obvious, but I hadn't pieced it together."

Pieced what? That the woman on his arm was the same one he'd spoken of three years ago?

Time to get the topic changed. "I understand you have children. That's so great."

Thomas beamed. Actually beamed. "Yeah, our daughter Skylar and our son Samuel. They're fantastic kids."

"Whom we were happy to get a night away from." Peter offered a sheepish grin. "Skylar turned three last week, and Samuel's turning one next month."

I remembered Cole mentioning their son had a disability. Two kids under the age of four was daunting enough, but more challenges? I had tremendous admiration. I indicated the two men. "And you met on the movie set?"

Thomas tucked his arm around Peter's waist and placed a kiss to his temple. Peter grinned.

Cole guffawed. "Have them tell you about tiger tail ice cream one day."

"Hey, you guys." Petite Julie Reyes joined our circle, holding the arm of a much taller redhead.

Cole grabbed Julie into a hug while the man offered me his hand. "Seamus O'Malley."

I cocked my head.

"Newfoundland."

Ah, yes. Seamus whose husband was a producer who was out of town and that's why Julie was attending with him instead of available to escort Cole as they normally did.

I shook Seamus's hand with some appreciation. If not for him, I wouldn't be here.

Wait, is that a good thing or a bad thing?

"You look lovely." His green eyes held a gentle admiration.

"Seamus also has a son." Peter grinned. "How is Jason?"

"He's fine. Wasn't pleased I was going out. He gets stressed when Val's out of town and I have to leave. But we've got a great babysitter who brings her dog, so his attention is easily shifted."

We all smiled.

"Lovely to finally meet you, Caressa." Julie Reyes was nearly a foot shorter than Cole and Thomas in the group and half-a-foot shorter than myself, Seamus, and Peter. The woman's white-blonde hair hung loose down her back, and her emerald-green eyes shone with warmth. She felt approachable—like just another person rather than a big celebrity. She rivaled Peter and Cole thanks to her major role on *VJ*.

I managed a smile, but words just wouldn't push past the lump in my throat.

"And you're recovered?" Julie eyed Cole.

Ah, right, she'd been the accidental cause of his injury.

He swept his hand along his left leg. "Pretty much good as new."

They'd been back to work for a week now, so Julie should have known that. Maybe some residual upset? Or maybe she felt he hadn't been honest on set but might be more candid in a social setting.

A stunning woman in a red dress approached us. The

dress should have clashed with her red hair, but somehow it didn't. Her height nearly topped six feet with those stilettos she wore. She pressed a familiar hand to Cole's arm. "It's time."

His grip tightened on me. I did my best not to wince at the pressure. Magically, Donovan and Michael appeared.

Cole pressed a kiss to my temple. "I'll be back soon."

Michael brushed against my right side while Donovan insinuated himself between Cole and me.

"Jennifer's got your number, buddy." Donovan grinned.

The redhead had taken off toward the microphone stand that stood on the mezzanine level. Cole shot me one more smile, and the little lines around his eyes crinkled.

As I watched him move away, Donovan introduced Michael to the group.

"So Donovan finally brings a respectable date." Julie's grin was nothing less than shit-eating.

Michael sputtered. Donovan pressed a kiss to his temple as Cole had with me. To give Michael credit, he didn't look disgusted. But he did give Donovan a *"what the fuck, dude?"* look.

"Michael, Cole, and I are friends from way back. He's here tonight…with us." I offered the words, not really understanding the potential message until I'd spoken them.

All eyes turned to me.

My face flamed with heat. "As friends."

Donovan coughed to cover his snorted laugh. Thomas and Peter exchanged a look while poor Seamus appeared genuinely confused.

Julie put a hand to his arm. "I'll explain it to you later, sweetie."

He started to speak, but the noise from the microphone caught our attention.

Donovan and Michael flanked me.

What the hell have you done? I could argue I was trying to save Michael, but he'd been okay. No, I wanted to stake my territory. Michael was mine as well.

Jennifer stood and offered a wide smile. "We're so glad you've joined us tonight. As you know…" She went on to list the charities benefitting, but my attention was elsewhere.

Michael kept brushing against my arm. Purposefully. And periodically, our fingers would touch.

Jesus.

My body tingled at the remembrance of our lovemaking just last night. And as his subtle masculine scent invaded me, I longed for him to gather me in his arms. As I surreptitiously glanced around the room, I felt even more like a fraud than I had before.

Most of the people here were glamorous. A few I suspected were recipients of the generosity—not so much because of their clothing, but because of their lack of comfort as well. A small group of teenagers stood off to one side. My heart ached for the young woman in an ill-fitting yellow dress. She kept fidgeting and nearly toppled off her high heels twice, even though they weren't high.

I could've been her.

She could've been me.

That day when we'd come to see Aida flashed to my mind. I'd borrowed one of my mother's few dresses. A pretty flowery number from before she'd hit the drugs hard. Before she'd become skeletal.

Except my body hadn't matured yet, so the dress had drooped precariously in the front. I'd spent the whole day with my arms plastered to my chest.

Michael'd asked what was wrong, but I was—surprisingly—too shy to explain.

Cole'd taken him aside. Whatever he'd said worked because the two remained glued to my side in case any boys made unwanted moves.

Even then, protecting me from myself.

I'd donated that dress to charity after my mother died of an OD. I couldn't fathom she'd been gone fifteen years. She'd been dead for almost as long as she'd been alive in my life.

Yet I still couldn't shake her from my remembrances.

At least I hadn't been the one to find her dead. I'd been home alone, in the apartment I was sharing with the guys and studying, when the police made the notification. Cole and Michael'd arrived home shortly after—Cole from his job and Michael from classes. I didn't remember crying, but I remembered being numb. I had never sunk to hating my mother—she kept me, at least, with a roof over our heads. That, in turn, had kept me close to Michael and Cole. I might not have hated her, but I'd never forgiven her the addiction. I'd studied that in nursing school. After graduation, I'd worked in the Downtown Eastside with many addicts, but I'd never truly understood.

Until now.

Because if someone demanded I give up Michael, Cole, or both, I wouldn't be able to do it. They'd become my world, and I'd do anything for them. Make any sacrifice. Climb any mountain. Challenge anyone who might try to take them away from me.

Applause pulled me from my reverie. Several people moved toward Cole, but he brushed them aside as he made a beeline to the group of kids in the back.

Clearly, they weren't expecting him to join them. Their wide eyes matched their starstruck expressions. Did they know Cole personally? Or did they just know of him? The young teenage girl finally, after what appeared to be coaxing on Cole's part, offered a shy smile.

His returning smile shone.

"Do you ever feel like we're the luckiest people on the planet?" Michael's whispered words brought a smile to my face.

"The Cole Hamilton jackpot."

"Would you like a drink?"

I glanced around to find most people had one. "Sparkling mineral water?" That sounded fancy.

Michael snorted.

I gave him a mock glare.

"Trouble in paradise?" Cole stepped up to me, snaked his left arm around my waist, and pulled me in for another kiss to the temple. With his right hand, he grabbed Michael's left.

We all stilled.

"I'm going to find a time—the right time—for us to come out. Just…not tonight."

Not ever my mind screamed. Cole would tank his career, Michael and I would be flung to the tabloid wolves, and nothing good could come of it.

"Hello, Cole." A husky voice caught my attention

147

while Cole released Michael's hand and turned to the newcomer.

She was a plump woman I judged to be in her mid-twenties. She wore a short black dress that, unfortunately, emphasized her short legs in an unflattering way. She'd used a heavy hand with her makeup, and her hair screamed bad bleach job. Clearly, she'd been trying to replicate Julie's white-blonde look but had failed utterly. Still, she had soft brown eyes which were laser-focused on Cole.

Michael gave a slight bow and headed toward the concession stand.

"Meggibeth, great to see you." Cole offered her a smile while tugging me closer. "Caressa, this is our caterer extraordinaire, Meggibeth. She also does first aid and took care of me after my injury."

Meggibeth stepped forward and, to my shock, ran her hand along Cole's left leg. She was so close she nearly touched me. And her breath nearly knocked me over. Sherry? Brandy? Something alcoholic and sickly sweet.

Cole's face remained impassive as she withdrew her hand. "I never got to thank you." He offered a smile that I knew to be strained but that I suspected would fool most of the world. His charm could woo anyone, but I knew he wasn't comfortable.

Michael sidled up to my other side. "Caressa, here's your sparkling mineral water."

Him handing me the drink meant I had to pull away from Cole, which didn't make me happy.

"And Cole, I brought you a ginger ale. I can get you something stronger—"

"Nope, this is perfect." He offered Michael an

appreciative smile. "Michael, this is Meggibeth. We work together."

Michael gazed fondly at her. "So you keep him out of trouble." He winked.

She barely acknowledged him, instead keeping her gaze on Cole.

"Well, I'm going to grab a drink for myself. Meggibeth, may I get you something?" Michael was all smiles and charm. Did he see what was going on?

For just an instant, she looked away from Cole. Her smile didn't reach her eyes. "A ginger ale?"

Somehow, I was pretty sure she didn't drink the stuff and was instead mimicking Cole.

"Got it." Michael headed back to the bar.

Before any of us could speak, Donovan appeared. "Meggibeth, great to see you. Cole, Lisette wants a word." He turned back to Meggibeth. "So how was your Christmas?"

"Can't make Lisette wait." Cole offered a shrug.

Lisette Grenier was Cole's director, mentor, and—in an odd way—a friend.

Cole nodded to Meggibeth as he guided me toward the little dynamo who had made his career. He let out a breath.

"Everything okay?" I took the arm he proffered, holding my clutch in that hand while balancing a drink I no longer wanted in the other.

"Everything's perfect."

Yet as we walked over to Lisette, I couldn't help the feeling of disquietude that settled over me.

Chapter Thirteen

Cole

I was still riding high Monday morning when Michael dropped me off at the old post office in downtown Vancouver. I'd considered taking transit—and then remembered I'm *the* Cole Hamilton, and although most people might play it cool, I might also cause a stir. I'd considered taking a cab—but Michael'd insisted he was coming this way for his job and yes, he'd be early. He'd then gone on to insist being early was never a bad thing because he could scope things out. I didn't know if that meant he expected nefarious things to be going on or if he was just trying to appease my conscience.

As I snagged a coffee from catering, I paused.

You're overthinking this. If he didn't want to drive you, he wouldn't have offered.

And I could've driven, but my leg still wasn't perfect, and I wanted to be focused on the work today, not whether I'd be strong enough to drive home. Given the hour was six in the morning and they'd scheduled the shoot to run all day, leeriness had set in. I had a follow-up with Zoey tomorrow at the studio, and I was looking forward to getting a clean bill of health. Well, she'd sign off, and I'd see the doctor, but I knew he deferred to Zoey, so she was the one I really needed to impress.

"You ready for a big day?" Julie grinned as she sipped her coffee from a chain store.

"How many espresso shots are in that?"

She shrugged. "Still recovering from Saturday. What was the final tally?"

"More than three million."

She let out a low whistle. "That's great. How much of that are you matching?"

I glared. Clearly undaunted, she appeared happy to wait for my answer.

"Half." I probably could've swung more, but I liked having a little bit extra in the bank these days in case Michael or Caressa wound up needing it. I didn't figure I could ever be too prudent.

"Well, I was happy to throw in a donation." She indicated she wanted my face closer.

Assuming she was about to whisper something in my ear, I bent forward. She fluffed my hair. I groused.

Clearly undeterred, she grinned. "Oh, you'll survive." She bumped my arm. "You're a good man, Cole."

"Being the center of attention drives me nuts."

"But raising money brings you joy. And I saw how those kids reacted to having you join them."

I couldn't argue. The one young woman reminded me so much of Caressa at that age—wary and weary beyond what a teenager should be. Untrusting of a world that had been nothing but cruel. If my presence and the money I raised offered some comfort, I'd take it.

And Caressa was back at work this morning. We'd had a blissful weekend, with the gala being the highlight of it. Raising money was just a bonus.

"Hey, you two." Donovan approached with a clear

bottle in his hand.

"Is that toxic sludge?" I shivered inwardly, suspecting one of his *special* drinks.

He gave me a mock glare. "How you two stay healthy drinking that shit is beyond me. This is a spinach protein shake with probiotics and—"

"I'll have you know this isn't shit." I held up my coffee. Then I pointed to Julie's sugar caffeine bomb. "That's shit."

She nudged me.

Donovan snickered.

"Hey, and what was with kissing Michael?" I tried to replicate Donovan's mock glare but totally failed.

"Just a peck." He ribbed me. "Don't worry, I'm not poaching."

Julie watched me intently. "Are you planning to come out as a threesome? You know how insane that thought is, right?"

I was about to answer when Meggibeth approached us. I held up my cup in salute, to thank her for the great coffee, when I realized she'd pulled a gun from her pocket.

On instinct, I let my cup drop, and I shoved Julie down and under me.

I figured Donovan could handle himself.

Several shots rang out, and for just a moment, I thought we were okay.

Then the searing pain in my chest registered.

Holy fucking shit.

"Cole?"

I had to be dead weight on Julie, but I wasn't going to move, wasn't sure I could move, until I knew she would be safe.

"We've got her." Was that Larry, our security guard?

Julie managed to get out from under me. "Cole's been shot. Oh my God, someone call an ambulance." She pushed me so I rolled onto my back.

More pain lanced through me, stealing me of breath.

Or maybe I couldn't breathe because she'd punctured a lung.

Jesus, for fuck's sake, don't panic.

Donovan's face loomed over me as he pressed something against my chest.

"Mother fucker." In my head, I shouted the words. In reality, I barely managed a whisper.

"To control the bleeding. Fuck, Hamilton, you just had to be a hero."

"Julie?"

"I'm fine." Julie knelt beside me and stroked my face.

Cold seeped into me, and I hoped it was just the frozen asphalt and not death creeping closer.

"Has someone called an ambulance?" Donovan's beautiful face screwed in concern.

"Elouise" came the response from someone I couldn't see. Was that Seamus with his Newfie accent?

"Donovan, you're bleeding." Julie tried to reach for my friend.

He waved her off. "A scratch, literally."

I tried to focus on his arm but found differentiating the blood from his dark-gray jacket difficult.

He pressed harder.

I winced.

Then in the distance, I heard sirens.

"Caressa." Oh God, were they going to take me to

St. Paul's? She was working the ER today. "Michael. Take care of Caressa."

I needed Donovan to understand.

"Let's just focus on you. We can deal with your lovers later."

No. Now. Michael needs to take care of Caressa.

Or maybe it was the other way around.

"We'll take care of them." Julie stroked my face. "You're going to be fine, and you're all going to come out as a throuple, and life is going to be perfect."

She thinks I'm going to die.

Maybe I am going to die.

Then after a moment, everything went dark.

Chapter Fourteen

Caressa

I glanced at the wall, disheartened to see Franklin's name on the board.

Four days away from the hospital had given me a bit of breathing room. Now, knowing I had to face him, the walls felt like they were closing in.

"Caressa, darling." Miles bumped my arm.

"Hey, how are you?"

"Oh, honey, you want to go there? My wife and my two kids are the center of my universe, but your love life comes a close second."

I scowled.

He yanked his phone from his back pocket, tapped a few times, and handed the thing to me.

A close-up of Cole and me. At the gala.

What did you expect? That no one would notice?

I handed the phone back to Miles. "It's not—"

"Don't say *what it looks like*. He admitted you were his girlfriend. I think it's adorable. Apparently, you were best friends and—"

Lynette poked her head into the break room. "Need you now. GSW to the chest. ETA two minutes. It's someone famous."

"What?" I tried to clear my mind. Gunshot wounds could range from a graze to a life-ending event.

"They were on set, and someone shot them. I don't have details." Lynette indicated we needed to hurry.

I flashed back to the news that a famous actor had discharged a weapon on set and killed a member of the crew—that news had made it even to my corner of Africa. Was this the same thing? Some kind of weapon discharge?

To the chest.

Miles and I stood at the ready when the paramedics wheeled in the gurney at breakneck speed. Another nurse had met them at the ambulance bay and was now repeating everything.

Everyone moved into action except me.

Despite all the equipment, blankets, lines, and monitors, I recognized Cole.

Icy dread enveloped me as I took in the scene.

He was deathly pale. All the heartiness was gone.

Words in staccato bursts hit me.

Blood loss.

Pressure dropping.

Possible pneumothorax.

No exit wound.

"Caressa." Miles hissed my name.

Franklin strode in. "Give me the rundown."

"Thirty-two-year-old male, gunshot wound to the upper chest, no exit wound…"

Thirty-two. Would Cole live to see thirty-three? Or was this the end of the road? Who had shot him? Was Michael hurt?

Michael.

"Get Caressa out of here." Franklin barked the order, and it stopped everyone in their tracks for just a moment.

156

"She can help." Miles looked at me imploringly.

"This man is her good friend. She needs out. Call security if you have to."

I wanted to argue. Wanted to rail against anyone sending me away. Except I'd been rooted to the spot for a good minute and hadn't helped—hadn't proven I was capable of stepping up and stepping in.

"I want her gone now."

Miles started to move toward me at Franklin's repeated bark.

Painfully, I held up my hands. "I'll go." I didn't want Miles to spend a single second worrying about me. "Just…save him."

I fled.

As I made my way down the row of curtains, I caught another voice.

"I don't give a fuck about myself. I want you to save Cole."

"Sir, your friend is in excellent hands—"

I yanked back the curtain. Donovan sat on a gurney without a shirt.

With a start, I realized I'd never seen him naked. He had a smattering of chest hair and beautiful mahogany skin.

And a nasty gash on his arm.

"I can take care of him, Trina. I think they need another set of hands in Trauma One."

Trina was in her first year out of school and still excited about medicine. She looked at me uncertainly.

"Tell Miles I sent you."

She bobbed her head, then took off in a jog.

I eyed Donovan's wound. "That's a nasty gash, and it's going to require stitches."

He tipped my chin toward him. "How bad?"

I blinked several times. "They sent me away. Franklin sent me away."

"Fucking Franklin is treating Cole?" Donovan's voice rose. "We've got to get someone else."

"Fucking Franklin?" I scrunched my nose. "Look, I know Cole and Michael don't like him—"

"They fucking hate him."

"But he's one of the best ER doctors we have. And yes, he's fucked up a couple of times recently, but there are enough nurses—"

"Are you listening to yourself? You need to go find another doctor."

"They'll call one in if they're needed." I grabbed gloves from the box and snapped them on. "I can clean the wound, and hopefully, someone can fix you up—"

"Caressa." He snapped the fingers of his uninjured arm.

I met his gaze. "If I think about what's going on, I'll completely lose my shit. I was useless, Donovan. I just stood there. And I thought about all the things I should've said before now. All the things I should've done. All the time I wasted in Africa while I could've been here. And I thought maybe I might've done something to prevent this, even thought I don't know what—"

He snapped his fingers again. "Meggibeth shot him. I don't know why. He protected Julie with his body. I think she might've bumped her head, but she stubbornly refused to let anyone look at her." His dark eyes penetrated my panic. "Thomas is driving her to pick up Michael and bring him here. He's listed as Cole's emergency contact, and Thomas remembered where he works."

"I…uh…" *Think, goddamnit.* "I think he's on a jobsite today."

"Well, then his boss will direct Julie and Thomas to him, right?"

"You've been shot, Donovan."

He grasped my arm. "I'm okay, Caressa. And Cole will be as well."

Yet even as he said the words, his eyes conveyed the worry. He couldn't promise that. No one could promise that.

Miles stuck his head around the curtain. "They've got him stabilized, and they're running him up to surgery. Williams is going to take over the case. I think he's consulting Dr. Graham."

Lance Williams was our trauma surgeon while Stephanie Graham was our cardiothoracic surgeon. Honestly, Cole couldn't have been in better hands.

And yet my panic hadn't receded.

Miles stepped into the area and drew the curtain.

"Don't you need…" He should be with Cole, not here with me.

"They have enough people. I assume you sent Trina? I pushed her to get in there."

"That little thing?" Donovan scowled. "She's what, twelve?"

Miles scowled back. "Twenty-three and one of the most levelheaded nurses I've ever met. She's got a combination of the best schooling out there and an ability to react quickly. She's doing great." He pivoted to me. "If Cole can't have you, he'll do okay with Trina to get him upstairs."

I would have preferred Miles stay with Cole, but he

also knew to come here. "We need to get Mr. Riggs stitched up so he and I…" My vision blurred.

"Need to get upstairs. I get it." Miles moved to set up to clean Donovan's wound. "Dr. Lipschitz is scheduled to start in fifteen minutes. Unless you prefer Dr. Caruso—"

"Fucking Franklin? I'd rather lose the arm to gangrene." Donovan spat the words.

I gaped at him. "You've never even met him."

"No. But I know what he did to you. He's made an enemy out of me. And Cole and Michael. If Cole makes it out alive and if he finds out Franklin worked on him, there's going to be hell to pay."

If Cole makes it out alive.

GSWs to the chest were serious. Many people died.

Miles held up his hands. "I'll see if I can find Dr. Lipschitz. Gangrene is unlikely, but let's get you treated and upstairs."

He disappeared, and Donovan indicated his jacket.

I picked it up.

"My phone's in there. I assume you don't have yours."

"In my locker. I should go get it—"

He shook his head. "Just check my home screen and see if I have any missed calls."

With shaking hands, I did as instructed. Every instinct had me wanting to run upstairs, but Cole would be in surgery for hours.

If he survives.

I was certain Donovan hadn't meant it the way it came out. Of course Cole was going to survive. He was young, healthy, and a fighter. He hadn't come this far in life just to be felled by a bullet.

"No missed calls." Even as I said the words, the phone vibrated in my hand. I held the screen over to Donovan as he read who it was from.

"Lisette. Likely wanting an update."

"Are they all going to come?" I'd encountered large families showing up. Funny, I saw Cole's show people as his family. With his father long dead and no mother in the picture for almost thirty years, he only had found family.

Dr. Evelyn Lipschitz poked her head in. "Ready for some sutures?"

Donovan managed a smile. "Yeah, that'd be great."

She turned to me. "Caressa, you might—"

"I'm staying."

"Very well. You know the gentleman?" She didn't look at me while she probed the wound.

Donovan sucked in a breath.

"I can hold his hand."

"He'd appreciate that." Donovan met my gaze. "He'll always appreciate your friendship."

After she applied the numbing agent, Evelyn set to work, and within no time, she was done.

As she was snapping off her gloves, Miles returned. He handed Donovan a green scrub shirt. "Might be a little tight."

I might have noticed Miles checking out Donovan. *Who wouldn't?*

But Miles had a loving wife and two kids, and I was one hundred percent certain he'd never risk any of that. So probably my warped imagination that was running amok today.

"Thanks." Donovan handed over a gray shirt with *Vigilante Justice* written across the front. "I don't wear that shirt often, but it's a favorite."

"I'm sure they'll find you another one." Miles took the shirt. Then he pivoted to me. "Grab your phone, knapsack, and jacket from your locker and head upstairs. I'll check in with you—"

I started to protest.

He waved me off. "You'd do the same if it were Darla in there and I was pacing the halls."

Yeah, he wasn't wrong.

Donovan tried to grab his coat, but I was quicker.

He growled.

I scowled.

"Look, I wasn't wearing the jacket. If I go up like I am, there's this big-ass bandage that everyone will see." He indicated his right arm.

He wasn't wrong. The scrub shirt didn't cover the wound.

"You'll overheat."

"I'll take my chances."

Gingerly, I helped him into his coat.

Miles and Evelyn had disappeared. Neither had given Donovan instructions on wound care—probably they assumed I'd do it.

Which I would. "I want you to wait by the elevators while I get my stuff."

He grabbed my arm. "Are you okay?"

His words caught me off guard. Of course I wasn't okay. What kind of a stupid fucking question was that? Yet even as I tried to find the words to formulate a response, I understood why he asked the question.

I wasn't in hysterics. I wasn't panicking. I wasn't giving any outward sign of distress. But this was eight years of working in high-pressure situations—be they

ERs or clinics on the front line or other war-torn countries.

After a moment, I bit my lip. "I need Michael."

"And if Julie and Thomas don't track him down, I'll go myself."

I eyed his arm.

"Cabs are a thing. I'll bill it to Cole."

That made me smile. Cole and Julie were the highest paid pretty much of everyone, but Donovan was likely making a decent wage—Cole would make certain of it. "Yeah, Cole's good for it."

God, please let him be okay.

I'd issued a few prayers in my life. Most had gone unanswered. Still, for the man I loved, I was willing to try again.

Chapter Fifteen

Michael

"Yo, Dubois, there's some hot chick here to see you."

I could remind Garth, one of our rebar guys, a hundred times a day that we didn't use sexist language on-site, but I'd be wasting my breath.

We were waiting to go up the tower to check on construction. I was finishing the last of my coffee and still wondering if I'd made the right decision about not raising a stink with Pamela Strickland's project. Waiting for city approval was driving me nuts. I kept hoping someone there would come back with concerns and I could use that as a pretext for shoring up the building the way I wanted to.

"Hot chick?" The only person I knew who fit that description was Caressa, and no way was she down here.

Unless something was wrong.

I hightailed it across the lot to the entrance only to come face-to-face with Julie Reyes and... I struggled for a moment. "Thomas."

He nodded. "Yeah. Met you on Saturday."

"What's wrong?" I searched their faces for some indication.

"Cole was injured. On the set." Thomas grabbed the coffee cup I almost dropped.

Julie grabbed my arm as I swayed.

Maybe it's nothing. Maybe you're overreacting.

And yet I knew I wasn't. No, if the injury was minor, then Cole would have called. Hell, he might even have waited until we all got home tonight. If he needed me, he would have reached out. "How bad?" The words came out as a croak as I pushed them past the tightness in my throat.

Thomas ran his hand through his hair. "We don't know—"

"Bad." Julie obviously felt sugarcoating things wasn't going to wash.

I appreciated that. "What happened?"

"Look, why don't you just come with us? I've got my SUV. Do you need to worry about your vehicle?" Thomas held up his keys.

My… I waved him off. "I can get it later." Honestly, I didn't give a shit. But I'd parked at the office and walked down. I had a remote that allowed me twenty-four-seven access to the garage so I could get in and out anytime I needed to.

I met Julie's gaze. "How bad? What happened?"

She snagged my hand and guided me toward an illegally parked SUV.

"Yo, Dubois, where you goin'?"

I turned back to face Garth. He was just a guy on the crew. I didn't report to him. Didn't owe him an explanation. I'd call Tyanna. I pivoted to Julie. "Are we going to the hospital?" Somehow, I didn't think they were snagging me so we could go the few blocks back to the day's shoot.

Julie nodded.

I met Garth's stare. "Someone I love has been hurt.

165

I have to go." I wasn't critical to the day's operations, and Tyanna would deal with the mess.

Garth waved me off, but not in a concerned way.

Does he have anyone in his life that he cares about? I'd heard he was dating someone, and I'd wondered what kind of woman would put up with such an asshole. Oh well, the world was full of people who made bad decisions. Maybe he wasn't so bad off the site. *Doubt that.*

When we reached the SUV, I started to open the door to the back seat. Julie nudged me to the front and hopped in the back.

Not wanting to argue, I slid into the passenger seat and secured my seat belt as Thomas did the same.

"You still haven't told me—"

"Is there anyone you need to call?" Julie's voice penetrated the encroaching panic.

I nodded. I tried Tyanna but got her voicemail. I left a rambling message that I was quite sure made no sense, but my boss had my number if she needed to reach me. She had a family of her own, and although she didn't know specifically that I had someone in my life, she'd gotten a glimpse the other day.

Thomas pulled up to the front of the hospital. Julie and I hopped out. I turned to thank him.

He waved me off. "Just keep me updated. We're anxious to hear news."

Part of me wondered why he wasn't coming in. The rest understood that the hospital wouldn't be able to handle that many people. "Thank you."

He inclined his head. When I shut the door, he pulled out.

"We're headed up to the surgical wing." Julie led me

in the automatic swishing doors.

"How do you…"

"Donovan texted me. Which is a good sign, because he got shot as well."

I halted.

She stopped and turned.

"Cole got shot?"

"Did I not say that?"

"Uh, no, you didn't say that." I had assumed some kind of accident. Like when she'd injured his IT band. Or maybe that he'd fallen. Crazy man did many of his own stunts. I pressed a hand to my chest. "How bad?"

She indicated the bank of elevators. "Serious, okay? But I'm not a doctor. I'm not even a nurse. I'm trying to get you to a medical professional who'll update you. Come on, Michael, Caressa's waiting."

"Is Donovan with her?"

Julie nodded.

That brought a modicum of relief. And Cole wasn't dead. Right? Because if Cole was dead, Julie would have said something. Right? Or maybe she was waiting for someone else to break the bad news.

Get a fucking grip. No matter what, you've got to be strong. For Cole. For Caressa.

The last thing any of us needed was me losing my shit.

The elevator was packed, and I lamented not having taken the stairs. Still, Julie held my hand and kept her head bowed.

Someone gave her a sideways look.

She wore a beret, but she was still drop-dead gorgeous and memorable—even if her distinctive hair wasn't visible.

Gabbi Grey

We exited and followed the signs until we arrived at a nurses' station.

A gentleman in scrubs passed behind us, then halted and came back. "Julie Reyes?"

She nodded.

"I almost didn't recognize you. I'm Miles. I work in the ER with Caressa." He cocked his head at me. "Michael?"

Clearly a guess, but an educated one.

"Yeah." I shook his outstretched hand.

"I'm just on a break, and I've come to check on Caressa." He nodded to the woman behind the counter. "They're with me."

She nodded and let us pass.

We entered a small room with a wall of glass facing the corridor.

Donovan sat in a chair with his head resting back against the wall, wearing a heavy winter coat.

The room already felt warm to me, and I was about to take off my own coat when I spotted Caressa.

She was in the far corner, looking out the window. The view wasn't anything impressive—just a bunch of condo and office towers. But with her arms wrapped around her waist and huddled in on herself, she looked cold.

I was about to remove my coat to offer it to her, even as I saw her own sitting on a chair with her knapsack.

Miles cocked his head at me, but I just stood there.

I knew I was supposed to go to Caressa, but I couldn't. I stood rooted to the spot, just inside the door. As if…maybe if no one spoke, then this wouldn't be real.

Miles approached Caressa and gently spoke her name.

She turned, at first looking at him, then looking over his shoulder at me.

Our gazes locked.

I'd thought I'd seen pain before, but everything previous to this moment paled in comparison to the abject misery and agony in her eyes.

"Is he…" I swallowed.

She shook her head.

Miles squeezed her shoulder. "Let me see if I can get an update." He nodded at me, then left the room.

Julie sat next to Donovan and whispered something to him.

He cracked an eye open. He looked at me, nodded, then closed his eye again.

Caressa stepped up to me. "He's been shot. I know he thinks a graze isn't a big deal, but they've given him painkillers and antibiotics."

"But he'll be okay?"

She nodded. "Yeah, he should be. As long as the wound doesn't become infected."

"At least Fucking Franklin didn't treat me." Donovan said the words in a singsongy voice.

"Is he high?" I whispered to Caressa.

She shook her head. Paused. Then furrowed her brow. "I wouldn't think so, but everyone reacts to painkillers differently."

"Fucking Franklin?" My mind was still processing Donovan's words.

"He was the physician. I was the nurse but—"

"Tell me you didn't treat him." *Oh, Sweet Jesus.*

"I didn't treat him. Not that I didn't want to." She winced. "I froze. As soon as I realized the patient was Cole, I couldn't move."

Finally, slowly, I reached for her. I'd been afraid to touch her because she looked so damn fragile—like she'd shatter into a million pieces.

She fell into my arms and clung to me like a koala holding onto its mother. There wasn't a breath of space between us.

"Is he going to die?" I whispered the words, not wanting the answer and yet knowing I needed to know. In case I needed to prepare myself.

"Likely not." A male voice came from behind us.

Caressa and I twisted to find Miles, who had just returned to the room.

He wore a guarded smile. "Quick update. The bullet missed all the major organs and lodged in a rib. Well, it nicked his heart, but the damage was minor." His gaze shifted between Caressa and myself. "No guarantees, and they're a long way from done, but he might just be okay."

"That's a relief." I barely managed to get the words out past the lump in my throat.

We turned, in unison, as two newcomers stepped into the room.

Detectives Gleason and McGillvary of the Vancouver Police Department. I flashed back to the night they had come to Cole's house—to interview Caressa about a toddler who died after ingesting marijuana-laced brownies that her negligent parents had left out. They had also had a question or two about Dr. Franklin Caruso's medical care of the patient.

Distractedly, I wondered whatever happened to that investigation. I didn't remember the parents being charged. Or it they had, news hadn't filtered down to us. I was positive Caressa would have told us.

"Tyson." Caressa nodded an acknowledgment. "Uh, everyone, this is…"

She's a mess.

"Detective Tyson McGillvary and Detective Mariah Gleason." Tyson offered a wave. "We're just here to check in on everyone." His gaze, however, honed in on Julie and Donovan.

Julie was still a terrifying shade of white, and Donovan's eyes were open but not particularly focused.

"We can take a walk." I held Caressa close.

"I need to get back downstairs." Miles gave a brief salute and headed out of the room.

"Actually, we understand you saw the suspect on Saturday night." Detective Gleason pulled a notebook out of her jacket pocket.

"Suspect?" Right. Duh. If someone got shot, then there was a shooter. "Wasn't this some kind of accidental discharge?" My head was starting to ache—a low throb at the base of my skull that would likely turn into a doozie of a headache if I didn't take something.

"Meggibeth." Donovan rubbed his hands over his face vigorously, as if trying to wake himself up. He met the detectives' gazes. "There's nothing to say, really. I knew she had a crush on Cole. Did I think she'd show up with a gun at work and shoot him? No."

"She took a shot at you as well." Detective Gleason pointed to his right arm.

He waved them off with his left arm, nearly knocking Julie in the process. "Sorry."

"You're a victim and a witness. We'd like to interview everyone—while memories are fresh. We've got a room down the hall." Gleason pointed to Donovan. "If you're up to it, we'll take you first."

He didn't look up to it. His normally dark skin had a weird and disturbing hue to it. He didn't look well at all, now I scrutinized him.

"Why don't we give him a rest? Caressa and I can speak to you. I don't think we know much beyond our brief encounter with…Meggibeth…on Saturday, but we'll try."

Detective Gleason didn't look pleased, but McGillvary offered a genial smile. "That'd be great," he said.

We followed him down the hall to a little side office. The four of us barely fit in the windowless room, but we didn't take long. I tried to keep calm, telling myself we were just having a chat with Tyson and Mariah. That this was a normal thing to do. All while a surgeon was fighting to keep my lover alive.

Caressa gave her impression of Meggibeth.

I said I'd barely spent moments in her presence and that Donovan had steered her away. "I didn't realize, at the time, he was separating her from Cole."

"That was unusual?" Tyson held his pen poised over the paper.

"Cole and I have never…" Caressa yanked at her ponytail. "I don't know about dates he's taken to previous events, so I can't speak to that. We were…affectionate."

"I saw the footage on CNC." Mariah's smile didn't reach her eyes. "Cole definitely made it clear how he feels about you."

Caressa blushed. "I wouldn't have chosen to be quite so…brazen. But that's Cole."

Mariah nodded.

I'd had the impression she was taken by Cole. And

why not? Tall, dark, handsome, piercing blue eyes, and a genuinely warm personality. Cole was the whole package, and people gravitated to him. I'd just never realized that geniality might cost him everything.

"We need to be checking up on him." I started to rise.

"One more question." Tyson shifted in his seat. "I understand you, Caressa, implied that you were a threesome. You, Cole, and Michael."

If she had, it had been subtle. Or not even in my presence. Or… "When she made the comment about the three of us being there together. She said *as friends*."

"She implied more." Mariah's sharp tone had me sitting up straighter.

"What Detective Gleason is trying to say is that we're trying to ascertain the nature of the relationship and how Meggibeth might've perceived it."

"I can't say how she perceived anything." Caressa met Tyson's gaze and held it. "We're friends. From way back."

"You seemed pretty cozy back there." Mariah indicated the waiting room.

"Comforting a friend." I held back the bite, but it nearly came through. Who was she to judge us? And even if we were all together, what business was it of hers?

"Look, you deal with law stuff. We need to get back to Cole." I managed to rise from my chair. I held my hand out for Caressa.

Before she took it, she met Tyson's gaze. "Is this my fault?"

"It's no one's fault. No one forced the suspect to shoot Cole and Donovan. Perhaps Cole can shed some

173

light on the situation."

"He's still in surgery, for Christ's sake." Now my temper frayed. "He'll need recovery time. He doesn't need you harassing him."

"It's not harassment," Mariah said.

Tyson put a hand on her arm, then met my gaze. "We'll wait until the doctors clear him. We won't impede his recovery."

I had to believe him.

I didn't have any choice.

Wordlessly, Caressa rose and let me tuck her into my side.

Fuck the cops and their judgmental attitude. If they couldn't see the love, then I wouldn't be the one to explain it.

When we returned, Donovan looked a bit better, and when Tyson asked him to speak to them, he nodded. As he rose, though, he swayed.

Tyson was there, at his side, to steady him.

Donovan looked at the cop almost as if seeing him for the first time—which, I supposed, was essentially the case.

Tyson was handsome, if a little on the short side. His close-cropped steel-gray hair didn't match the line-free face, and he had penetrating brown eyes.

And I wouldn't have noticed any of that particularly before Cole made the move on me. Now I looked at other men with an odd curiosity. *Is he attractive? Am I attracted to him? If I didn't have Cole, might I consider him?*

The answer was usually *no*. Donovan had flirted shamelessly. And although the Black man was gorgeous, I didn't go for brash. I had no idea if Tyson was gay or not, but he was certainly attractive.

Donovan and the detectives left.

Julie rose and stretched. "I need to do a coffee run."

Caressa reached out to touch the woman's cheek. "You're bruised."

The woman's green eyes dulled. "He pushed me down. Cole. He protected me even as she was shooting him."

Not surprising. Cole'd always been the hero.

"And Donovan got hit in the crossfire?" Caressa grimaced.

Julie shook her head. "He rushed her. Went at her and tackled her to the ground. She got off a shot at him before he hit her. It's a miracle she only grazed him. I think he caught her off guard. She didn't see him as a threat."

I wanted to say *more fool her*, but she'd been smart enough to hit Cole.

"I don't know if she would've shot me or not." Julie adjusted her beret. "It all happened so fast. I barely registered the gun before the first shot. I just…never thought I'd be shot at. I mean, aren't handguns illegal or something?"

"Or something." I couldn't remember exactly. We'd had a government dedicated to getting guns off the streets. I recalled that much. Where the actual legislation stood, I had no idea. "Even if they ban them, they're still around. I suspect it's not hard to get one. Don't they have them in the studio?"

Julie winced. "Maybe—in the armory. But those would be under lock and key, and they wouldn't have live rounds anywhere near them. I wouldn't think anyway. No…" She waved her hand. "I have no idea

175

where she got the gun. Or why she felt shooting Cole was the only alternative." She probed her cheek and winced.

Caressa stepped forward to examine it. "Nothing appears broken. But that's going to be a hell of a bruise. Did you hit your head?"

"Well…"

Immediately, Caressa swept the beret off Julie's head and began probing. White-blonde hair spilled everywhere, and Julie winced.

"You should get an MRI. You might have internal bleeding."

"In my head?" Julie scrunched her nose. "I'm fine."

"You're not fine. You might also have a concussion."

Julie snagged the beret back. In an impressive move, she had all her hair shoved back under it and was well out of Caressa's grasp in just a heartbeat. "Either of you allergic to anything?"

"Uh…" Caressa frowned, like she couldn't compute the question.

"No." I met Julie's gaze. "I have cash to pay for the food—"

She waved me off. "I'll be back." With that, she was gone.

Caressa looked at me. "What the fuck is going on?"

I didn't know if she meant with Julie or with everything that had happened since we all rolled out of bed together this morning.

Since I had no idea how to answer her, I merely shrugged and pulled her back into my arms again.

Chapter Sixteen

Cole

A persistent beeping pulled me out of wherever I'd been. Some nebulous place between happiness and despair. I couldn't grasp on to the dreams as I was rudely dragged into consciousness.

"Go ahead, open your eyes."

My eyes felt gritty and my lids leaden. I didn't want to open them. I wanted to sink back into Caressa and Michael's embraces. Back into our bed where we could enjoy ourselves. Wasn't Zoey supposed to clear me today?

So why…

Everything flooded back. All of it. With the speed of a bullet.

"Julie? Donovan?" Was I saying the words or only thinking them in my mind? My mouth was parched, and I couldn't lick my lips.

"Relax, Cole." A hand on my shoulder soothed, but only a little bit. "I think you're asking about your friends, and I can tell you that everyone's fine. You're the one who's going to need a lot of rest to heal."

Heal?

Oh, right, the bullet to the chest.

"Not gonna die?"

A chuckle reached my ears. "No, Mr. Hamilton,

you're not going to die. Not on my watch."

The shock of cold air hitting my skin as the blanket was yanked down slapped me hard. I'd been nicely cuddled. Then a cold object pressed to my chest.

Oh, a stethoscope. Well, all right, then.

"You do need to follow Nishita's orders and open your eyes." This woman's tone was no-nonsense and not all that gentle.

I cracked an eye. The light pierced my retina and shot to the back of my skull. "Jesus."

"It's not that bright."

"Says you." Again, the word came out as a croak.

"Try again."

I obeyed. Basically because I didn't want to be an asshole. A recalcitrant patient, Caressa used to call them. They fucking drove her nuts. I didn't want to be *that* guy.

The woman who came into focus had a gentle grin. Her gray hair was pulled back into a bun, and the widow's peak accentuated a strong forehead. Her blue eyes sparkled as she gave me a more dazzling smile. "I'm Dr. Stephanie Graham. I operated on you a few hours ago."

"Wanna sleep."

"And I'll let you. You're probably not going to remember all of this. I've got a chest tube in to drain the excess fluid. You took a bullet to the lung that nicked your heart and lodged in your rib."

I winced.

"You're going to be okay. I chose to remove the bullet, and I've patched you up pretty good. Recovery's going to be a long road, so don't go thinking you can play superhero again anytime soon."

"Julie? Donovan?" Keeping my eyes open hurt like

hell, but I needed to know they were okay. I seemed to recall them hovering over me, but I wasn't sure if that was an actual memory or something my mind conjured.

"Another man was shot in the arm, but he's fine. And I haven't heard anything about a woman being injured. Just you." She pulled the blanket back up. "Nishita's going to escort you from recovery to the ICU in a bit. Just rest."

"I have to pee."

"You have a catheter."

I managed to give her my most imperious look.

It apparently had no effect. "Look, Mr. Hamilton. I suspect your instinct is going to be to push the recovery. You can't—it's as simple as that. And I understand you're a friend to Caressa Klein."

Friend? "Yeah, something like that."

"Well, Ms. Klein knows I'll be very disappointed if you don't follow my instructions to the letter."

My head was still fuzzy, but I understood what she was saying. If I pushed and made things worse, Caressa might get in trouble. That didn't seem fair to me. On the other hand, blackmail was known to be an effective weapon. I'd never do anything to jeopardize Caressa or her career.

"Yes, Doctor."

She patted my shoulder. "I'm amazed you're so lucid. I've got you on the good stuff for now. If you have breakthrough pain, tell your nurse. I'm going to check on you before I go home. If anything feels wrong, tell your nurse."

I wanted to tell her that everything felt wrong. I'd been shot, for Christ's sake. By someone I'd known for five years. By someone I'd trusted. Yeah, I'd known

Meggibeth had a crush on me. So did countless other women.

You're lucky she didn't go after Caressa.

That thought hit me in the gut. Some obsessed people did that—went after their perceived rival. At least she'd come after me. I was sorry to hear someone else got shot. I struggled to recall…Donovan? If that was the case, I'd have to find a way to make it up to him.

My breath caught.

The doctor, who had been stepping away, came back. "You okay?"

"When can I see them?"

"Your friends?"

I nodded.

"We allow one at a time and only for a few minutes. You're riding on a bit of a high right now, but you're going to come back down at some point."

"Pain?"

"Probably. We'll keep up the meds, but this isn't going to be a snap-of-the-fingers recovery."

"If Caressa's a nurse, then she doesn't count as a person, right? So she and Michael can come see me together?"

Dr. Graham pursed her lips. "You're going to be a difficult one. I can tell."

I tried to shake my head, but the motion caused nausea to roil. "I promise I'll be good."

She held my gaze, those blue irises flashing. "Fine. I'll leave instructions that Caressa can be with you while one other person visits. ICU isn't a place for chitchats. You're still at risk. At least for the next day or two."

I intended to heed her warning. "I'll behave. I promise."

"This is Nishita."

I turned my head to see a beautiful woman with tan skin, black hair, and dark-brown irises. I managed a smile.

She smiled back. "Do what I say, and we'll get along just fine. Give me trouble, and you'll regret it."

I believed her.

Then as a feeling of well-being overtook me, I closed my eyes and sank back into oblivion.

I awoke later, having no sense of time or place. Except more beeping, but it seemed muted.

A soft hand feathered through my hair.

"You need to wake up, Cole. If only for a moment." Caressa's voice.

My eyes snapped open. At least this time, bright lights didn't greet me. The room was in semidarkness, and I could barely make out Caressa's features.

She offered a soft smile. "There you are. We were wondering when you might come back to us."

"How long…" I cleared my throat. "How long have I been out?"

"Quite a while. And although sleep is good, Nishita needs to check you over." She started to pull away.

I tried to reach for her, but my arms were tucked under the blanket. I started to thrash.

"Whoa, Cole, relax." She cupped my cheeks. "Breathe, okay? I'm not going anywhere. I just need to give Nishita space to do her thing." She held my gaze until I finally relaxed.

You're a big boy.

Except I wanted to crawl into Caressa's lap and have her hold me forever.

Nishita lowered the blanket and gave my chest a

thorough examination. I didn't want to look, but I snuck a peek. Nothing to see but bandages.

"Might I have some water?" My throat was still parched, and making saliva was proving difficult.

"I'll give Caressa a few ice chips." She adjusted something with the IV. "She's a good woman."

"She's the best. And a good nurse," I quickly added. I had no idea who knew what about our relationship.

Nishita regarded me. "That she is. She wanted to treat you, but Dr. Caruso ordered her out of the room."

"Dr. Franklin Caruso?"

She nodded. "He treated you in the ER. Got you stabilized and up to surgery."

"Does that mean I have to thank him?"

"Well, he helped save your life." She eyed me speculatively. "But he can be a…" She glanced around.

"Asshole," I supplied.

A ghost of a smile passed across her lips. "I give him a wide berth."

"Oh, glad to hear he's up to his old tricks. Still married?"

"No." Nishita pressed her fingers to my wrist. "His wife left him. Nasty divorce. She hired a detective to query pretty much every attractive woman in the hospital."

"Did you ever…"

She snickered. "Uh, no. He's so not my type."

"Married?"

"You bet. Eight years with three daughters. He'd never catch my eye. My husband would kill him. Which would be just fine with me."

"Oh. Fair enough."

She indicated a gold wedding band around her ring

finger. "And he knows I'd eviscerate him if he ever cheated."

I laughed. Then winced.

"Pain meds doing okay? We've got you on a high dosage."

"Is that why I'm so sleepy?"

"You need rest. Your body needs time to heal."

"I need Caressa."

She rolled her eyes. "Always with the dramatics." She tucked my arm back under the blanket before probing something in my side. "Chest tube."

"Ah. When does that come out?"

"Pretty soon. If you rest and recover."

"Ah. Yeah, okay." My eyes drifted shut. "Tell Caressa to wake me."

Nishita chuckled as she pulled the blankets back up. "Sure thing, big boy."

I was out again before she even left the room.

The next time I crawled into consciousness, a rough hand stroked my cheek. Well, rougher. "Michael?"

"Nah."

I cracked an eye at Donovan's word.

He looked absolutely wrecked. His eyes were red-rimmed, and his face bore creases I'd never seen before.

"I'm not going to die, am I?"

A small smile crept across his face. "You're the most stubborn son of a bitch I know. Of course you're not going to die."

I lifted my hand to my chest.

"Hey. What do you need?"

"To assure myself I'm still in one piece."

"Are you in pain? I can call a nurse."

I waved him off. "I'm okay. Really. Thirsty."

He took a cup, fished out an ice cube, and put it to my lips.

Effectively silencing me.

Damn man.

"Caressa and Michael went home for a few hours. She's tough, but even she realized she needed to get some sleep or she'd be useless."

I searched for a clock. "Time?"

"About nine a.m." Without blinking, he continued, "Caressa had to do some sweet-talking to get them to let me sit with you. Julie went home at the same time I did last night, but I came back when Caressa texted."

I tried to melt the ice cube faster.

He held up his hand. "Caressa insisted they check Julie for a concussion. Seems she hit her head on the pavement when you knocked her down."

My eyes widened.

Donovan puffed out his chest. "I might've tackled Meggibeth." He indicated his arm. "And she might've shot me."

My chest constricted. Confirmation of my earlier guess.

"I'm just fine. Patched up. They wanted me to wear a sling, but I promised to keep the arm fairly immobilized. Unlike certain other pigheaded men I know, I'm good at obeying orders."

Finally, I spoke. "Julie's okay?"

He nodded. "Yeah, no concussion. Bit of a bruise to the back of her head, but she's okay." He took my hand. "Thomas managed to keep everyone at the studio apprised. Everyone wants to come, but the doctors have been clear—even when you're out of the ICU, the number of visitors is going to be limited. Can't have the entire cast and crew traipsing through."

I narrowed my eyes.

"You think they wouldn't? Lisette, I think you'll have to see. I can put off Thomas and Peter—they're big on respecting privacy. Val, as producer, will probably want to come. He might try to bring Seamus, and I'd let him."

I quirked an eyebrow.

"He was the first to hear the shots and come running. Goddamn man ran toward the gunshots."

Yeah, that was Seamus.

"He also administered first aid while Elouise called an ambulance."

Another wince.

"Yeah, Kelci was doing her makeup. They waited until Seamus gave the all clear. Tanya secured the weapon. By standing on it and daring anyone to come near her. Larry helped me subdue Meggibeth—although she was pretty compliant at that point."

"Is she…"

"Under arrest. Crown prosecution is sorting the charges. I don't…" He drew in a sharp breath. "I'm wondering if we should've seen this coming. The armorer at the studio confirmed the gun didn't come from the show. Val was hella relieved to hear that. Talk about liability."

"I would've never—"

Donovan put another ice chip on my lips. "I know you wouldn't have sued, but there might've been a police investigation and charges." He rubbed his face. "It's been a crazy twenty-four hours."

I didn't question him. And I'd been unconscious for most of it. I worried about Caressa and Michael. Neither needed this kind of stress in their lives. And for fuck's sake, they had just spent most of the last month caring for me. Since I'd convinced them to move in, they weren't likely to take it well if I asked them to leave me alone. "Caressa and Michael?" Maybe my friend would tell it like it really was.

"They're okay." Donovan rubbed his face again. "Well, okay is a relative word. They're holding it together. Thomas arranged to have Michael's car driven back to your place, and I understand you commuted with him this morning. Uh, yesterday morning."

I nodded.

"Okay, so all that's sorted. Trust Thomas to keep things on track."

Thomas was the head production assistant on *VJ* as well as husband to one of the most famous actors in the industry and father to two little kids.

I swallowed the last little bit of the ice. "I don't want—"

Donovan placed another chip on my lips. "No one gives a shit what you want. They all wanted to help. Let them. They can do little things to make things better for you. That's not such a big ask—that you accept their help. Because they don't just want to make your life better. They've pretty much accepted Caressa and Michael as a major part in your life, and they're circling the wagons to protect them as well. I don't think everyone knows you're not just living together as friends, but it's none of their fucking business anyway." He waggled his eyebrows. "But this is going to put a crimp in your BDSM. Hard to be a Dom while hooked up to IVs and monitors."

I closed my eyes for a moment. Then I swallowed

the ice and met his gaze. "Intrigue does not a relationship make. So Caressa and Michael are intrigued. That might mean next month, next year, or never."

He cocked his head. "You okay with never?"

I considered. "Yeah, I really am. I'd always used BDSM as a way to connect with people—physically and psychologically. But none of those relationships ran deep."

"They couldn't." Donovan scratched his stubbly chin. "You weren't looking for a full-time submissive. You kept things casual."

I flashed to my photo album. Those hadn't felt casual in the moment—I'd formed some genuine bonds. But they had only lasted for the length of the scene or the length of the relationship—which was never long. Maybe Caressa hadn't always had my heart.

Maybe.

But I'd always kept myself away from long-term relationships. I'd told myself I'd done so because of my celebrity status. That I couldn't take the risk of someone telling the tabloids about my exploits.

"They mean more to me than all of it."

"Then I guess you have your answer." Donovan placed another chip on my lips. "And I suspect you'll never resent them for it, if you do wind up giving it up. Man, I've never seen you so happy. Even when you landed the role of Montgomery, you weren't as glowy as you are these days."

I arched an eyebrow.

He waved me off. "Okay, that probably isn't a word. But you know what I mean. And I didn't mean to be a shit disturber."

I nearly guffawed. Somehow, though, I knew my

chest would hurt too much. I blinked a couple of times, trying to maintain focus.

He brushed a lock of hair out of my face. "They'll be back soon, and you need to be at your best."

Did he mean my hair or my fatigue level? I'd never felt so exhausted in my life, yet I wasn't sure if I'd be able to sleep again before Caressa and Michael returned.

Yet even as I had the thought, my eyes drooped. Within moments, I was back under again.

Chapter Seventeen

Caressa

Despite my best intentions, Michael and I crawled into bed for a couple hours' sleep. I didn't want to, and neither did Michael, but neither of us was fit to drive back to the hospital and, by logical extension, to sit by Cole's bedside.

Donovan's offer had meant everything, and once we relieved him, he could go home and get some solid rest. Or get on with his day. Or do whatever the studio needed him to do.

I hadn't thought I'd be able to sleep, but with Michael clinging to me, sleep came hard and fast.

We got a solid three before I awoke. A dream chased me into consciousness. But I knew where it ended, and I didn't want to go there. So I forced myself into wakefulness. After a moment, I tried to slip from Michael's grasp.

"Don't you dare."

"You can sleep some more. I'll take a cab."

"No way. Give me a second. Once I'm awake, I'll come with you." He rubbed his face. "I remembered to call Tyanna, right?"

Knowing he wasn't fully awake, I didn't panic over his confusion. "Yes, you called your boss. She's given you as much time off as you need. And you might've also come out to her. About Cole and, in a roundabout way, about myself. Pretty impressive."

He moaned and scrubbed his hands across his face. "I did not."

"Oh, you absolutely did. Things'll be interesting when you go back to work."

"Tyanna's progressive."

"But I doubt she's in a threesome." I rolled out of bed. "I'm going to my room. I'll meet you in the kitchen in twenty. We can do drive-thru."

"No, I'll whip something up quick. I don't trust drive-thru at…" He squinted at his phone. "It's already eleven? Ugh, they'll be serving lunch."

"Yeah, we got some solid sleep. I want to get back to Cole. Plus, I love those little maple-syrup-infused breakfast-sandwich things. They serve all-day breakfast. That's a thing."

He managed a small smile as he rose. "Yeah, I can see that about you." He rounded the bed, and despite morning breath, he kissed me deeply. "I'm also going to text Donovan to see if we can bring him anything."

And to see how Cole was doing. Something I should have thought of myself.

"Kitchen in twenty." I trudged through the house, up the stairs, and into the spare room that was sort of mine. I loved sleeping in Cole's room, but I appreciated having my own shower and closet space. Not that I had many clothes. Michael'd insisted I add to my wardrobe when I returned from South Sudan. Also, I was aware of Cole bristling at me not letting him buy me more stuff. Didn't Michael just essentially buy me five new pairs of scrubs? Since I spent half my life at work, I truly didn't believe I needed anything else.

I debated about washing my hair but decided it needed to be done. After my shower, I added some gel so it wouldn't frizz, then I put it up with a clip. I dressed in my jeans and the soft pale-blue blouse I loved so much and that Cole said matched my eyes. I hadn't thought he meant that as a come-on, at the time, but now I wondered. I often replayed the entire relationship in my mind—searching for the moment when things had changed.

For just another moment, I looked at the blouse in the mirror. I'd worn it our first night getting together after I'd returned from Africa. When we three had gathered together at our favorite pub on Commercial Drive. The night I delivered a baby in the washroom of said pub.

I had, through the manager, received another thanks from the woman I'd helped. And she'd confirmed she'd named her son Michael Cole. Again, I wondered if I'd said I was with my friends Cole and Michael, if she would have reversed the names. And finally, I wondered if this kid would ever know he was named after someone semi-famous.

Oh, who was I kidding? Cole was famous. Between *VJ* and his various movies, he was making a name for himself in the industry.

I made my way to the kitchen, not quite trudging, but not with much enthusiasm either.

Michael had toast in the oven and eggs in the fry pan.

I cocked my head.

"Old habits. Coffee should be ready soon."

"Did you shower?" I didn't care one way or the other, but I was curious.

"Quickly," he confirmed. "I skipped my hair."

And since his hair was fine, I offered a small smile. "What did Donovan say?"

He pulled his phone from his back pocket and handed it to me. Then he rattled off the password.

As I entered it, I frowned. "Is that…"

"Yeah, your name. Now you'll always know it."

His openness, and lack of guile, never ceased to amaze me. He didn't have any secrets.

While I held too many to keep suppressing. "He woke for a bit but is asleep again. The nurse says she's happy with how he's doing."

Michael buttered the toast. "How is he not in pain?"

"Well, they're giving him painkillers."

"Yeah, but remember when I had my wisdom teeth out? They gave me painkillers, but it still hurt."

"They're giving him the good stuff." I shot off a text to Donovan—letting him know I was the one responding and letting him know we'd be there within half an hour. "And they gave you the crappy stuff. If you'll recall, I wanted to complain. You wouldn't let me."

He gazed at me. "I totally forgot about that."

"Yeah, not surprising." I poured the coffee into the two mugs. "You were in so much pain, and Cole and I debated taking you to a clinic, but they don't like doling out painkillers any more than your stupid dentist." I added appropriate milk and sugar to each. "But you persevered, and we decided to let you ride it out."

"Gee, thanks."

His dry tone made me smile because I knew he wasn't actually upset. If it had gotten worse, then I would have taken him in. I hated seeing people suffer. In fact, I'd become a nurse to help alleviate pain and suffering.

How naïve was that?

Way too much.

Michael put our breakfast sandwiches in little baggies, I secured the lids to the mugs, and we headed out.

I'd debated bringing something of Cole's to make him more comfortable, but the ICU didn't really have room for stuff like that. I also suspected there would be plenty of flowers and gifts once we got him moved to a regular room.

We made our way to Michael's SUV, which the *VJ* production staff had arranged to return. We'd driven home in my car last night.

Or early this morning.

Grogginess overwhelmed as I sipped my coffee wordlessly as Michael drove us through the bustling streets. Vancouver had been awake for hours, but I felt like I'd been hit by a truck.

"Donovan texted that the story's made international news. He wondered if there might be press." Michael tapped the steering wheel.

"You're worried about me."

"Yeah, I am. Cole was pretty public about claiming you on Saturday. Those interviews are being shown again with talking heads speculating you're the reason he got shot."

"They're letting that story run?"

He turned us north onto the Burrard Bridge. "They can't let the rumor it was an armory accident stand. That would bring down a world of hurt for the studio."

Yeah, it would.

"So that leaves mugging or some kind of deliberate action. I doubt anyone on *VJ* said anything, but word's bound to filter out that Cole was targeted."

True. Whatever privacy bubble we'd enjoyed for the past few weeks, that was now completely burst. "Are they speculating about you?"

"Donovan didn't say anything—and I trust he would. No one knew you'd moved in with me—"

"Except Kendall. And Miles."

He shot me a glance before returning his attention to the road. "You think your former roommate or your co-worker might talk?"

"I…" I swallowed hard. "No?"

"That doesn't sound certain."

I cleared my throat. "No, I don't think so. Neither has anything to gain."

"Except money. Tabloids pay big bucks for scandals like this."

"I don't see why it has to be a scandal."

Michael turned us into the parking lot. "A threesome involving one of the most famous actors on network television?"

Arguing that television wasn't what it used to be, or that it was a Canadian production, wasn't likely to garner any points in the debate. Cole was big. Yes, he kept a low profile. But people knew who he was. If *VJ* had set tongues wagging to begin with, his turn as Peter Erickson's gay lover in the little studio film that went big and garnered Peter an Oscar had pushed him up to the elite. We might live in Hollywood North, but we still had an active press corps who liked to report on the goings-on.

No one hung out by the back door of the hospital. I swiped my badge and ushered Michael inside. We hustled to the elevators, hoping not to spot anyone.

Luckily, we didn't, and soon we were in the ICU. I didn't know the charge nurse, and she didn't look thrilled to see us, but she got Donovan and brought him out.

He looked like shit. After a moment, he reached for me.

For just a moment, I worried something had happened to Cole. But no, he just sought some assurances. That I wasn't mad? That I didn't blame him?

I wasn't, and I didn't.

After a moment, I coaxed him into Michael's arms. Not a bro hug, but a real clinging. Our friend hurt, and apparently only we could comfort.

Finally, he pulled back. "We had a good few minutes of lucidity. He says he's not in pain, but I think he's trying to put on a brave face."

"I'll get him to admit the truth."

Donovan cupped my cheek. "Yeah, I'll bet you will." He turned to Michael. "I'll be back tonight."

I wanted to tell him that we'd be okay, but he needed to be here. I understood that.

"Oh, and when Julie comes today, convince her she has to go to LA."

I cocked my head.

"The Golden Globes are on Sunday. Cole's nominated for *VJ*. He's not likely to win, but in case I'm wrong, we need someone from the show to be there. Who better than Lyric? And she's nominated as well. She'll tell you she's not going to win, but there's always a chance."

"Julie's not going to listen to me." Donovan's reasoning was sound. If we really cared about the awards show. "When were the nominations announced?"

He looked back and forth between Michael and

myself. "Typical fucking asshole. He didn't even tell you. Was he just going to sweep you off to LA?"

"Maybe he didn't want us there." That thought hurt, but it rivaled the panic as I contemplated one of the most glamorous nights in Hollywood.

"I want to say he might've forgot, but that's unlikely. He's been nominated three times for *VJ*. Biased as I am, I think he should've won by now." Donovan suddenly gave me the once-over. "Pretty blouse. Are you supposed to be working today?"

"Yes." I hesitated. "The head of HR came down to see me yesterday and told me to take all the time off that I needed. I'd hate to think I was being given special treatment—"

"But if you screw up patient care, they'll claim you were distracted." Michael pulled me into his side. Then he met Donovan's gaze. "My boss gave me the same lecture. I don't know what the studio said to her…"

"That your best friend nearly died yesterday and that he and your other best friend need you right now? Seems reasonable they give you a few days off."

I didn't remember Michael telling me this, but yesterday was a blur. "We should get in to see him."

Donovan took my hand and squeezed. "He's going to be okay."

"You say that like you have the inside track." I couldn't keep the sarcasm from my voice.

"Look, your boyfriend is the most stubborn man I know." He yawned. "I am going to get some sleep. I might swing by your place later. Cole asked me to do a couple of things."

He was lying. I wasn't sure how I knew, but he was lying. Still, he had a key and could come and go as he pleased. He was doing the polite thing by giving us the heads-up.

"Whatever." Michael grasped my hand. "Thanks, Donovan."

The man saluted us and headed out.

Michael gazed down at me. I nodded. We headed into Cole's room.

Chapter Eighteen

Michael

The next five days passed in a blur.

Every day we went to the hospital.

Every day Cole got a little better.

Every day I worried about the tabloids.

Not for my sake. Well, or so I told myself. My boss might be progressive, but I wasn't certain a threesome with a famous actor would fly. Most of my worry was for Caressa. Cole and I were strong. Or at least Cole would be once he recovered. Caressa still felt fragile to me. Like a breath of wind might knock her over. And I struggled to find the words to express my concern.

Cole saw it. But Caressa never left us alone for more than the five minutes it took her to go to the bathroom. She insisted I go for coffee and food runs. Prying her away from Cole's side at night always proved challenging, but even she understood she'd be useless if she didn't get some sleep.

Each night, we cuddled in Cole's enormous bed and didn't talk about the future.

Our bed.

They moved Cole from the ICU to a regular room— a huge relief to me. I couldn't pinpoint an exact reason, but I assumed it meant they didn't think he was in danger any longer.

The room was full of balloons, stuffed animals, and flower arrangements. Cole kept quietly asking Miles to re-home the extras—the stuff from people he knew wouldn't come and visit and so whose feelings wouldn't be hurt. Miles dropped by frequently, despite his hectic schedule in the ER. He pointed out if his wife Darla was in the ICU, Caressa would do the same thing.

He wasn't wrong.

Caressa.

At times I sensed she held on by a thread. Other times, she appeared perfectly in control. Although the medical staff didn't defer to her, they listened to her comments and suggestions. I knew my lover well enough, though, to see her fraying around the edges.

If I tried to broach the subject, she'd wave me off.

If Cole and I tried to talk, she'd reappear in the room before we could get out two sentences.

If Donovan approached her, she'd become as prickly as a hedgehog.

I couldn't find a way in. I told myself over and over that once Cole was fully recovered, or at least safe and home with us, then we could deal with whatever Caressa was enduring. Her silence, though, ate away at me. I might not be the most sensitive guy, but even I could see things were going sideways.

As we settled in for what I hoped would be a quiet Saturday, a doctor breezed in. At least their name tag proclaimed them as a doctor.

"I'm Dr. Winston." She removed her stethoscope.

Cole obligingly let her lower his gown so she could listen to his heart. There had been a lot of that over the last few days. How he hadn't lost his temper before now, I wasn't sure. Possibly just grateful to these people for keeping him alive?

"I understand we've removed the chest tube and you've even been up a couple of times."

"Finally letting me pee on my own." Cole might have grumbled that.

Caressa grabbed his hand.

"I want to consider moving you to a rehab hospital. A step down in care, but somewhere you can continue to be monitored."

"I want to go home."

Cole's jaw took on the mulish look I was so familiar with. Twenty-seven years of that stubborn expression.

Dr. Winston considered. She was an attractive woman in her late thirties with spikey blonde hair, multiple piercings in her ears, and the hint of a tattoo around her collarbone.

I couldn't decide if that made her more relatable or more untouchable.

Her brown eyes narrowed. "You nearly died five days ago."

"And I've done every single thing you've told me to do."

"You still require around-the-clock care."

"He has me." Caressa met the doctor's gaze. "He also has a physical therapist who can work with him to regain his strength. I don't think she's particularly qualified in cardiac care patients, but I'm sure she'll figure it out."

That was, to my recollection, the nicest thing she'd ever said about Zoey.

"I'm not a cardiac care patient." Cole huffed.

Caressa glared. "You're lucky she used a small caliber bullet that didn't do more damage and only lodged in your rib instead of splintering it and sending shards all over your chest."

My breath caught. I hadn't known this. Which made me wonder how Caressa knew. Yes, Cole'd been lucky the damage hadn't been more severe, but I hadn't stopped to think how the caliber of bullet would have played a role in all this.

"If you can arrange care, that should be acceptable." The doctor put her hand on her hip. "But that means doing everything by the book. You can't give him an inch of leeway."

"Oh, trust me, she won't." I eyed Cole.

Caressa, Cole, and the doctor all turned to me.

I felt my cheeks heat. "Just…she's stubborn. So's he, but I'd pick her if I had to lay odds."

That appeared to satisfy the doctor. "I'll prepare discharge papers, and tomorrow, if you're still improving, you can go home." She pivoted to Caressa. "He'll need a medical bed and—"

Caressa held up her hand. "We'll get that all arranged."

I didn't know what *all* meant, but I assumed she did.

The doctor nodded and headed out of the room.

Before any of us had a chance to speak, Detective Tyson McGillvary entered the room. Hesitantly, he approached the bed.

My hackles rose.

I must have made some kind of sound low in my throat, because Tyson held up his hand. "Just here to ask Cole a few questions. I promise I won't be long."

I almost made a smart-ass comment about his partner, but frankly, I was glad Tyson was here alone. Mariah Gleason fawned just a little too much over Cole.

And although that might stroke his ego, it didn't get done what needed doing.

"Should we leave?" *God, please let him say no.*

He shook his head. "No. Since we've reviewed your statements from—"

"You interrogated them?" Cole growled. Might have come out as more of a whimper, but he conveyed his message clearly.

"We asked them about the gala last Saturday night."

Cole didn't appear to have a snappy comeback for that, so Tyson began his questioning.

I only listened with half an ear. I was curious about Cole's acquaintanceship with Meggibeth, but I didn't feel I needed to know all the details. In the end, he acknowledged suspecting she had a crush on him, that he'd never done anything to encourage her, and that he still didn't understand why she shot him.

We probably all assumed some kind of jealous rage possibly triggered by my appearance on the scene, but that would be up to the cops and lawyers to sort out. And I supposed a doctor...if they questioned her sanity.

"You've spoken to Donovan?" Cole spoke quietly.

His question caught my attention. I glanced over at the police officer.

Who flushed.

"Uh, yes, I've spoken to Mr. Riggs. Several times. He's been...most helpful."

I nearly snickered. Then I eyed Cole. Did he see what was so obvious? That the cop was taken with Donovan? If I knew Donovan better, I'd consider razzing him. As it stood, though, he'd been here every day watching over Cole so Caressa and I could take breaks.

"So you're going to be released soon." Tyson tucked

his notebook into his jacket.

Cole nodded.

"The watch commander will add a couple of drive-bys in your neighborhood. If anything suspicious happens, don't hesitate to call."

Caressa's gaze sharpened on him. "What are you suggesting?"

"That word's gotten out about where Cole lives. We've had police cars driving by, and that seems to have deterred the press. But if they know Cole's home, then it might take more…persuasive measures."

"Fuck me."

Caressa's invective startled me.

Tyson shrugged. "We'll do what we can." He closed his notebook and pulled out a card.

After a moment, I grabbed it.

"If you think of anything else."

"I doubt I will." Cole's brow unfurrowed.

A bit.

"Uh, thanks." Tyson met my gaze. "If you see Mr. Riggs…"

"We'll tell him you said *hi*." Caressa didn't try to hide her amusement.

This cop was so genuinely serious and concerned that having him…crushing…over Donovan felt awkward. I meant, if Donovan returned the feelings, then more power to them.

How would that work?

Donovan was an unabashed Dominant. A Top, as Cole had explained. Wouldn't a cop be the same way? Always needing to be in control? What happened when two Tops got together? According to Cole, he'd occasionally bottomed for Donovan—in the beginning.

Gabbi Grey

As he'd been learning. But now? Apparently, neither man ever took the submissive role.

Tyson nodded and headed out.

Caressa let out a long sigh. Cole shifted. Both Caressa and I moved to assist him.

He waved us off. "I was just fucking shifting. I can't have you hovering." He turned to Caressa. "Not that I want you to, but you need to consider returning to work."

Her chin rose. "Who's going to take care of you when you come home?"

"I can bloody well take care of myself."

Judging by the fire in her pale-blue eyes, I was quite certain Cole'd said the wrong thing.

Clearly undaunted, he turned to me. "And I'm sure you have some construction to oversee or some plans to—"

I held up my hand. "I haven't taken a real vacation in years. Tyanna has forbidden me from returning to the office for at least another week."

Cole cocked an eyebrow.

"Well, she figured it out. She's a pretty smart woman. Two people show up wearing *Vigilante Justice* jackets and asking for access to the garage to retrieve my car on the same day that Cole Hamilton gets shot?" She might not know the extent of my involvement with Cole, but she'd put two and two together and come up with just how important the man was in my life. "And what are we going to do about the reporters?"

"Nice dodge, Dubois." Caressa's voice dripped with sarcasm.

"I was planning to hire a nurse." Cole tried to cross his arms, but the action was clearly too painful.

Pointing out he could barely take a piss by himself

204

wasn't going to earn me any favors.

"I've arranged to have a medical bed delivered to the house later today." Caressa rubbed her brow wearily. "Seamus is taking delivery and getting everything set up in your bedroom."

"Our bedroom." Cole growled.

"Our bedroom." Caressa echoed the words but didn't put much enthusiasm behind them.

"I'd prefer to be in the main room." Cole fidgeted with his blankets. "I want you guys to get a good night's sleep, and you won't get that with me in the room."

"We need to be near you, Cole."

"That's what the nurse'll be for. God knows I can afford one."

Even if he wasn't relatively rich, his insurance plan would cover many of the expenses. I'd looked it over while trying to sort out the myriad of forms to get Cole's private room secured. Not that the hospital wouldn't have given him one anyway. Security had already been enhanced since several reporters and a couple of fans had tried to sneak in. I thought we should hire a full-time security guard for the door, but Cole'd put his foot down.

No arguing with him—and I couldn't have paid the out-of-pocket expense myself anyway. Not working didn't mean no expenses. We'd done a lot of takeout, and parking around here was ridiculously expensive. Plus, I had to make certain Caressa had enough to cover the bed and everything else we'd need. Insurance would, hopefully, reimburse her. I appreciated universal healthcare, but plenty of stuff wasn't covered.

"Are we agreed on a nurse?" Cole tried to fidget with his blanket.

Caressa stopped his movements. "No, we're not,

okay? I get it. I really do. I wouldn't want you and Michael to see me vulnerable. Weak and needy."

"Gee, thanks."

She smacked his hand lightly. "We're not going to tolerate you trying to pretend you're okay. You're not okay. You almost died, Cole—"

"As you keep reminding me."

"Hey." This time, I moved in on his other side. "I get you don't want to be here. I get you don't want us to take care of you. Here's the deal—if we take care of you and you do everything they tell you to do, then you'll get better sooner."

He wrinkled his nose.

I smiled. "Is that acquiescence?"

"I love you guys."

Caressa angled herself so she could gently lay her head on Cole's arm. "We love you too. Just don't get shot again, okay?"

He offered a wry smile. "I'll do my best."

Chapter Nineteen

Cole

Whoever tipped the press that they were releasing me from the hospital deserved a horrible and slow and painful death. The doctor even released me in the evening, to try to cut down on possible detection. Most people were released in the morning to early afternoon. So later at night should have bought us privacy.

Truthfully, I could have done without the whole mess. Even the wheelchair ride down to the ground floor hurt.

Michael pulled up to the back door. He, Caressa, and Miles all helped me into his SUV.

Even that little step up hurt.

The ride home proved uneventful, but we hit a couple of potholes that jostled me, and I might have cursed.

Caressa, from the back seat, put a hand on my arm.

That helped.

All that supposed calm vanished when we pulled up to my driveway. Numerous cameras, both still and video, followed us as we drove up to the garage. In the moments it took for the door to open, some enterprising photographer put their camera up against my window and took several shots.

"That's trespassing." Caressa was indignant.

"Even if he gets arrested, his photo will make him so much money that it'll be worth it. And the odds of the charge actually sticking and being prosecuted are almost zero." I let out a relieved breath when the garage door shut.

Michael cut the engine.

We all sat in stunned silence.

"Should we call Tyson?" Caressa was the first to find her voice.

"I'm pretty sure my neighbors will have called the cops by now, but just in case, it wouldn't hurt."

We sat for a moment before Caressa pronounced, "Done."

Michael turned to look at her.

I was completely incapable of moving that way. I tried to look in the rearview mirror, but the angle was off. "You texted him?"

"No, I texted Donovan to call him."

I snickered. "Are you matchmaking? Because it'll never work between them."

"Matchmaking is such a strong word. I'm just giving a job to someone who's always whining about being left out." She squeezed my shoulder and then hopped out of the car.

Michael unclipped my seat belt.

I scowled.

"You'd just fidget with the left hand. I want to be in bed before midnight."

He was only half joking—I was truly terrible with my left hand while he was nearly ambidextrous.

Caressa opened my door.

"I want Michael."

"Fuck off, Hamilton. I'm trained in how to help

people without injuring myself. I've moved guys far larger than you."

I wasn't going to comment. I let her guide me out of the car, even as I pressed a hand to my chest.

"You should've stayed a couple more days." Caressa scowled.

"I'd have lost my mind, and the doctor agreed I could come home." I might have applied a fair amount of pressure to the doctor, but I figured she could hold her own. Despite my best efforts, I was becoming the recalcitrant patient I didn't want to be. "Sorry."

She cocked her head as she gently helped me around the front of the SUV.

Michael grabbed my overnight bag and shut the door.

I'd arranged to donate all the flower arrangements, and the various stuffed animals had been shuttled over to the children's hospital on the other side of town. And apparently St. Paul's had an uptick in donations to their foundation. I intended to make one myself. The place might be old, but it had done its job in keeping me alive.

Leaning more heavily on Caressa than I would have liked, I let her guide me through the house to the master bedroom.

Why did I think having the bedroom so far from the front door was a good thing?

Once in the room, she pointed to the medical bed.

"I've got to pee."

"And this is where I come in." Michael dropped the bag on the bed and came to my side.

"I can help him piss, for Christ's sake. I'm a nurse." Caressa's jaw set in the mutinous way I was so familiar with.

"It's a matter of pride." Michael's chin tipped upward.

"Oh, hang pride."

"Dignity," I interjected. "I don't want you seeing me with…" I indicated my crotch.

"Seriously?" She put her hands on her hips. "You're thinking I've never seen you deflated before?"

Oh, how I hated that word. "It doesn't matter what you have or have not seen. I'm saying, in this moment, I don't want you looking at my dick." I pressed my hand to the bed to keep from toppling over.

"Fuck." Michael was by my side in an instant, holding me upright. "Do you want to get his coat off? He's sweating."

Caressa didn't look any happier, but she helped me remove my coat. "Michael can untie your laces while you're sitting on the toilet."

"Sitting?" Both Michael and I exclaimed the word at the same time.

"Oh, wait until you see what we have for you."

I could totally wait, but my bladder wasn't happy, so with Michael's help, I shuffled toward the bathroom.

Twenty minutes later, I was in bed. A sheen of sweat coated my body, even as the cotton pajamas and flannel sheets rested cool against my heated skin.

Caressa pressed a cool washcloth against my forehead.

"I don't feel good."

She offered a small smile. "You overdid it. You can't be doing that, Cole. My heart can't take the stress."

I was quite certain she could withstand any amount of stress, but guilt that I'd put her through that swamped me. "I'll try harder."

210

"I know you will." She raised the side of the bed so I was essentially trapped, or protected, depending on how I wanted to approach the situation.

She snagged her knapsack, which I hadn't seen arrive, and she pulled out a stethoscope.

"Seriously?"

"Yes, seriously." She undid several buttons of my pajamas.

"Oh, this could be interesting."

She swatted my upper arm. Then listened to my chest. I tried to breathe slowly and deliberately—tried to slow my heart rate.

After a moment, she pulled back and put the stethoscope around her neck. Likely, she didn't even realize the reflexive action. "It sounds okay, but I'm going to keep an eye on your heart. The damage has been repaired, but you've been through a hell of a trauma—"

"I know."

"Do you? Sometimes I wonder."

"I'm the one with the hole in my chest. And the scar to prove it."

"In time, it'll heal."

"I do a lot of scenes with my shirt off."

She quirked an eyebrow. "Well, you were, admittedly, naked with Peter Erickson in that movie."

"Don't remind me."

"What, you don't like to think back fondly upon being naked with another man in bed?"

"Well, frankly…" I scratched my nose. "He was thinking about Thomas, and I was thinking about you."

She took a step back, nearly knocking into Michael who had changed into pajamas.

"That was more than three years ago, Cole.

Surely…"

Did I really want to open this can of worms *now*?

"We both realized we loved you—in that way—when you left." Michael slowly wrapped his arms around her from behind.

She leaned back into the embrace.

I nearly lost my shit for wanting to be the man holding her. Michael doing it appeased me somewhat—but only a bit.

Caressa angled her face back so she could see him. "You never said anything." She turned to me. "You never said anything."

Michael nuzzled her neck—but not in a sexual way. "We kept thinking you'd come home and…" He met my gaze. "I didn't know how Cole felt, but I knew I'd try to find the right time to convince you to stay home. If you hadn't met someone over in Africa."

She'd mentioned having a relationship with a guy in logistics—whatever that meant. It hadn't sounded serious, and she certainly hadn't seemed like her heart was broken. Not like what Fucking Franklin had done to her.

Something we still hadn't talked about.

But Miles had let me know, when I asked, about all the nurses and doctors who had helped save my life. I'd been galled to learn Franklin was one of them. I wouldn't have been surprised if he'd let me bleed out—especially after the *talk* Michael and I had given him when we discovered he was married and only saw Caressa as a side piece whom he could keep in the dark. I still wasn't clear on all the details, just that Caressa found out about Caruso's wife and two kids, and one night she'd broken down with Michael and me, confessing the truth. In return…Michael and I'd given Franklin a *talking to* that he'd likely never forgotten.

Or so I hoped.

Knowing he helped save my life disconcerted. Still, I'd sent him a thank-you card as well. Not wanting to involve Michael or Caressa, I'd enlisted Julie to help. I was pretty sure she'd been glad for the task. She and Donovan were the only two I permitted to visit me in the hospital. They had struggled—and they knew me. I worried about what others might think.

Lisette likely couldn't be put off much longer. Val, as producer, would want to see me. He'd likely try to bring his husband Seamus. I was pretty sure Peter and Thomas would be happy to receive an invitation. Finally, I should consider inviting Elouise. She'd been there that morning and had kept a cool head. I owed her as much as everyone else. Whether seeing me would be considered a reward, I wasn't sure. But I could at least express my gratitude.

"Cole," Caressa whispered.

Her voice yanked me rudely from my inner thoughts back into the present.

She placed a hand to my forehead. "You seem okay, for now anyway. I'll need to give you pain meds soon and antibiotics in the morning."

I wanted to insist I didn't need either, but shit like that would land me back in the hospital. "Thank you."

My easy acquiescence didn't fool her for even an instant. Her eyes narrowed.

"No, truly. I would've preferred a private nurse, but you might prove to be more entertaining." I couldn't have gotten hard for a million dollars, but that didn't bother me.

She glared.

"What? I'm allowed to watch."

She slashed her hand through the air. "That's total bullshit. And even if I felt like putting on a show—which I don't." She turned to Michael. "Sorry."

He held up his hands. "The last thing I'm thinking about right now is sex."

Even as he said the words, he cut me a glance. Oh, he could totally think about sex if not for my predicament.

"I'm getting changed and getting into bed." She gave Michael a peck on the cheek. "Make sure Shithead doesn't get up to anything while I'm gone."

I wanted to put up my hands in protest, but sleep was already dragging me under.

I didn't even hear them settle into bed.

Chapter Twenty

Caressa

The next few days passed in a blur.

Despite my worst fears, Cole proved to be a…reasonable…patient.

Zoey came to start him on gentle exercises.

Dr. Graham made an unheard-of house call to check on her patient's progress.

I couldn't pin down the exact reason for her visit, but I certainly knew she didn't do this with any of her other patients. For all that Cole was just another person coming through St. Paul's doors, and how we were committed to treating everyone equally, his status earned him certain privileges. I downplayed these because, frankly, I knew he'd hate it if he was aware they were going an extra mile because he was *the* Cole Hamilton.

Michael, reluctantly, returned to work. He worked from home a couple of days during that first week, but he had a critical project that really needed him on-site.

On leave from the hospital and not wanting to hover, I set about putting away the Christmas tree and trying to make the house feel a little less…sterile. Cole'd lived here for years, yet I didn't sense much of his personality. He used the views to speak for the magnificence of the house, but hadn't done much, aside from keeping the windows clean, to enhance his home.

Although I was loath to spend his money, I encouraged him to pick out a few art pieces by local artisans. A few pieces from northern artists as well. He couldn't articulate why, but he always felt a kinship with the Arctic dwellers in our country.

I tapped Michael as well. To my surprise, he picked a couple of pieces by Indigenous artists. He never talked about that part of his heritage. He chose to remain, I was certain, rooted firmly in the present. Thinking about his parents—or even long-dead ancestors—never improved his disposition.

After a week of being home, Cole was getting restless. Although Donovan and Julie'd come to visit, I hadn't allowed anyone except medical professionals.

Today, almost two weeks after he'd been shot, I allowed him two guests.

He groused…then asked for Lisette Fortier, his director, and Elouise Hynes, his co-star.

I didn't stick around for his time with Lisette. Instead, I left him settled on the couch with a cup of decaffeinated tea and headed to the grocery store to pick up a couple of things. We'd had deliveries made several times, but I wanted to handpick a few items.

And although I didn't know Lisette personally, within thirty seconds of meeting her, I knew Cole'd be in excellent hands. The woman was petite, compact, and no-nonsense. With her close-cropped gray hair, incisive eyes, and lined face, I spotted wisdom and experience in putting people in their place. She'd worked in the film industry for more than forty years.

Cole confided she'd started from the bottom—in a male-dominated industry—and worked her way up the ladder until she was finally able to helm her own productions.

After meeting her briefly, I understood why Cole found her so compelling and why, every time she tapped him for a role, he eagerly signed up.

When I returned from shopping, I parked in the driveway behind where Cole's SUV sat in the garage. We had yet to figure out how we'd maneuver three vehicles, but Cole claimed it wouldn't be a big deal to jockey the cars around so everyone got charged. This felt like way too much effort.

On the other hand, I was grateful for the ride. With the paparazzi often lurking, I liked being able to get in my car and drive away. Not to say they wouldn't follow me—but I felt less exposed than when I walked.

Which drove me nuts because I loved walking.

For now, we'd moved a treadmill into the increasingly crowded living room. Eventually, when Cole was strong enough to do stairs, we'd move it.

Up to a spare bedroom or down to the dungeon?

I just didn't know.

Upon exiting the car, I noticed someone getting out of a vehicle across the street. I was about to bolt when I recognized the stunning woman crossing to me.

Elouise Hynes was beautiful—luxurious blonde hair, stormy gray eyes, and a killer body with just the right hint of curves. I didn't lean that way, but even I could appreciate how gorgeous the woman was.

She waved.

I waved back and beckoned her over. "You could have gone in."

She shook her head. "I'm early. I just didn't want to be late, you know?"

I did. A very Canadian trait. "Help me with the

groceries?"

A quick bob of the head and she smiled when I handed her several bags. I'd gone a little overboard, but I'd enjoyed the freedom of being out of the house.

No wonder Cole was ready to bust out.

I couldn't ever remember being confined like this before. Even when I had pneumonia, back in university, I hadn't been so restricted. Probably should have taken it easy more, but that hadn't been my nature.

Still wasn't.

After unlocking the front door, I ushered my guest inside.

Given the unseasonably warm January, we wore only light coats and running shoes—all of which we shed before heading into the kitchen.

"You can go through to Cole."

"Uh, I've never been here."

"Ah."

"And I think he's still talking to Lisette."

I craned to listen. "Yes, her French accent is quite distinctive." Words were impossible to make out, but her voice was much louder than Cole's.

"She intimidates me a little."

I grinned. "Yeah, me too."

Once we had everything stowed and I'd returned the cloth bags to their place under the sink, Elouise and I took the coffees I'd brewed into the living room.

Lisette rose when she saw us. "Perfect. I will leave."

Neither Elouise nor I dared argue.

Cole's eyes flickered, and I couldn't tell if he was happy to see us or relieved his boss was leaving.

I put my mug down on the coffee table. "Let me see you out."

The woman looked like she might argue. Since I needed to lock the door behind her, I was prepared to wait until she left and then go. She nodded and indicated I should lead the way.

After she put on her steel-toed work boots, she gave me the once-over. "You're good for him."

I hesitated.

"He told me. I'd known he pined for someone. He told me everything."

"Ah." But had he—

"And about the other man. Michael? That's…quite an arrangement you have going." She cleared her throat. "I lived with two women for most of the nineties. We pretended to be roommates. I'm not sure I'd be up for such pretense these days. Not that I'm suggesting my girlfriend would allow another. She's very jealous." She nodded, opened the door, and headed out.

I stood in stunned silence for a moment. Closing the door, I then engaged the lock and headed back to the living room.

Elouise sat close to Cole on the couch. I liked that she felt comfortable with him. Sometimes people didn't react well to being around the sick.

"Oh, good timing." She indicated my coffee. "I didn't want it to get cold, and I was just about to share my news."

"I can—"

She shook her head. "I mean, this is so not for public consumption…but I trust you two won't say anything. Like, you can tell your man, but I trust he's big on secrets too. Although, if things go as planned, I won't be able to keep things a secret for much longer."

Slowly, I retrieved my coffee. I sat in the lounge

219

chair and prepared myself for what I feared was coming next.

Elouise placed her arm on Cole's. "So Kelci and I have decided to start a family."

"That's...quick." Cole shot a quick glance to me.

She shrugged. "In some ways, sure. I mean, I've only just come back to Canada. But on the other hand, we've been *dating* since last April. That's, like, forever."

Cole rolled his eyes. We were about half-a-dozen years older than Elouise, but I seemed to recall her girlfriend was older as well.

"Well, congratulations." Cole pressed his hand over hers. "I'm sure you and Kelci will make brilliant parents."

Was I supposed to say something? Because even I, having been out of polite society for five years, knew two women couldn't make a baby without help.

"Oh, I haven't told you the best part."

Cole grinned. "I assumed you had more to share."

"Seamus has agreed to be our sperm donor."

I didn't sputter my coffee, but it was a near thing.

"That's...good of him." Cole met my gaze. "And a hell of a lot of responsibility."

Elouise nodded solemnly. "We had a long talk with Seamus and Val. I mean, Val's great and all, but Seamus is from Newfoundland. I'm from Newfoundland. It just...felt right. I mean, I offered to return the favor—"

This time I did choke.

She looked at me. "Are you okay?"

I nodded. "Wrong pipe."

"Oh, I've done that. Anyway, I offered to be a surrogate for them, but Seamus and Val said they love being foster parents to their son Jason. They especially love that he's older. They don't have a burning desire to raise an infant."

"Well, then it's all working out."

She nodded again at Cole's words. "Yes, right? And Kelci doesn't want to be pregnant—she feels she has faulty genes." She winced. "Well, but her mother and aunt died of breast cancer, and there's…other stuff."

This time, Cole nodded.

I cocked my head.

"Oh, Kelci has alopecia. I mean, I don't care. But it'd be rough for our child—"

"Yes, I can see that." Being bald would be tough for most people. Our society was way too judgmental.

"Anyway, once we've finished this season of *VJ,* then Seamus will do his thing and the doctor will do her thing and then…" She pressed a hand to her belly. "Kelci wants a child as much as I do but worried about being around for him or her to grow up."

"She's not guaranteed to get breast cancer." Although with two close female relatives, she certainly had a much greater chance.

Elouise pulled her lower lip through her teeth.

I waited.

"She's going to have her breasts removed and reconstructed. I mean, I so don't care about what she'll look like post-surgery. I just want her healthy and not stressed all the time, and if this will make that happen, then yeah, for sure. But she's worried I won't find her attractive anymore, which is such bullshit." She pressed her hand to her lips. "Sorry."

Despite myself, I laughed out loud. "Uh, I live with one guy who works in the movie business and another who spends much of his life on construction sites—trust me, I've heard it all."

Her cheeks pinkened. "Okay, but still…"

"You have a reputation to uphold."

She winced. "Yeah, a little. Although my most recent movie will dispel some of those rumors, I think."

I tilted my head.

Cole winced.

She straightened. "My ex-fiancée isn't…a nice person. She spread rumors about me. I try to ignore them. As best I can."

"Ah." Curiosity over these rumors gnawed away at me, but I figured I could later satisfy my curiosity by looking up stuff online. Although that felt like a gross violation of her privacy. Still, she appeared to assume most people knew.

"Okay, enough about me." She turned back to Cole. "Have you thought about what you're doing for the Globes?"

Again, I cocked my head.

"Golden Globes," he said quietly to my evident curiosity. He turned to Elouise. "Even if my doctor said I was up for it—"

I began to object.

He held up his hand. "Even if I were, I wouldn't be jetting off to LA mere weeks after being shot. I don't want to set up unrealistic expectations for people in my situation. I've had top-notch medical care." He indicated me. "Everything I could possibly need to make a full and speedy recovery. Not everyone's as lucky. And—" He gave me a warning look. "—my injury wasn't nearly as bad as it could have been."

I wanted to call *bullshit*, but he wasn't wrong. Many victims of gunshot wounds to the chest didn't survive.

And even if they did, their recovery could be perilous. Cole'd been damn lucky—in so many respects.

Elouise nodded. "Okay. Just…it'd make a great story, you know? Overcoming a grave injury to show up on one of the most important nights of the year."

He waved her off. "I'm nominated for *VJ*. You know I'll never win."

Hadn't he said something to me about superheroes never winning?

"Angelo, from that other show, can't win forever." Elouise tilted her chin.

"Actually, he can. He's fucking brilliant, Elouise. He deserves every nomination, and he deserves every win."

She scrunched her nose. "He's a jerk."

"Doesn't diminish his acting skills."

I noted that Cole didn't actually refute the *jerk* allegation.

"You should win." Elouise jutted her chin.

"I won't."

"Doesn't mean you shouldn't. Oh, but you could come to the Academy Awards."

"I'm not nominated." His brow furrowed.

"But you…oh…"

He cocked his head.

"I was going to say you had been in the past, but that was Peter."

"Yes, that was Peter."

She poked him in the shoulder. "You should've been nominated as well."

"No." He grinned. "Peter gave the performance of a lifetime. My role in the film was important but nothing compared to what he put into it. I was so grateful they

223

recognized him." He tapped her nose. "You're going to blow them all away, Elouise."

She blushed. "I don't want to get my hopes up."

"Completely understandable." I rose. "More coffee?" Mine had grown cold as I watched the byplay between two of the most famous actors in the world.

Elouise waved me off, but Cole held up his mug sheepishly. "Please?"

He shouldn't have caffeine, but half a cup wouldn't kill him.

"Half a cup."

He grinned.

Yeah, he had my number. Saying *no* to him, even when he needed to hear it, was getting increasingly difficult. He was healing nicely, and eventually, he'd be allowed more and more things.

I collected his mug and headed to the kitchen. Making more coffee wouldn't take long, and although I knew I shouldn't, I crept to the edge of the kitchen so I could hear what they were talking about.

"Are you going to come out?" Elouise.

"My agent thinks it's a terrible idea." Cole.

"Well, he doesn't know everything."

"*She* is fucking brilliant and has landed me some amazing gigs over the years. I've always trusted her judgment, and she's never steered me wrong."

She clucked her tongue. "I thought coming out with Kelci would be tough. People really liked Rosa, and after all the horrible things she said about me…well, I worried people might think Kelci was with me for the wrong reasons."

I couldn't hear Cole's reply, but my curiosity piqued again. *Wrong reasons?*

"Yeah, that's true. But what about when Caressa has a baby? If it's not yours, questions might be raised. And before you argue, you know I'm right. You and she have distinctive coloring—a baby with blond hair and hazel eyes would raise all manner of questions. Are you ready to deal with that? Is she?"

I pressed a hand to my belly as my ears roared. I couldn't have a child. Having a child was inconceivable.

Have you told Cole or Michael that?

More roaring. Suddenly, panic encroached. This space, which had previously calmed and soothed, now terrorized. They didn't know my truth. No one did. Well, almost no one. And I couldn't consider telling them. But I would also have to give some kind of explanation if one or both men suddenly wanted babies.

Babies.

Oh God.

With that, I fled.

Chapter Twenty-One

Michael

As I entered the house, a weariness settled over me. To my delight and Tyanna's annoyance, the City of Vancouver had come back and asked us to rejig the plans. I'd pulled out my old ones, and reluctantly, Tyanna had approved them. I'd submitted them, Pamela had thrown a fit, and all was right in the world.

I still couldn't afford to buy a condo in that building, but at least I could recommend, for example, that Cole buy one.

As I caught sight of the twinkling lights of Vancouver looking out of his stunning vista, I questioned if he would ever move.

Movement caught my eye. "Why are you sitting in the dark?"

He growled.

I moved to turn on a light. "Couldn't reach?"

He growled.

In the light, I caught dark shadows in his eyes. "What is it?"

"You said I wasn't allowed to panic if Caressa disappeared."

My senses went on high alert. "What do you mean, disappeared?"

Yet another growl. "Elouise was over. We were

talking. Caressa left the room to make coffee and never came back."

I stared, not comprehending.

He waved his hand. "Eventually, we wondered where she'd gone—if she was okay. Elouise found the makings of coffee, including milk on the counter, but Caressa was gone. Boots, jacket…and hopefully gloves. Her cell phone is sitting on the counter, so there's no way to reach her."

My first instinct was to throw on my coat and boots and to head out to search for her. But in a city the size of Vancouver, and the fact she had a car with a range of more than a hundred miles, she could be literally anywhere.

Wait. "The car's parked out front."

"Shit."

"Yeah." That might have technically limited our search parameters, although cabs and public transit were a thing, but it also meant she didn't have the protection of her own vehicle. "You're worried."

"Aren't you?" His tone was sharp. Angry.

"Well, sure. But she's got a good head on her shoulders—"

"It's been five hours."

I winced. And almost demanded to know why he hadn't called sooner, all the while knowing I'd been the one to insist we give each other breathing room. Admittedly, that had been before Cole got shot and he and Caressa had come out as a couple. Our girlfriend had a much larger target on her back than ever before.

"What were you and Elouise talking about? Might Caressa have overheard something? Or did she get a phone call? I think I have her code memorized…"

Cole's eyebrow arched.

"No secrets, she said." I scratched my scalp. "But looking feels like an invasion of privacy."

"Elouise and I were talking babies. She and Kelci have asked Seamus to be a sperm donor."

My mind spun as I pieced together Elouise, Kelci, and Seamus. So many people in Cole's life were permeating into mine—in a good way. I loved seeing how supportive and caring his friends were of him.

"And you think babies scared her off?"

"We also might've talked about what'll happen if one or the other of us is the father. What that might look like. What kind of strain that might put on the relationship."

All things I should have considered but, frankly, hadn't. "It's too soon, Cole. Caressa doesn't have her sea legs. She's barely been back a month. Then you promptly get injured and now get shot—"

"You say that like it's my fault."

Ah, extra sensitive tonight. I held up my hands. "Not saying that at all. Just making the point that we haven't had ten minutes of what normal might look like."

His eyes took on a bleak expression I didn't see often from him. "There is no normal, Michael. That's the point."

"But there could be." I wracked my brain. "What if we got a place…away from here? Where we spent weekends and holidays? Away from all the craziness?"

"You and your country dream."

That stung. It shouldn't have—but it did. "There's anonymity in the country, but you're right. It's just a dream. What do you suggest I do about Caressa?"

"I don't know. I considered calling Donovan, but he

wouldn't know. I considered calling Tyson, but he'd not have any answers either."

And calling the cops could complicate things.

"Why don't I…"

He held my gaze.

"Start dinner? Go driving around? Head back to my old condo?"

"You still haven't rented it?"

"We've been a little busy."

"I don't want you to. I think it's important you have your own space."

"Kicking me out?" I said the words in jest, but they were always in the back of my mind. That Cole, and possibly Caressa, would grow weary of me and want me gone. God knew their lives would be much simpler without me.

"Fuck, Michael, I don't need you questioning…this." He spread his arms wide, then winced and pulled his left arm back to his chest.

"Have you taken your painkillers?"

"Fuck my—"

But I was already heading for the bedroom where we kept his pills organized. Sure enough, he hadn't taken his afternoon ones. But if I gave them to him now, would that interfere with the night dose? Damn, I needed Caressa to advise me.

He needs pain relief now.

And food.

Fuck.

I snagged the pills and headed back to the living room. After placing the pills in his palm, I headed for the kitchen. At least I remembered that milk was okay if he didn't have food but food was better. I poured a glass of milk and took it back to him.

He crossed his arms.

"You want chocolate?"

He nodded.

Jesus fucking Christ, I was dealing with a toddler. Still, I marched back into the kitchen, pulled out the chocolate powder, and set about making a glass. "Did you want it heated up?" I yelled the question.

"No." Equally loud.

Fine. I went back into the living room and watched as he downed the pill. "I don't know what that'll do for your evening dose. Hopefully, Caressa'll be back in time to advise us. Now, you need food."

He grabbed for his phone.

I snagged it. "We don't have time to wait for takeout. What kind of soup do you want?"

"Cream of mushroom."

I managed not to gag, but I nearly did. "Fine. And I'll have tomato. Caressa can pick what she'd like when she gets back."

Because she would be back. She had to be.

Fifteen minutes later, I presented Cole with a steaming-hot bowl of soup and some crusty garlic bread. I wasn't convinced the two went together, but frankly, I didn't give a shit. Apparently, neither did he because he'd consumed half the meal by the time I returned with my bowl.

We ate in silence, looking out into the dark of night.

The temperature had dropped all day, and the forecast was for snow.

"Do you want to watch the news?" I eyed the garlic bread and took another bite.

Cole cut me a glance I couldn't interpret.

I continued to eat.

Once we'd both consumed our meals, I took the dishes back to the kitchen. I put the leftover soup in the fridge, and then I loaded everything into the dishwasher.

The front door remained stubbornly shut.

I went back into the living room. "You must have to piss."

Cole glared.

"Well, unless you got up while she was gone…"

Almost six hours, but my calculation. With an empty water glass by his side, it didn't take a genius to—

"Yeah, I need to piss."

"And we might as well get you into your pajamas."

He scowled. "What if she needs me?"

"Cole, you know I love you, right? So I'm going to give it to you straight—you're in no shape to help anyone. Physically, at least. Emotionally, I know you'll be a rock for her. Whatever set her off, or whatever called her away, if she needs to talk about it, you'll get her to talk." I maneuvered myself so I could help him rise. I'd learned a lot about caring for someone in the past few weeks. And truthfully, I enjoyed it. Not to the point where I could do it every day all day like Caressa, but enough that I wasn't totally panicked being left alone with Cole.

We managed to get him up, and he leaned heavily on me as we made our way to the bedroom.

He insisted he could manage on his own, so I left him be. I sorted out pajamas for him, all the while plugging in our phones and checking them repeatedly.

Nothing.

That feeling of unease settled low in my gut.

"Michael."

I hotfooted over to the bathroom and found Cole leaning against the sink. I leaned him against me. "Have you brushed your teeth?"

He nodded.

"Then let's get you undressed and into bed. We can watch television."

"You need to find Caressa."

We hobbled into the bedroom.

"If I knew where she was, don't you think I would've gone after her?"

I tried to keep the exasperation out of my voice, but the sharp look he gave me assured me that I hadn't succeeded.

Still, we managed to get him into his pajamas and onto his medical bed. I was about to raise the head when he waved me off.

"Just need a quick nap."

He looked like he needed to sleep for a hundred years, and the painkillers had a sedating effect. Apparently, he was losing the battle.

I tucked the blankets around him, and within moments, his breathing deepened.

At odds of what to do with myself, I grabbed my phone and headed back to the living room. Pacing wouldn't help, so I flicked on the television, keeping the sound as low as I could while still being able to hear it.

The eighth story on the news was about Meggibeth and her request for bail being denied. The reporter suggested her defense team might try for insanity. The claim rarely worked in Canada, from the research I'd done on it, but she had the right to try. Personally, as long as she went away for a long time, I didn't care how it happened. I wanted to keep Cole and Caressa safe. I couldn't do that if this woman roamed the streets.

Hell, I couldn't do it anyway.

I wandered over to the windows and spotted the first flakes of snow. They were followed by more, and within about fifteen minutes, the snow was heavy. Within thirty, it stuck to the ground.

Where the fuck is Caressa? I'd do anything to know the answer, but the world didn't work like that.

The television station had switched to some kind of British soap opera. Instead of changing the channel, I shut the thing off. I had enough chaos in my life right now. Work appeared, for the moment, to be calming down. My personal life, though? Total chaos.

Just over a month ago, Caressa'd blown back into my world, and now I recognized almost nothing. I couldn't regret the changes…but I also couldn't fathom them. Was this how our lives were always going to be? Cole injured? Caressa running? Logically, my mind said *no*. Emotionally, though, I worried this might be our new normal.

Deciding I couldn't sit still any longer, I checked on Cole, who was dead to the world, and headed for the front hall. I donned boots and a jacket and headed out to my SUV. Soon, I was on the road.

Driving aimlessly for an hour didn't improve my outlook on life. The snow was thick, and spotting Caressa's wool coat in this weather proved impossible. Every pedestrian I sighted was hunched against the snow and ever-increasing wind.

Eventually, I went home. I hoped for some sign of her, but everything was exactly as I'd left it.

Was I supposed to wait up? Go to bed?

The clock read barely eight thirty, but a weariness

settled into my bones. Cole would undoubtedly be up in the night. Was I supposed to wake him now to give him his pills?

I snuck into his room and found him lightly snoring.

Deciding against waking him, I headed back upstairs to my room where I shed my clothes, took a quick shower, and donned pajamas.

As I descended the stairs and headed back to the other side of the house, I couldn't help but glance forlornly at the front door.

Part of me was angry. She had to know we'd worry. She had to know we might even panic. What if we called the police? Then what? We wouldn't, though, and she likely knew that as well.

I settled onto Cole's side of the bed, snagging my e-reader. I planned to stay awake until Cole needed his meds.

That wasn't meant to be, and within moments, I nodded off.

Chapter Twenty-Two

Cole

I awoke suddenly, momentarily disoriented. My shoulder ached, and my chest itched, but that wasn't what had pulled me from slumber.

Slowly, I turned my head.

And caught sight of Caressa shedding her clothes.

She's safe.

I'll throttle her.

Yeah, right.

I could barely brush my teeth and couldn't walk without help—the likelihood of me throttling anyone was next to impossible.

Didn't mean I wasn't willing to try.

Since she and Michael'd worn pajamas every night since we got home, I expected her to locate hers and put them on.

She didn't.

In fact, she went over to my side of the bed—where Michael slept, completely oblivious. Before I could say anything, she grabbed his e-reader and put it on the bedside table.

Then she yanked the covers down.

Michael awoke in alarm, with his eyes wide.

My nightlight cast a low glow in the room, but the naked panic on his face was clear to see.

I wanted to say something, but words stuck in my throat.

She grabbed the waistband of his sleep pants and tugged.

Out of sheer preservation instinct, I was certain, he canted his hips so she could drag them down and off.

She pounced. She literally crawled on top of him and dove in for a kiss.

He appeared stunned, but after a moment, he thrust his hands in her loose hair, tugging her closer.

My cock stirred.

Huh, hadn't thought it would be capable of that. The doctor had been very specific about no sexual activity until she cleared me. She obviously hadn't predicted my two lovers putting on a show. I wanted to say for my amusement, but I got the feeling neither of them was thinking about me as they rutted together.

Caressa fumbled as she unbuttoned Michael's top.

He fumbled as he palmed her breasts and squeezed her nipples.

She rubbed against him.

He bucked up against her.

Friction. I didn't doubt they both sought friction.

Then she eased back. She grasped his now hard cock and impaled herself.

He groaned.

She gasped.

I palmed my own cock, willing it to not react.

A losing battle, if ever I saw one.

Michael bucked again and again while Caressa rode him.

She raked her fingernails down his abdomen as he gripped her thighs with bruising strength.

Then without warning, her breathing stuttered. She held herself still and then, if I could guess, came.

Michael pushed up twice more, then stilled as well. He closed his eyes and arched his neck back.

Caressa turned her gaze to me. "Don't come."

Normally, I'd have seen that as a challenge. That maybe she was edging me from a distance.

She wasn't.

For just a moment, she was Caressa the medical professional. The one who knew I might hurt myself if I gave in to the passion snaking through my body.

I stilled my hand, which had been rubbing my cock through the sleep pants. I pressed, none too gently, and willed my body into submission. Priding myself on having an iron will, I staved off the impending orgasm, and slowly, my body calmed. My heart rate lowered. My breathing steadied.

Michael opened his eyes. "Caressa?"

She scrambled off him and fled the room.

"Am I..." He hadn't even caught his breath, and he was trying to rise.

"Leave her." I wasn't sure how I knew she wouldn't run again, but I was certain she wouldn't. "She just...needs time."

He groaned. "She's not the only one." He looked over at me. "Are you okay?"

"Yeah."

"You're flushed."

I chuckled sardonically. "You try watching that show and not get aroused."

"But—"

"It's all good. I'm...evening out."

His eyebrows lifted.

237

"Yeah."

A slight smile ghosted his lips.

I winced.

"Your chest?"

I nodded.

He rose, and his sleep pants fell to the ground. He stepped out of them. On unsteady feet, he headed for the pills. He flicked on the lamp and squinted as he sorted them out.

Within moments, he had pills in my hand and a glass of water at the ready.

"I'm sorry." I might have mumbled the words before downing the pills and half the water.

"What are you sorry for?" He looked down at his deflated cock. "I need to clean myself. Do you need to go to the bathroom?"

I shook my head.

"Okay, I'll be right back."

Waiting for him to return was agony.

Worrying about Caressa was just as hard.

I'd told Michael to give her space, but was that the right thing to do? What if she wanted him to follow her? What if she wanted private time with him? Because no way would I be able to follow her—wherever she'd gone.

And she'd know it.

Michael returned a few minutes later. He took the empty water glass from my hand and put it back on the dresser. "Did you need more?"

"Nah, I'm good." I squinted—I couldn't read the clock radio from this distance. "What time is it?"

"Just before midnight." He checked his phone. When he put it down, I assumed he hadn't missed a call or a text. "She was…cold. And her hair was damp."

"Doesn't have the sense God gave her," I grumbled.

He looked up sharply at me. "I wouldn't let her hear you say that."

"Duh."

After a moment, he sorted his pajamas and put them back on. Then he turned to look at me.

"I don't know, Michael. I just don't know."

He started to move toward the door when Caressa flittered in wearing thermal pajamas.

I couldn't think of a better word to describe her movements.

She came to me, gazed into my eyes, then leaned over for a kiss.

Where I expected a peck, she gave me a full-on tonsil-hockey tongues-clashing kiss.

As I started to react, she placed her hand over my cock. Then she pulled back and met my gaze.

In the low light, the blues of her irises were translucent and her pupils were blown wide. "Don't even think about it."

"Okay." The words came out a little strangled.

She held my gaze for another moment before releasing me. "You take your pills?"

"Just now."

"Good." She pressed her hand against my forehead.

I reveled in the touch—even if I understood she was doing it for medical reasons.

Eventually, she stepped back. She arranged my covers just the way I liked them. Then she got into bed.

Michael still stood by the bed, clearly a little dumbfounded.

"You can hold me. Or I can hold you. Or we cannot

touch. I don't give a fuck."

Yet even as she said the words, I saw the lie. She wanted contact. Hell, she needed contact.

And never more, in my life, had I felt an ache down to my bones that I wanted the same thing. "Can't I—"

"No."

"Just for one—"

"No." This second no wasn't as harsh. She sighed. "Cole, you're one week post-op on major surgery. We can't risk it. Know that I want to say *yes* more than anything, but I won't risk your recovery. I'd never live with myself if something—" She swallowed hard.

And didn't finish the statement.

Michael climbed into bed, scooted over to her, pulled the covers over them, then tucked her into his arms. "What…"

"Tomorrow, Michael, okay? I'm tired."

"And you're still cold. Do you want me to turn up the heat?"

"I'm fine. Don't fuss." Her voice bit.

Michael winced.

He met my gaze, and I offered what silent reassurance I could. Whatever had just happened, we *would* talk about it. We couldn't go on like this.

Caressa conked out first, followed quickly by Michael.

I was the one who lingered in consciousness far longer than I would have liked. I tried to clear my mind, but thoughts kept ricocheting around in my brain. Somehow, I was missing a sizeable piece of the puzzle that was Caressa. I'd believed Africa was the key, the one thing we didn't know about, but I was starting to wonder if whatever demons drove her hadn't begun earlier. Back when she was in Vancouver. Back to whatever had pushed her to go to Africa in the first place.

On that thought, I drifted off.

Michael's alarm pulled me into wakefulness.

He silenced it. "Sorry."

I waved him off.

Caressa burrowed farther under the covers.

Michael rose and made his way over to me. "You need a hand?"

I tried to act like I didn't, but we both knew I wasn't strong enough to get out of this bed, and yeah, I had to piss.

He helped me up, and while I sat on the toilet, he had a quick shower. Then after drying himself off, he helped me into jeans and a Henley.

Slowly, he walked me to the living room where he let me slide into my favorite spot.

"I'm going to make you some breakfast. You want pancakes?"

I eyed the time on the mantel clock. "You don't have time for that."

"I do, if you want them."

"A bagel with some cream cheese would be amazing. And a coffee."

He hesitated.

"Caressa was making me one yesterday, I swear."

"I'll make you a decaf."

Had I been stronger, I might have argued. Or followed him into the kitchen. As it was, I remained in the living room while he prepared a delicious breakfast for me.

He sat in the chair opposite me and wolfed down his bagel.

"You going to be late?"

His shrug irked me.

"You didn't have to fucking stay."

His amused grin also irked me.

He took a swig of coffee, then rose, collected my plate, and headed to the kitchen. Three minutes later, he was back to give me a kiss.

That somewhat mollified me.

Finally, he handed me the remote. "Oh shit."

I barely had time to ask what was wrong when he darted from the room. Ten seconds later, he was back with our phones. He handed me mine and pocketed his. "Call if you need anything, okay?"

"And you'll come running home?" No point hiding the sarcasm.

He pressed another kiss to my lips. "Yeah, if you need me to." He stood up straight.

God, he took my breath away. Today he wore jeans and a T-shirt with a plaid shirt over top. I assumed he was headed to the construction site.

"I'll be okay."

"Do you need me to leave the front door unlocked?"

I pulled up my phone. I had a notation in my calendar with a name I didn't recognize. "I'd love to say *no*, but you better leave it unlocked. I need to get one of those automated things."

"Except they can be hacked." Michael touched his hand to my foot. "Keep your phone close. I love you."

I managed a nod, not being able to push words past my clogged throat. Would I ever tire of hearing him say that? Or of Caressa echoing the sentiment? I hoped not.

He left, and I snagged the remote for the television. I didn't really want to watch anything, but Julie'd been scheduled to be on a late-night talk show yesterday, and I'd promised to watch.

By the end of the interview, I grinned. Damn, such a smart woman. The host had tried to get her to talk about the shooting, but she'd deftly avoided the topic altogether and, at the end, had graciously accepted well wishes on my behalf. It pissed me off that I hijacked part of her interview without even being present. This had been her moment—and she deserved it. This was her first year being nominated for a Golden Globe, and I hoped she might be up for an Emmy as well in the fall. I'd won that one a couple of times already, but the Globe was always just beyond my reach.

VJ was much bigger than I liked to admit—both a critical and fan success, which could be tough these days. The show was smart, sexy, funny, dramatic, and thought provoking. It didn't allow viewers to sit on their laurels. Instead, it demanded they think about what crossed the line between right and wrong. How far would they be willing to go? How far, in the end, was too far? And could a villain be the hero of their own story? Julie's character, Lyric, was definitely on the wrong side of the law, but she wasn't evil. And she had strong motivations for doing what she did. Which made my job, as Justice, much tougher. More often than not, I empathized with her. That push-pull made the dynamic so fucking strong and kept viewers tuning in week after week. Given the power of streaming, the fact we brought in people at all, seeing as we were episodic, meant even more.

My phone buzzed with an incoming call.

"This is Cole." I rarely bothered to screen—this number was buried pretty deep, and few people had it.

"Mr. Hamilton? My name is Hamish McAllister. I

have an appointment with you at ten. I'm in front of your house now. Is there someone who can let me in?"

Right, the name in my calendar. The reason I'd had Michael leave the door unlocked.

Ten?

God, I'd been sitting here ruminating for a long time—and Caressa had yet to make an appearance.

"Uh, the door's unlocked. I'm in the living room."

The pause was infinitesimal. "I'll be right in."

Within a few moments, I caught the sound of the front door opening and closing.

Just as footsteps sounded toward the living room, Caressa came careening into the room.

Disheveled, sleep-rumpled, and clearly addled, she nonetheless took my breath away.

"What…" She gazed around.

The man I assumed to be Dr. McAllister stepped into the space.

I was vaguely glad, for her sake, that Caressa wore pajamas.

"Oh, excuse me. I'm Dr. Hamish McAllister. I have an appointment to see Mr. Hamilton." He looked back and forth between Caressa and myself.

He didn't look like any doctor I'd ever met. The tall, gangly man wore dark-brown corduroy pants, a blue plaid flannel shirt, a camel-colored cardigan, and the brightest red socks I'd ever seen. Were those…yep, with little white hearts. His light-brown hair was overlong and desperately in need of either a trim or a style. His green eyes, behind his wire-rimmed glasses, though, were incisive. In mere moments, he seemed to have taken in the situation.

Stepping forward, he offered me his hand and kept

his gaze on mine. "Dr. Hamish McAllister." He finished shaking my hand, nodded, then made his way around the sectional to approach Caressa.

With caution.

Smart man.

"Caressa Klein."

I had to crane my neck, but the two shook hands.

Something in the doctor's demeanor had Caressa warming up, and she even offered him a small smile. "I should get dressed."

Hamish grinned. "I leave that up to you. I ask that you give me a bit of time alone with Cole." He held up his hands. "I promise no harm will come to him. I'm just here doing my job."

"And what is your *job*?" I cursed myself for not having noted in my calendar who the man was.

He offered an apologetic grin as he made his way back to my line of sight.

With gratitude, I adjusted my neck a little so as to work out the crick.

"I'm the caseworker assigned from JEAP—Johnson Employee Assistance Program. I know you've had a lot going on, but I assumed they told you I was coming."

I winced. "They did. I mean, I have you in my calendar. I just…JEAP? I don't know what that is."

"Ah." His gaze flicked to Caressa.

She sighed. "I'm grabbing a coffee, and then I'll go have a shower and get dressed. I can also do some stuff on my laptop—"

"Can't she stay?" I might have whined that.

Hamish considered me. "Why don't we say you and I talk for fifteen minutes? If you want Miss Klein—"

"Caressa." No-nonsense and firm. Staking her

territory, as it were.

"Caressa," he repeated. "If you're comfortable with her joining us after that, then by all means. My job is to help you—in whatever form that takes."

She huffed but headed toward the kitchen.

Since I still didn't know what had set her off yesterday, I worried she might eavesdrop. I pointed to the chair. But also indicated over my shoulder.

Hamish nodded. He pulled his messenger bag over his shoulder and sat in the chair. He pulled a notepad and pen from his bag and set them on his lap. "I'll explain why I'm here."

"That'd be appreciated."

"I'm a psychologist. I've worked for Johnson for most of my career."

"What, about ten days?" The guy didn't look a day over twenty-five.

He chuckled. "I turned thirty about seven years ago."

My jaw dropped.

"Yeah, I get that a lot. I'll say it's good genes—or it'll feel that way when I'm older. These days, I still have to fight to be taken seriously."

"You have a PhD?"

He nodded.

"Well, I would've taken you seriously if you just had a bachelor's degree in social work. Anyone who's willing to listen to other people's problems has my admiration." I grinned. "Although part of me is tempted to ask to see your driver's license."

He began to reach for his back pocket.

I raised my hand. "Kidding." *Mostly.* "You said you have been assigned to me?"

He nodded yet again. "Yes. The studio hired my firm. We specialize in helping deal with the aftermath of workplace violence."

"So you've done this before?"

After holding my gaze for a moment, he then brushed his hair out of the way.

That man really needs a haircut.

"Yes, I've done this before. Unfortunately, too often. Our team has mobilized several times in the past few years. Not that long ago, we helped a company deal with something similar. They had an employee who stabbed six of his co-workers. Two died."

My first instinct was to demand to know why they didn't fight back. I always believed, in a knife fight, that I wouldn't be taken down.

Except if the person uses a machete and is bigger than you…

I was being arrogant. I'd also always believed I would lunge after a person shooting. Protecting Julie had been my instinct.

Donovan's had been to step toward the shooter and try to take her down.

"Are you seeing other people?" I needed to know.

Without breaking eye contact, he nodded. "Ms. Reyes, Ms. Hynes, and Mr. Riggs."

Julie, Elouise, and Donovan.

He continued. "I have other co-workers who are fanning out to speak to anyone affected. We understand everyone processes things differently." He offered a gentle smile. "Often my boss, Alessandra MacLean, takes the lead. She had a baby a couple of months ago, though, and so is a little busy."

A baby.

Was that what had set off Caressa yesterday?

"All is well with her?" I wasn't going to open up this line of inquiry, but it seemed the polite thing to do.

"Mother and baby Wesley are doing great. She owns the company with her husband, Smith MacLean."

And the penny dropped. Smith owned the most prestigious BDSM club in Vancouver—Club Kink.

I met Hamish's gaze head-on. "I've met Smith."

Only once, but he needed to know.

Or I believed he did.

He tilted his head, apparently read my meaning, and pinkened a little. "Mr. MacLean has many businesses. And does much in the way of philanthropy."

"I met him at Kink."

"Ah." He looked down at his notepad. "I don't believe that makes this a conflict-of-interest situation, but if you prefer I refer you to someone outside of the company—"

I held up my hand. "I enjoy BDSM. I've met your, uh, boss. I don't see an issue here. Unless you—"

He cleared his throat. "No." He tapped his pen against the pad of paper.

Oh, interesting. His face showed every expression, and I enjoyed guessing. He appeared curious. He was probably dying to ask. But he likely wouldn't, because he was a professional.

I longed to tease him, but at that moment, I heard Caressa's footsteps up the stairs. "We don't have much time."

"If you want Miss Klein—Caressa—to join us. Usually, counseling is one-on-one."

"I have nothing to hide from Caressa. She's my girlfriend. As I'm sure you know. Our partner, Michael, is at work at the moment. If you felt it might be beneficial to have him here, he'd come home."

Hamish's hesitation was momentary. And also noticeable. "You're in a triad?"

Again, naked curiosity.

"Yes. Our circumstances are…unusual. We grew up together. Literally. We've been friends since we were five years old. We did everything together and, somehow, managed to get away from the hardscrabble life of the Downtown Eastside." I ran my hand through my hair. "But I'm not telling you anything you don't already know."

Slowly, he nodded. "I read the article written about you a few years back. I understand sometimes such things are embellished—I didn't get that sense from you."

"Nope." I popped the P. "If anything, I downplayed how bad things were. And I didn't mention Caressa and Michael—who both had it worse than me. Michael, most especially."

Hamish didn't betray much emotion, but I caught the flicker in his eyes.

I'd been pretty honest with the reporter. I wanted kids who had grown up in abject poverty, and who had suffered abuse, to see there might be a way out. I also acknowledged, freely, that my success was as much about luck as about hard work. And that some people, no matter how hard they tried, wouldn't be able to escape their grinding poverty. That was why I gave back. That was why I attended the gala.

Hamish cleared his throat.

Might as well be honest. "I was thinking about the charity gala."

He sat a little straighter.

"I don't know why she shot me. Honest to God. And I want to say that if I'd known she'd do that, I wouldn't have taken Caressa, which I believe was the trigger. But the truth is I would have taken Caressa—because I didn't believe the woman capable of that level of violence. I don't know why she shot at Julie and Donovan. Maybe because she knew how much they meant to me?"

"She never showed any tendency toward jealousy?" He held up his hand. "I'm not saying you should have seen warning signs—just asking your recollections."

"Okay, so I kind of guessed she had a crush. I mean…" I cleared my throat. "I get the looks thing. Honestly, I do. I wouldn't say I'm vain, but I do look in the mirror and appreciate that I'm an attractive person. Do I think women, and men, should be fawning over me? Hell, no. But I'd be naïve if I didn't understand that people see me, in my role as Justice in particular, and think I'd be a good catch. But they don't know me. No one does." I glanced toward the stairs. "Except my two best friends. And I get that friends to lovers might be a little creepy. Truthfully, I didn't see it coming. We just went along as we always had until the day Caressa announced she was heading for Africa. Was supposed to be six months, but that six months turned into five years. Five long years. And I realized I loved her. In the romantic sense."

"That must've been challenging."

"I wanted to fly to Africa and demand she come back to Canada. And Michael felt the same way. But we didn't."

"Were you and Michael…"

He made some odd gesture I couldn't interpret.

"Oh, yeah, no." I squinted against the ever-increasing sunlight that backlit Hamish. "I mean, I was attracted to him. But I convinced myself that was all kinds of wrong as well."

"But now…"

"Well, frankly, when he and Caressa got together romantically, all bets were off. I decided to finally be honest and tell everyone how I felt. Let the chips fall where they may, so to speak."

"And it turns out, Cole can be very persuasive." Caressa's sultry voice caught me off guard.

Chapter Twenty-Three

Caressa

I'd thought I made plenty of noise, tromping down the stairs, but the look on both men's faces assured me I hadn't.

Hamish started to rise, but I waved him back down.

"I was very rude and didn't offer you a coffee earlier. I have a pot. Would you like some?"

"I would." Cole's eagerness couldn't be overstated.

My gaze turned to him, and I scowled. "You already convinced Michael to give you a cup."

He held up his mug. "Decaf. Surely, one cup won't hinder my recovery."

Swear to fucking Christ, the man batted his eyelashes at me.

I took his cup and swore under my breath.

The doctor, who truly looked like a Hamish, chuckled. "I don't drink coffee, but thank you for the offer."

"Water? Tea? We've got two dozen varieties."

"We do?" Cole scrunched his nose.

He looked adorable.

"Grocery shopping? I bought several multi-variety packs. We've got plenty of choices."

"I'll take a water, if you don't mind." Hamish swept his hair back from his face.

I bestowed a radiant smile on him. "I never mind." With that, I skedaddled to the kitchen. I didn't want to be out of earshot for long. If the men were talking about me, then I wanted to be there. I nearly sloshed the coffee in my haste to pour it. I did a small mug for Cole and another large one for myself. Despite having slept well, or perhaps because of it, I was sluggish this morning.

After placing the mugs and glass of ice water on a tray, I headed back to the main room.

Hamish stood at the windows, looking out. "The view is breathtaking."

"Yeah." Cole took the mug from me. "Thanks." Then he clearly noticed my larger one. "Bitch."

"Did you just…"

"Oh, fuck no. I absolutely did not—"

Hamish spun. "Not that I would ever excuse your behavior, but you have been under a lot of stress. Still, I think—"

"It slipped out." Cole's eyes widened, and panic overtook his features. "I swear, I didn't mean it. Like…a bad joke or something…and that's just sinking me farther, isn't it?"

Finally, I smiled. "I can be a bitch, Cole, when it comes to your health. Just be grateful I'm letting you have any caffeine." I handed Hamish his glass.

He took it with a smile. After putting it on the coffee table, he picked up his discarded notepad and pen and resumed his seat.

I tried to glimpse the paper but couldn't see if he'd written anything at all, let alone what he'd written.

"Hamish is a psychologist."

"Ah." This, I hadn't known. Might have guessed but hadn't been certain about.

"The studio hired him to talk to several of us. About what happened."

With my mug in my right hand, I reached out with my left to grab Cole's hand. Cold and clammy. "Why don't you drink your coffee while it's warm? Do you need a blanket?"

He cut me a look that wasn't hard to interpret—*don't baby me*.

I nodded in acknowledgment.

"Cole was just explaining about your...unconventional relationship."

"Yeah, I caught that part. Care to tell me what I missed?"

Hamish indicated Cole should speak.

"Just about what signs I might've missed."

Ah. Meggibeth.

"Unless she said *I'm going to shoot you if you get a girlfriend*, I'm not certain what signs you might've missed. At least I assume that's what the police concluded. That she did this from some kind of jealousy." I pivoted my attention back to Hamish. "We are unconventional. Michael and I worry about that constantly. I mean, I doubt my employer's going to care—as long as I keep my private life private." To his raised eyebrow, I added, "I'm a nurse. They never have enough nurses."

"Yes, that's true enough. And not an easy job." Hamish smiled.

"Caressa works in the ER at St Paul's."

I cut him a glance. He didn't need to go into that much detail. He said it like we should be making a big deal of it. I didn't want that. I was just doing my job—nothing more and nothing less.

"She was on duty when they brought me in."

Ah. Shit. So that's why…

Hamish pivoted his attention to me. His green eyes bore both compassion and curiosity. "What was that like?"

"Horrible." My hands tightened around my mug, seeking the little warmth that remained. "Close to the worst day of my life."

Cole's gaze shot to me.

I didn't meet his eyes.

Shit.

That shouldn't have slipped out. I needed to be more careful. Needed to make sure those walls were back up and impenetrable. They had nearly failed me yesterday, and I had to make sure that didn't happen again.

"Anyway, I froze. I had to be ordered out of the room."

"By the asshat." Cole muttered the words.

"I'm sorry? I didn't catch that." Hamish leaned forward.

"By the doctor who helped save Cole's life." God, defending Franklin made me want to hurl, but he was owed credit. I'd checked in later with Miles about everything Franklin had done—and it had been by-the-book perfect. Cole likely would have survived anyway, but Franklin had ensured that fact. I fidgeted. "But we're not here to discuss me. What are you expecting from Cole?"

Hamish's smile lit his pretty eyes. "I'm here to talk through what happened. To help Cole, and whomever he chooses to bring in, deal with the trauma. He might feel okay today. But these things have a habit of sneaking up on us when we least expect them to. We're going along

Gabbi Grey

with our lives, and something happens—a sound, a smell, something someone says—and we're right back into the situation. Sometimes we can cope with that, and sometimes we need help."

"Like post-traumatic stress."

"Yes, some clients develop PTSD. Many don't, though. They can mostly cope, but they just need that extra little bit of help—a sounding board to assure them that everything will be okay."

"Will it, though?" I put my half-empty mug on the coffee table. "Cole, and the rest of his people, have been through hell. Do you honestly believe a few therapy sessions will solve all that?"

"I believe that talking about what happened, realizing it wasn't your fault, can be very powerful." He tapped his pen on the pad of paper. "I'll be honest. What happens in this room stays in this room. But letting the other cast and crew know that Cole's talking to someone will give them permission to do the same. And you never know what this event might trigger. Someone might be perfectly fine but have some event in their past that this brings to the fore—something they haven't dealt with."

"You told me you're speaking to Donovan, Julie, and Elouise." Cole shifted.

Whether from physical or psychological discomfort, I couldn't tell.

Hamish nodded. "Yes, I've spoken to all of them. And all of them gave me permission to acknowledge as much."

Cole's eyes narrowed. "You've spoken to Donovan? And he gave you permission to tell people?"

I understood his skepticism.

"He did." Hamish shifted. "But only to you, Julie,

256

and Elouise. He's…an interesting man."

Did he just… Yep, the good doctor blushed. Quite pink, in fact.

"Donovan is an interesting man." Cole put his mug down on the coffee table, then resettled. "He's also intensely private. He's a tough nut to crack."

Hamish cleared his throat. "Well, I can't discuss specifics—"

"Tell him to get his head out of his ass and to be honest with you. He's carrying on like being shot was no big deal—that being a hero doesn't mean anything."

"Well, if your positions were reversed, wouldn't you be doing the same thing?"

My breath caught on Hamish's insight. Of course, Cole would be downplaying his role. Just saying he was doing his job. And of course he wouldn't want acknowledgment of his wound or his heroism. That wasn't how he rolled.

"What if she gets off?" I threaded my fingers. "What if she, I don't know, pleads insanity? And they let her off?"

Hamish appeared to consider, his gaze steady on me. "That's a tough plea to make, and it doesn't mean someone gets *off*. They might spend years in a psychiatric facility. I can't speak to her mental state—"

"She's nuts." Cole shot out the word.

I shot Cole a glance.

He shrugged.

"Well, there might be more clinical ways of putting it." Hamish again tapped his pen.

I'd yet to see him write a single word.

"But she's in jail for now, so you can rest easy on that score. If she has a trial, I can help you prepare for that."

"How long are you going to be in my life?" Cole glanced at me. "In our lives?"

"The contract doesn't have a stipulated end. If you need us, be it me or someone else in our company, you need only call. We have a twenty-four-hour crisis line, so even if I'm not available, there's someone who can help."

"This sounds way too simple."

"Perhaps." Hamish tilted his head. "You likely haven't begun to deal with everything. You're still very much in recovery mode."

"You know my medical issues?"

"I wasn't briefed on specifics, no. Privacy and all that. But I was told what happened and have followed your progress through...other means."

"Don't always believe what you read in the papers." This time, the warning came from me.

Hamish smiled. "No...I meant other people have shared. I didn't ask, but they spoke up. You have a lot of people who care about you. Who want you to make a full recovery."

"I have to piss."

My gut clenched—this was Cole's way of shutting things down. Hamish had hit a sore spot, obviously.

He rose. "I should be going." He pulled out his wallet from his back pocket and procured two business cards. He handed one to me and tried to hand the other to Cole.

My boyfriend looked toward the ceiling.

So I grabbed it. "I'll see you out."

"That would be appreciated."

To my relief, he didn't dawdle. His notebook and

pen were quickly returned to the messenger bag. He gave Cole a long, level look. "I'll be back."

Cole grinned, and I knew the movie he was thinking about.

Yet I was certain Hamish didn't get the reference. Well, he was quite young. Older than us, but…less world-weary.

I escorted him to the door where he shoved his feet into his loafers, tossed on a wool coat, wrapped a scarf around his neck, and offered me a smile.

"Tell Donovan I say to mind his own fucking business." Cole's voice carried right through to the front hall.

Hamish's cheeks reddened. "Uh, yes, I'll do that." He met my gaze. "Although maybe not in those exact words."

"Oh no." I wagged my finger. "You need to quote Cole exactly. He's going to check up on that."

He cleared his throat. "Thank you for the warning. This isn't my first rodeo."

I cocked my head.

"Thirteen years."

"You were what, ten?"

He grinned. "No, more like twenty-four." He nodded. "Lovely to meet you. Please, call anytime."

I had the distinct impression he would answer—no matter what time we called.

At my hesitation, he offered a more measured smile. "He's going to go through some rough times between now and…whenever."

"Cole's strong."

"As are you. But we all have a breaking point. I hope neither of you reaches it, but I'm here to help if you do."

Without another word, he slipped out of the house.

I stood, a little stunned.

"Uh, Caressa? I really do have to piss. I can try to make it on my own—"

Within moments, I was by his side, helping him rise.

"I fucking hate this."

"I know you do." I smoothed away his hair from his face. "But just for a little bit longer, okay? Just a little bit longer…"

Unfortunately, I wasn't sure any of us were going to make it.

Chapter Twenty-Four

Michael

The house was quiet when I stepped through the back door. I managed to juggle the Thai food, the milkshakes from the local burger joint, and the cheesecake I'd picked up at the grocery store on my lunch hour that I stored in the car.

"Here, let me help you." Caressa offered a wide smile as she entered my field of vision.

"Yeah, that'd be great."

She grabbed the tray of milkshakes. She grinned. "You think this measly old milkshake is going to make that spicy food more tolerable."

I winced. She and Cole loved spicy...I did my best but wasn't always able to hide the chagrin. "I chose a few less spicy options—I wasn't sure what Cole could tolerate."

"Cole wants as spicy as he can get." His voice rang clear through most of the house.

Caressa caught my gaze. "He's in a mood."

"I'm sorry for that."

"Why are you apologizing?"

"Because you're stuck here with him?"

She waved me off. "I've dealt with far worse in my time. He'll come around. Or I'll have you kick his ass."

"There will be no ass kicking." I couldn't fathom

touching Cole in any way other than loving care. He was still so fucking fragile—like a gust of wind could knock him over. And not a gale either. Just a strong breeze off the Strait of Georgia.

"You might change your mind when I tell you what a pain in the ass he's been today." She went to the kitchen, deposited the drink tray, then returned for the cheesecake and takeout.

"That bad?" I removed my boots, hung up my coat, and put my briefcase with my laptop on the dining room table. I didn't actually need to do work tonight, but I'd been trained to never leave it in the car—even if the car was locked and in a locked garage.

She sighed as she set about opening the containers. I grabbed plates, and soon we had everything organized.

"He needs to tell you about Hamish."

And with that little confusing piece of information, she took Cole's plate, as well as her own, and flounced out of the room.

I managed the drink tray and my plate as I made my way to the living room.

We had yet to eat at the dining room table—Cole was still too weak to hold himself up for that long. At least on the couch, he had full support.

"This is fucking delicious." Cole's only pause was to say the words before he started shoveling food again.

"Don't talk with your mouth full." Caressa's admonishment of Cole was only half in jest.

He looked sheepish. "I'm hungry."

"Well, if you'd eaten the sandwich I made for lunch—"

"I wasn't hungry."

She glared.

He tilted his chin up.

Ah, so that's how the day had gone. Good to know. "Other than that…"

"We met Cole's psychologist."

Cole glared.

"What? Hamish said he was willing to counsel all of us." She glanced between the two of us. "I've stopped seeing the counselor at work—"

"Hey."

"What the hell?" I spat out my question at the same time as Cole made his exclamation.

She shrugged. "I've been busy and, you know…"

"No, I don't know." I eyed my savory food with less enthusiasm than before. "Caressa, we all agreed you needed counseling. Whatever happened in Africa—"

"Nothing happened in Africa—"

"Bullshit."

Both my lovers turned to me at the force of my words.

"You told me some of the horrible things. Those stories alone would have given me nightmares. But you would have stayed. Honestly you would have—"

"I fucked up."

Her eyes flashed, and that naked pain seared me right down to my core. "Okay…"

She rose, gave us both a long look, and headed into the kitchen.

"Well, that was distinctly unhelpful." Cole eyed his food. "But I'm hungry."

"So eat. She'll come back or she won't. She'll tell us or she—"

"I will." She reentered the room with a bottle of beer in her hands.

Since we rarely drank recreationally, I understood the Dutch courage she was needing. More than a few times since Cole got shot, I'd eyed the beer in the fridge or thought about the liquor in the bar downstairs.

"You want one?" She pointed to me.

I shook my head. No, I suspected I needed a clear head tonight.

"I'd love one." Cole offered a sheepish smile.

We both turned to him.

"Barely a week out of surgery?" I eyed Caressa.

She sniggered. "Not in a million years, Hamilton. And you'd known I was going to say that. Now, do you want seconds—"

"I want you to tell us what the fuck happened."

After a moment, she dropped into the lounge chair.

My hope that she'd sit between us on the couch vanished. Between sitting in the chair and the beer, she'd put an effective barrier between us.

And I still didn't know what had set her off yesterday.

We waited. I used the bread to mop up the rest of my food and was debating whether to go for seconds— Cole had cleaned his plate as well—when she spoke.

"The day was ordinary. Hot, yes, but ordinary. I had a woman come to me. Well, more like a girl—but old enough to understand she needed help."

My gut clenched. Caressa's stories always seemed to involve women.

"She wouldn't let me take her to the doctor. We normally had a woman doctor, but she'd been called away on a family emergency, and until they found a replacement, we just had a man. He was the gentlest soul you could imagine, and I would've been there the whole time, but she was adamant." She toyed with the label on her beer. An IPA, if I had to guess. And likely a local brew. Cole was all about supporting people in the region.

"What happened?" Cole asked the question gently.

"She let me do an exam to confirm the pregnancy. She was adamant it'd only been a month. I believed her. Well, mostly. And as much as I needed her to see the doctor, she swore she'd never go. She also said she'd been raped."

Cole drew in a sharp breath, but Caressa'd told me a similar story the night she came home. Hearing another desperate story hurt, but it didn't shock.

"I gave her the abortion pills. They're safe, effective, and the possibility of severe side effects is so low that it's negligible. And since the alternative was…" Her voice trailed off.

She didn't look at me. Hell, I wasn't even sure she saw me. She was likely back in the camp. Back in that horrible place.

Finally, she drew breath. "I thought I'd taken a complete history, but I'd missed her family history of clotting. Or something like that. Only when she was bleeding out did she ask if she was going to die like her mother."

"Jesus." Cole said the word, but I echoed the sentiment.

"Did she…" I didn't want to ask the question, but I also needed to know.

And Caressa needed to talk.

She shook her head. "The doctor was able to stop the bleeding in time. I can't stress how safe these pills are." She rubbed her face with her hand. "I was fucking arrogant. I believed I knew what I was doing."

"Sounds like you were doing your best." How she'd been mistaken was obvious—getting her to forgive herself would prove difficult. If not impossible.

"And they sent you home." Cole's words were quiet. And sure.

"Yeah, they sent me home. Swept everything under the rug, looked at my record, and decided I needed some R&R."

I tilted my head. "Record?"

She fidgeted. "I worked for two agencies—each thought I was on vacation while I worked for the other."

"So you didn't take any time off? Like, at all?" Cole's tone bit just a touch.

"I told you this."

Had she? Maybe she'd mentioned it to me and I was now befuddled. That wouldn't surprise me—more and more about her past was coming out. Between that and Cole's shooting, it felt like life was getting away from me.

She shot him a look. Then took a long swig of her beer.

Discussion over.

"Who's up for cheesecake?" I rose.

Caressa held up her beer, but Cole gave me an eager look as he handed me his plate.

I went to the kitchen, loaded the dishwasher, and cut two slices of creamy cheesecake, then added the blueberry topping. I preferred fresh, but in the dead of winter, in Canada, one took whatever one could get.

After getting everything organized, I moved back to the living room.

Caressa'd risen and had made her way over to the massive windows. We'd had snow earlier, and although it had been heavy, it also hadn't lasted long. Tonight we were forecasted to get a walloping. Our work crew had been put on alert—more than a foot and they had the day off. Much more than that, and the executives weren't expected to make an appearance either.

For some places in Canada, a foot was nothing. In Vancouver, that little snow could bring the city to a standstill and paralyze everything. I had winter tires, as did Cole and Caressa, but that didn't save us from the yahoos who didn't. And just about everywhere we went, we'd find some kind of incline or decline. Vancouver had flat areas, Point Grey was one of them, but most of the region had hills of various sizes.

I handed Cole his cheesecake.

He offered me a grateful smile.

A smile I'd never tire of seeing. It lit something inside me and burned bright. We'd been friends for more than twenty-five years and lovers for mere weeks, and I couldn't imagine my life without him.

Without Caressa either.

"Snow's starting." She laid her palm against the glass.

Embarrassingly, my first thought was fingerprints. And that someone would have to wipe them away.

Cole has staff for that. Or, hell, you can do it yourself.

Yeah, I could. I made a note of the general area and packed away the notion that I'd do just that on the weekend. Or even tomorrow—if we had a snow day.

"Okay, so you're back." Cole's words had Caressa stiffening. "That still doesn't explain why you left."

Ah, back to the dog with the proverbial bone. He just wasn't going to let this story die. And maybe he was right. Maybe we did need to clear the air once and for all.

"I was pregnant."

I'd been in the process of sitting down, and I nearly spilled my cheesecake. How was I supposed to deal with her revelation? Go and take her in my arms? Sit and blithely eat my cheesecake?

I caught Cole's gaze, and he looked equally perplexed.

"While you were in Africa? You said the logistics guy was a couple of—" I struggled to do the math.

"Five years ago."

I dropped to the couch. Then I immediately put my plate on the coffee table. My appetite was completely gone. Fled in the wake of the one word.

Pregnant.

Cole handed me his plate, and I put it on the coffee table as well.

He reached for my hand.

I gave it willingly.

We'd figure out what was going on and then offer whatever comfort we could to Caressa.

"Did you…" Cole cleared his throat. "Did you have a miscarriage?"

Because that was the only logical explanation. Something had happened, and she'd lost the baby—

"I had an abortion."

The word hit me like a gunshot to the chest. Was this how Cole'd felt? A piercing pain through the heart?

"I don't…" Nope, I couldn't find the words.

She didn't turn. "I was young."

Nearly twenty-eight. That didn't feel young.

"I was naïve."

But she'd had several boyfriends…hadn't—

"Fucking Franklin." Cole muttered the name quietly.

I barely heard it, and I was pretty sure Caressa hadn't.

"I…" She traced her finger along the glass. "I couldn't cope. I'd just found out I'd been having an affair with a married man—"

Fucking Franklin.

"His wife threatened me. I don't know…I just didn't know how to cope."

You could have come to us. We would have taken care of you.

"And I blamed myself. How could I have been so stupid, you know?"

No, I don't know. It takes two to tango.

"I just kept thinking I was going to wind up like my mother. On welfare, unable to support a child. My child," she corrected.

We would've helped. You never would've been alone.

"It felt like the only way out, you know?"

No, I don't know. Why didn't you tell us?

"Before you left or…" Cole swallowed hard before he could finish the question.

"Before I left Canada. I applied to go overseas while working out the logistics of the abortion, quitting my job, and finding someone to sublet my apartment. No matter what, I was leaving Vancouver."

"You could've sued him for child support. He was a doctor, for Christ's sake. If he could afford to take you to those hotels—"

She turned at my words.

Shit.

Cole shot me a glare, and I wanted more than anything to take back those words. But I was too late.

She wrapped her arms around her waist. "How did you know about the hotels?"

"We…"

Cole's glare intensified as if to say *don't throw me under the bus. You started this mess. You fix it.*

"We, uh, might've…"

"Had me followed?"

I scratched my scalp.

"Followed me?"

I squinted. "Sort of?"

Her rage was incandescent. She went from apathetic and pained to luminously rageful in a heartbeat. "You fucking bastard."

"I—"

"You knew he was married, didn't you?"

"Well…"

"And you didn't tell me?"

"We figured you knew." I rubbed my face. "By the time we discovered you hadn't known, you did know, and we'd, uh, threatened him—"

"His wife came to confront me."

"That wasn't our doing." Or at least I was pretty sure it hadn't been. We'd *threatened* to tell his wife—but we hadn't actually done it. Whether he'd done it himself for the sake of self-preservation, I wasn't sure.

"Caressa…" Cole tried for a placating tone. Then, because he could totally be a manipulative bastard, he pressed his hand to his chest. Over the bullet hole.

She narrowed her eyes.

He held her stare. "Would it have made any difference? We didn't beat him up or anything… Just

270

recommended that he only use his hand or his wife's—"

"Jesus, Cole." Her face scrunched in utter revulsion.

"We didn't know you were pregnant." I scratched my scalp again. "Would you have wanted him to leave her? To leave their daughters? Would that have made you stay? Made you keep the baby?"

She pressed her hand to her lower abdomen. "I wasn't going to chase him for child support. My mother tried that with my father for years—and look where she wound up."

We would've supported you.

The words were on the tip of my tongue, but I knew, instinctively, they were the wrong words for this situation. They might be true, but they might also destroy her. Abortion was such a personal decision, and I knew, without an iota of doubt, that she hadn't made the decision lightly. Hadn't chosen that path without careful consideration.

"The thing is…" She rubbed her face. "I still don't understand how I got pregnant. I was adamant about condoms—"

Cole coughed.

We both turned to him.

A man more conflicted, I didn't ever remember seeing. His brow knit, but his mouth set in a firm line that I didn't often witness.

"You know something." The words came from me, but Caressa could have just as easily said them. We both saw something.

"I, uh…" This time, a throat clearing. "There was another woman. A medical secretary. Her boyfriend worked with me on a show, and we got to talking and figured out that her ex-lover worked with you and…all the pieces fell into place."

"What do you know?"

Cole flinched. "He stealthed her."

My stomach bottomed out. Okay, yeah, I'd heard about guys who did that. Claimed they were using a condom and then removed it at the last moment—usually when his partner didn't realize, which was horrifying. "That's shitty. That's—"

"Rape." Cole met my gaze quickly, before turning to Caressa. "It's unwanted sexual contact. You would never have agreed—"

She shook her head violently, her long hair swaying.

"Then it's a form of rape. He took something from you that you didn't give willingly. That's rape."

Cole must have known the impact the word would have. On me, for sure, but mostly on Caressa.

"I need—" She tried to bolt.

I leapt off the couch to waylay her as she headed toward the exit. "Not tonight. We've had enough of this running shit. You're going to stay and deal with this once and for all. And if that means you sit alone in a room and I sit on the outside and keep watch, then that's fine. But you're not going out in the middle of a snowstorm. Jesus, you were freezing last night when you came home."

"Was that what triggered you?" Cole gazed at her.

She winced at his question. Even the word triggered was loaded, but I understood what he was getting at. After a long moment, she nodded.

I tried to arch an eyebrow. And failed miserably. But Caressa's small smile soothed my battered ego.

"Yes. Elouise talking about babies and..." She let out a whoosh of air. "How was I supposed to react? I wanted to be happy for this woman I barely knew. But then she started to talk about you and us and…"

"You having our child." Cole uttered the words softly.

"I have an IUD because I never want to get pregnant again."

My heart seized.

"But with you…" She looked back and forth between the two of us. Then wrapped her arms around her waist again. "What would that even look like? Do I marry one of you and have the other one's child? What if Cole and I continue to be seen in public, but our child has blond hair and hazel eyes? My mother was a blonde, so it could happen. Or…"

"Or what if the child has tanned skin?" My voice caught in my throat. "Because that could also happen."

Cole let out a long breath. "Yeah, we need to talk."

Chapter Twenty-Five

Cole

We need to talk.

Possibly the most ominous way of addressing the elephant in the room.

But that oversized animal wasn't going to go away if we just ignored it.

Caressa sighed.

Michael guided her over to the couch. He positioned her next to me and then tucked himself beside her so barely a breath lay between them. Then he angled himself so he could see both of us.

And we could see him.

Both of them looked at me.

I took Caressa's hand.

Michael rested his arm on the back of the couch and fingered the ends of my long hair.

"We haven't talked about the future." I kept my voice steady.

Caressa stiffened against me.

I held her hand tighter. Then I cleared my throat. "I always thought I'd be a shitty father—"

Caressa made a noise low in her throat.

I sensed Michael's automatic denial.

"We none of us had good parents." I rushed on. "Alcoholics, drug addicts, abusers—we really lucked out in the shitty parental units."

Michael made a murmur of what I assumed was agreement. Of all of us, he'd had it roughest.

Caressa's mother had been too high, or too low, to pay any attention to her.

My father was mostly absent and—mostly—kept his fists to himself.

Michael, though? Present parents who liked to take their fists to him. Frequently. Even now, all these years after their death, I still wanted to kill them. I remembered every single one of those bruises. He'd try to hide them, but Caressa and I would insist on seeing them. As if we could somehow judge if they were bad enough to require medical attention. God, we hadn't even turned ten.

"What I'm trying to say is…until Peter and Thomas adopted Skylar, I didn't know the first thing about kids. Babies in particular. But they'd brought me into their little family—Julie and me and even, on occasion, Donovan."

Caressa snorted.

"Yeah, I know. Go figure—he's great with her. And now Samuel. He's thriving, being with the Erickson-Walsh clan." Peter, being the mega star, still used his last name. But Thomas and their children used his last name. Protected the kids from being linked to the Erickson name even more.

What would the Hamilton name do?

"Then Val and Seamus took in Jason, their foster son, and I saw how happy that made them. Seamus is happy to donate sperm to Elouise and Kelci without the need for reciprocity because the men don't feel a driving need to have an infant—but they're considering another foster child. So many kids…" I exhaled. "And I keep thinking that I want that. I want to give a kid a home and loving parents and…" Damn it. I swallowed hard. "I don't know that I'd ever be good enough."

Caressa tucked herself against my shoulder, and Michael continued to feather his hand through my hair.

Still, I didn't look at them. "So part of me thinks I should let you two go."

"No." Caressa wrapped a gentle arm around my waist. "If I can't go, then you can't either."

I continued on as if she hadn't spoken. "And part of me can't bear the thought of you having a child and it not being mine."

Michael's hand stilled.

Finally, I looked at him. "I've had a lot of time to think since Elouise left. And yes, much of that was worrying about Caressa."

She made a little whimper.

"But a lot of it was trying to sort out how I'd feel if the child wasn't mine. I mean, my genes are shit anyway."

"Fuck, Cole, you say the stupidest things." Michael held my gaze with his intense eyes that sparkled gold in the lamplight. "If anything, I'm the one with the shitty genes. Your mom took off—mine stuck around to beat the shit out of me. My parents were equal-opportunity abusers."

"I remember." I said the words quietly.

Caressa tightened her grip on me. She reached back her hand to grip Michael's thigh.

Thank God, my chest didn't hurt. Or rather, not much more than it had been. I was due for some painkillers soon.

I closed my eyes. "And it's probably way too soon

to be talking about kids. With what you said…" I pressed a kiss to the crown of Caressa's head. At least, finally, I had some understanding of why she'd taken off for Africa. I'd assumed it had something to do with Fucking Franklin. I'd never, not in a million years, guessed she was pregnant.

Probably why she had an IUD now—their failure rate was infinitesimal.

Still…the idea of her growing my child inside her. Or Michael's child. That filled me with a longing I felt deep into my soul. At the same instant, I thought of all the kids out there in need of a good home. All three of us could have wound up in foster care as kids—probably should have. But we'd been terrified of the system and had done everything in our power to stay as far away from it as we could. That had meant squirreling Michael away when the bruises couldn't be hidden. That meant hiding the fact we often went to school hungry. Or that meant taking care of ourselves and each other at a time in our lives when our greatest worry should have been getting good grades—not how to scrounge enough food to eat.

"We don't have to decide today." I gripped Caressa. "And if you're never okay with it, then that's okay too."

It might break me, but I'd learn to live with it.

"I want…" She tipped her head up to face me, glanced back at Michael, then fixed her gaze back on me. "I know I can never make up for the baby I…" She swallowed. "But I don't want to write off having a child." Her eyes hardened. "But you have to be okay with it being Michael's. Just like he has to be okay with it being yours. If we do this, we do this together as a team. Or we don't do it at all."

Her words struck me. Hard. She wasn't closing the door on us having a family of our own. But this wasn't an enthusiastic yes either. Just a…perhaps.

I could live with that. I angled my head so I could capture her mouth.

She came willingly.

Michael grasped my hair and pulled.

Just the way I liked.

Her pliant lips against mine kicked my libido into gear. My body ached for the kind of relief that sinking into her—into either of them—would bring.

She stroked my cheeks, rasping her fingers through my stubble. My facial hair grew pretty fast, and I was in need of a shave. Unless I grew slovenly and let a beard run wild.

Nah, that wasn't me. I liked to be clean-shaven. I liked Michael the same way—although I sometimes found a little scruff sexy. Hell, I'd take him any way I could.

Caressa pulled back. "I think I want some cheesecake."

My cock didn't agree, but my stomach wasn't going to argue—we'd had a hell of an intense discussion. Sometimes things like that upset my stomach. Other times, that intensity made me hungry.

Michael tugged on my hair one last time before releasing it. He continued to rest his hand on Caressa's back as he reached over to snag my plate.

Then he grabbed his own and tried to hand it to her.

She shook her head. "You guys can share."

He grinned, settled back on the couch, and offered her the first bite.

Watching her eat cake off his fork did nothing to

cool me off, and after a moment, I gave her a piece of mine.

In the end, I was pretty sure she'd consumed more than anyone, but I wasn't complaining. "I need to piss."

Michael moaned, but Caressa popped up.

"I think we all need an early night." She angled herself to help me up.

"I want to sleep in the bed with you tonight." I was so goddamn raw that I didn't even want to think about sleeping alone in that hospital bed.

She gave me a sympathetic look, with her eyes softening. "I know you do. But, Cole, you were shot a week ago. You're already making significant progress and—"

"More than a week and I'm tired of everyone telling me how great I'm doing."

Michael, who had collected the plates, cocked his head. "You really want to risk your recovery? I want you in bed more than anything, but I want you healthy too." He indicated Caressa with his head, even though she couldn't see as she faced me.

In his own way, he was letting me know that I had to put her needs first. And for tonight, that meant doing as she asked. He'd take care of her. In the way I wanted to.

Time. We have time.

Yet I wasn't convinced we did. We'd faced so much in the last six weeks that I couldn't fathom any more.

"Oh, Susan Miller called." Caressa eyed me.

Her offhanded comment had me scrunching my nose. "What does the studio boss want? And why didn't you tell me?"

She held up her hand. "You were, shall we say,

otherwise occupied."

I squinted.

"Napping."

"Oh." Yeah, I seemed to do that a lot.

"She wants you to record an acceptance speech in case you win the Golden Globe."

I snickered.

"Hey, last season was amazing." Michael's hazel eyes glittered. "Your best yet. And you might get the sympathy vote."

"First, all my seasons have been amazing." Although he wasn't wrong, season four had rocked. "Second, there's no sympathy vote. The Hollywood Foreign Press voted a long time ago." This much, I was certain about. "And finally, I wouldn't want the sympathy vote. And you know it. I want to win on the merits of my work. And although I did stellar work, they don't pick superheroes."

"Even complex ones?" Caressa cocked her head.

I tilted my head toward her.

"Well, I started by watching season one and am through to season three. But, oh my God, Cole—you were so young."

I wanted to point out she'd left for Africa just a few months earlier—and therefore had also been that young. Now that I knew her reasons for returning home, however, I vowed never to bring up her time away again. Knowing meant I could support her if she needed it, and give her space when that would help. "I really need to pee."

Michael chuckled and headed to the kitchen.

Caressa helped me rise and then guided me to the bathroom. "I'll get your pajamas."

"Thanks." I held her gaze for just a moment. "For everything. I know I've been a recalcitrant patient—"

She attempted to wave me off.

I persisted. "You can call me out on my shit. I hate being sick. First the IT band and now…" I swept my hand up and down my body. Even though the injury was to the chest, the fatigue seeped into every pore. Pain radiated from everywhere.

Gently, she grasped the back of my neck and tugged me down for a kiss. Just as things started to get interesting, she pulled back. "We've got time, Cole. Time for you to recover. Time for us to bond properly."

Again, I wanted to argue. But she was expressing her sentiments—and I had to respect that.

"I feel like we're running out of time." My words didn't make any sense, but I needed to express them.

"You've just faced death." She cupped my cheek. "Facing your mortality at thirty-two sobers you. Michael and I haven't had that. But we almost lost you, and that aged us differently." She managed a smile. "The threat has been neutralized—at least in parlance you can understand."

Ah, so she'd gotten to episode four of season three at least.

"We don't have to worry about that woman. And we'll face new challenges in the years to come, but we'll do it together."

"I like how you say *years to come*."

She snickered. "You need a shave."

"Tomorrow?"

"Before the crew comes to record the video."

"It's pompous and presumptuous."

"What if you *do* win?"

I blinked. I honest to God hadn't thought about it. Because I never won. "Elouise is nominated for her film. She stands an excellent chance of winning. You haven't seen the movie yet…"

She shook her head.

"Well, I've got a copy. We're doing that tomorrow. And you'll understand why I'm hawkish about her winning."

"Okay, but what does that have to do with you?"

"She's now my co-star on *VJ*. Her accepting the award on my behalf makes sense. Then even if she doesn't win, she'll have had her moment on that stage."

"Won't that make her sad?"

I laughed. "You need to really get to know Elouise. She'd enjoy the recognition for her brilliant work, to be sure, but she's just as happy at home hanging with Kelci and their dog."

"And soon a baby…"

For the first time since Elouise told me her news, it really sank in. "Yeah, her baby. If she can work the timing, she'll have this infant during the hiatus."

"You needed to pee."

Sore topic?

"I won't be doing *VJ* forever. We've had a good run, but Julie and I have discussed calling it quits after season seven. I want to go out on a high, and fans, I think, are going to tire of Justice and Lyric's…relationship."

"Do they wind up together?"

She asked the question innocently; I could tell.

"Uh, no one knows."

Her brow knit.

"Okay, I know and Julie knows and the executive producer knows. But the writers and Lisette—"

"And Donovan—"

"And Donovan have no idea."

"You're not going to tell us?"

"Tells us what?" Michael appeared in the doorway to the bathroom with my pajamas. "Have you peed yet?"

"He was just about to tell me if Lyric and Justice wind up together."

Michael laughed. A full belly laugh.

The sound warmed my heart.

"Caressa, I've been begging him to tell me for almost five years." He narrowed his eyes. "If you tell her—"

I held up my hands. "No one's being told. I love you both, truly, but I made a pact with Julie that we wouldn't tell anyone. I trust her to keep that promise. And I'll do the same. Now, my bladder is about to—"

Both my lovers held up their hands.

Michael dropped my pajamas on the counter and ushered Caressa out.

Phew.

At least she gave me this much privacy, which afforded me a touch of dignity. And even getting undressed and into nightclothes was a big deal.

Doing everything took longer than I would have liked, and I found a frowning Caressa standing at the door—already in her pajamas.

Gratefully, I leaned on her as we made our way over to the hospital bed. Hell, I was just grateful this room was large enough to accommodate it. We had it turned so it ran parallel to my bed but faced the opposite direction. So I could see my bed clearly. If I couldn't be in it with my lovers, at least I could see them.

"Just a few more nights." Caressa secured the

railing. "If the doctor gives you the okay, we can move you."

"Dr. Graham is a tyrant."

"Dr. Graham is one of the best surgeons in the city," she corrected. "And you're going to show her respect."

"Yeah, okay." I put no heat behind the complaint, but I put vehemence behind my agreement. Well, I attempted to.

Caressa's arched eyebrow assured me I hadn't quite succeeded.

Michael chuckled as he pulled back the covers. "Try again, Hamilton."

I held up my hand in the Boy Scout salute. "I promise, on my honor—"

Caressa cut me off with a swift and brutal kiss. She thrust her tongue into my mouth as if to swallow my pledge. Which worked in so many ways. I'd give her anything—anything—she asked for. If my acquiescence on this was her request, then I'd give it. I *did* want to get better. Anything that would get me out of this bed and back into the marital one.

I stilled.

Caressa pulled back. Concern shone in her eyes as she stroked my forehead. "What is it?"

The words caught in my throat. I wanted to marry her. But I wanted Michael to marry her. And I wanted to marry Michael. Viscerally, in my gut, I wanted this more than anything.

I flashed to the purchase I'd made at the jewelry store back on Christmas Eve. How naïve I'd been. But my gift giving had been derailed by Caressa's discovery of the dungeon, and we hadn't discussed BDSM in weeks. I'd anticipated missing that release valve intensely, but I didn't. We were, as a throuple, so busy living our lives that I barely gave a second thought to my former pastime. Not that I'd ever spent that much time down there, but it had been an integral part of me.

"Cole, you're scaring me."

"No—I'm fine. Just…" *Find the words.* "I wish we could all get married."

I expected panic from her, but she didn't balk. Instead, she eased me back down to the mattress. "Well, that's something to talk about. Often, when a third joins a pair, there's a handfasting ceremony. Our society isn't progressive enough to accept triads for legal marriages, but we can find a creative way around it." She winked. "But I'm more interested in what happens behind closed doors."

"We need to come out."

"Shush, Cole, you're stressing about something far in the future. Maybe after *VJ* ends—"

"No, now." I wasn't even certain where the vehemence was coming from, but I knew we couldn't wait three more years.

Michael made his way over to the other side of the bed. "Okay, Cole, we can figure something out. But I think you need to talk to a couple of people before you make such a big decision. Like, I don't know, your agent, your publicist, and your counselor?"

"What does Hamish have to do with this?" Funny how, after just one session, I saw him as an important person in my life.

"We have an appointment on Saturday with him. The three of us." Caressa offered a smile. "I think we can hold the discussion until then."

She's right. You need sleep. So do they.

Both looked weary, so I desisted and relaxed back into the bed. "Okay, fair enough."

Caressa pressed a kiss to my cheek.

Michael did the same to the other and feathered his hand through my hair. "Let Caressa shave you tomorrow."

"All right." Giving in was easy. My face already itched, and I didn't like the slovenly look. I looked unkempt. I needed to feel more like myself.

Caressa and Michael got into bed, and Michael turned off the lamp so we only had the glow of the nightlight.

One of these days, I'd cease needing it. Tonight, though, I did. I needed to see my lovers as they cuddled.

They spooned at the edge of the bed closest to me.

I could almost reach out and touch them.

Caressa offered a smile as Michael drew her closer.

As much as I wanted to fight sleep, I surrendered, and it quickly dragged me under.

Chapter Twenty-Six

Caressa

Saturday dawned, and, as I snuggled with Michael, I sensed Cole waking.

"I'm thinking pancakes." I sighed.

Michael nudged my lower back with his erection. We'd tacitly agreed that while Cole was out of commission, it wouldn't be fair for us to do more than sleep in each other's arms.

The night I came home after wandering the streets for hours and wound up in a coffee shop before walking home had been the aberration. Desperation had clawed at me, and I'd needed to connect with someone. And although Michael'd been inside me, I'd felt Cole's stare. His warmth. His virtual embrace.

His jealousy.

So I hadn't made love to Michael again. Oh, I was quite certain Cole'd encourage us. But he might also enjoy the show a little too much, and he wasn't ready for that.

Yet.

Dr. Graham was due to visit Monday, and I had high hopes for some good news.

"Hamish will be here in an hour." I pushed back against Michael's morning wood.

"I want a shower." Cole sounded as petulant as ever.

Gabbi Grey

"You won't be able to keep your dressing dry."

"What about cling wrap?"

"I can help him." Michael whispered the words in my ear.

"You're making pancakes. With chocolate chips."

He nibbled my ear.

"He should fuck you first." Cole met my gaze. "You know you want him to."

I snorted. "Michael will survive."

"Michael's going to go jerk off in the shower." Before he did, though, he reached around and tweaked my nipple.

Hard.

Cole grinned unrepentantly.

"You two." I evaded Michael's grasp and tumbled out of bed, barely righting myself in time.

"You know you love us." This from Cole.

"I'll get the cling wrap." I stalked out of the room.

By the time I was back, Michael had Cole out of his pajama top and looking vaguely pleased with himself.

Actually, they both looked pleased with themselves.

Forty minutes later, three showered lovers plopped onto the couch with coffee, OJ, and pancakes. Well, Michael and I plopped.

Cole eased down gently. "Should we warn Michael about Hamish?"

I cocked my head as I looked at Cole.

"Well, the guy doesn't take any notes, and he has a thing for Donovan."

I nearly sprayed my coffee. "And how do you know that?"

"Oh my God, Caressa, it's so obvious. Mention Donovan, and the guy blushes." He grinned

288

unrepentantly. "And mention him to Donovan, and you get much the same response."

Ah, so that's what they had discussed yesterday while on a video conference call. I'd made myself scarce by going for a walk while Cole and Donovan chatted. I didn't think Cole was missing all the LA excitement, but I appreciated Donovan looping him in. Tomorrow was the big night, and although Cole maintained he'd rather be home with us, I couldn't help wondering who he'd have taken with him to LA if he hadn't been shot.

I cocked my head. Somehow, I couldn't see the elegant Black man blushing. "Are you sure?"

"Oh, yeah. He got all..." Cole gestured. "Worked up. They've only seen each other a couple of times, and Donovan's smitten."

"You're thinking about teasing Hamish." I put on my stern expression. "Just don't. Neither man will thank you for it."

"I'll do it." Michael grinned devilishly at my death glare.

Goddamnit, I needed to work on my angry looks.

Except a small part of me wanted to see Hamish's expression. I couldn't decide if the psychologist would be a good match for our friend or not.

Breakfast dishes were neatly tucked into the dishwasher as it did its job when Hamish arrived.

Michael greeted him at the door, and they conversed a bit in the entryway before Michael ushered him into the living room.

"That view is still spectacular." Hamish pointed. "And I can see so much farther."

"Clear days give you the best view." Cole grinned as I settled against him.

He claimed he felt well enough to sit between Michael and myself.

That might be true, but I intended to have him lean on me as much as possible. As such, I positioned myself on his left side.

Hamish dropped into the lounge chair, letting his messenger bag fall to the floor beside him. He didn't even bother to retrieve a pen and paper.

Something told me he had perfect recall and the pad and pen had been a prop earlier in the week.

Michael took up his place on Cole's right, and we each gripped his hands.

Hamish offered a broad grin. "You're looking well today. All three of you."

"Have you ever counseled a throuple before?" Michael's tone wasn't sharp…but it wasn't kind either.

The psychologist offered a wide smile. "Actually, I have. I met an interesting throuple a while back—a Canadian woman, a gentleman from Texas, and an Argentinian man."

Cole whistled.

Hamish smiled. "Yes. Their employer is one of our clients, and the two gentlemen work there. They asked for a counseling session as a group. The men were having a few issues adjusting to life in Canada. And they wanted to make certain the third member of their triad was happy. I'm pretty sure they could have done things less formally, but they wanted her to see they took the relationship seriously. Of course, moving to Canada is pretty serious to start with."

"I know you can't divulge private information, but how did that work out?" Cole tilted his head.

"They're very open about their relationship—with

friends and colleagues. I'm not a betting man, but I predict a solid future for them."

"So you think we might be able to pull this off?" Again, Michael asked the question.

"Depends what you mean by *pull off*." Hamish met each of our gazes. "Living a lifestyle that moves beyond the hetero-normative couple always has risks. We've made great strides in the past twenty years. Gay marriage, gay adoption, trans awareness…but society hasn't quite grasped that someone might be able to romantically love more than one person at the same time. We were, as a species, designed to procreate."

I winced. For just a heartbeat, I flashed to my decision to terminate my pregnancy.

Cole's hand tightened in mine.

After a moment, Hamish continued. "Look, you're aware you'll face greater scrutiny—"

"I think Cole should wait until he's finished with *Vigilante Justice*." I blurted out the words. "Or that Cole and Michael should come out as a couple. I mean, yeah, Cole might get fewer roles if he comes out as gay—"

"Bi."

"Whatever." I scowled at his interruption. "But that's better than being in some kind of sordid threesome. And if—"

"We've already come out as a couple." Cole turned to face me. "I'm not walking away from you. That'd do more damage to my reputation than anything else."

Shit.

He had a point.

"Then Michael's on the outside?" I tried to keep the despair from my voice, but I struggled with it.

"No. We come out. As a throuple. End of story. I'll

get my agent and publicist to set us up with a friendly reporter. I can't see Lisette or Susan Miller, the head of the studio, firing me. Wouldn't look good."

Michael cleared his throat. "You're risking everything."

Cole shook his head vehemently. "I'm gaining everything. The money, the fame, the show…they mean nothing if I don't have the two of you."

Hamish grinned, making him look far too young to be the thirty-seven I knew him to be. "Why don't we talk logistics?"

A strangled sound escaped Michael.

Cole chuckled.

I flushed as heat raced up my cheeks.

Hamish held up his hands. "I don't need to know about that—unless you choose to share. I mean the rest of it…"

We spent the next hour discussing exactly what we might do. We tried out several scenarios, leaving Cole with plenty of options to discuss with his agent and publicist.

By the time Hamish left, I sensed a calm settling over Cole.

Michael prepared another round of coffees while I curled into Cole side, always mindful of his wound.

"Monday I get my two-week checkup."

"She's not going to clear you for sex."

"But she might clear me to sleep in bed with you."

I met his gaze. "We'd really like that. We were careful before—"

"Fuck."

"What?"

I tried to pull away, but he gripped me tighter.

"It's just…you've been here a month, and I've been injured the whole time. You and I have barely…and Michael…"

I pressed a kiss to his cheek. "Michael and I didn't move in so we could have sex with you."

He arched an eyebrow.

"That's just an added bonus." I blinked. "No, we moved in, purportedly, to take care of you. Somehow, though, I think you would've coped on your own."

"But this is so much more fun."

No missing the dry tone.

I gave him my bravest smile. "Cole, you're not going to be injured forever. Michael has the patience of a saint."

"True."

"Are you guys talking about me?" Michael entered the room carrying a tray laden with coffees—decaf for Cole, much to his chagrin—as well as some shortbread cookies he'd baked last night.

I'd have been too tired at the end of the week, but Michael insisted he loved cooking and baking. That they relaxed him.

That would be the opposite of my sentiments.

"I was telling Caressa how great your cookies are."

Michael met Cole's gaze.

"And she pointed out you have the patience of a saint." He snickered. "And the sexual habits of a monk."

I laughed at Michael's expression of outrage with his mouth dropping open.

"What are you—"

"You haven't fucked Caressa in days."

"Well, you know, you…and…you know…"

"No, I don't know. If I had a beautiful woman in my

bed every night—"

"She has to be willing."

Cole looked at me.

I glared back. "We're not doing anything that might rile you up sexually." His pretend look of hurt, all puppy dog eyes, had me laughing out loud. "Goofball."

"Promise me you'll have sex tonight."

Michael's pupils dilated. "Oh, I think something can be arranged."

"And I get to watch," Cole added.

Now Michael tapped his index finger to his lips. "Not sure about that. Nurse Caressa?"

I pressed myself against Cole and grazed my hand over his crotch.

He sucked in a breath.

Nonchalantly, I leaned over to grab my coffee and a cookie.

Cole glared.

Michael snickered.

Hours later, after Cole was settled for the night, I removed my pajamas before hopping into bed.

Likely assuming I knew what I was doing, Michael followed, crawling in behind me.

I pulled up the covers as he snuggled in behind me.

"No way. I want to see." Cole's petulant voice had both Michael and me chuckling.

I slid the covers down to expose myself almost to my knees. I groused, "It's cold."

Michael nuzzled my neck. "I'll warm you up."

Cole growled.

I arched a warning eyebrow.

He pressed his hand to his crotch.

Yeah, maybe this wasn't the best idea. That being

said, I'd checked with a doctor friend of mine, and he'd said that as long as Cole didn't show any signs of weakness or excessive fatigue, he was well on the way to recovery.

Michael slid his hand around my waist to my belly.

My breath caught. What would it be like? To be pregnant again? To have one of them father my child? They had both assured Hamish that they didn't care who wound up being the father—if we decided to have a child. But how would a child explain three parents when they went to kindergarten?

He slid his hand up to cup my breast.

All thoughts of kids fled.

As he tweaked my nipple, he nibbled my ear. We'd learned that was truly one of my erogenous zones—and he made full use of that knowledge.

Frequently.

I didn't mind.

We hadn't made love, except my night of desperation, since Cole'd been shot. And I hated thinking of that awful day, but it also made me more grateful every day that he still breathed. He still lived. He still loved.

"Her pussy needs attention, Michael."

I caught Cole's lascivious grin. Oh, he had my number. I'd been mindlessly rubbing my thighs together—trying to create some friction.

Michael slid his hand over my hip, across my abdomen, then to my thigh where he gently eased it back, catching it over his thigh.

Completely exposed—emotionally and physically.

He delved between my thighs, seeking and finding my clit. He flicked it.

I moaned.

Cole grinned.

Even as Michael worked it, I grew wetter.

His insistent erection pressed against my back.

"Please."

"You begging?" Cole's grin widened into a full-on smile. "I'd eat you out if I could."

"That day will come." And I looked forward to it—something told me Cole had an exceptionally talented tongue.

Michael nibbled my earlobe. "Do you want me to, you know—"

"I want you to fuck me. Here. Now. As soon as possible."

He stilled for a moment. "What the lady wants," he murmured in my ear. He guided himself to me and, after a moment, thrust in.

My gaze met Cole's. Holding it, though, was difficult. I wanted to close my eyes. I wanted to revel in the feel of Michael inside me. Usually, this position was my least favorite. I wanted to look into those glorious hazel eyes when I came.

When he came.

But this was the next best thing—having Cole eat me up with his eyes while Michael fucked me.

Cole moved his hand to his crotch.

Damn.

Did you really believe we could fuck and he wouldn't become aroused?

Well, I'd hoped.

But he pressed down on what I assumed was his erection and did nothing to further the pursuit of an orgasm. If he kept his heart rate steady, we should be okay.

And I so didn't need to be thinking of Cole's cardiovascular health while Michael thrust in and out of me.

His breathing quickened, and I refocused.

Then he rubbed my clit.

I tumbled into the abyss—hard and fast.

Michael followed me over as he stuttered, then held himself still.

Waves of pleasure continued to wash over me even as Michael continued to massage my clit. Part of me felt overly sensitive while another part of me yearned for a second climax. To come while having him nestled and still inside me.

"You can do it." Cole whispered the words urgently.

Whether he was speaking to Michael or myself didn't matter as that second climax hit me—hard and fast.

I bit my lip so hard that I likely drew blood.

This time, as I drifted back to earth, Michael soothed me with long strokes down my belly and thighs. He'd brush the lower part of my breast but never make it up to my nipples. Probably just as well—I was overly sensitive in all the right places.

"Michael." Cole cleared his throat. "I want to smell her."

In my befuddled state, his words took a moment to register. Then they did, and my cheeks flamed.

My lover, for his part, nodded. He withdrew from me, then gently ran his hands through my labia. He brushed my pussy, and I nearly yelped.

Then he rose, a little unsteadily, and headed over to Cole. He held out his fingers, and Cole inhaled deeply.

This might have felt weird…but it didn't. The action cemented us.

Finally, after the men held their gazes for a long time, Michael headed to the bathroom.

"I should check your heart—" I tried to rouse properly.

"I'm fine, Caressa. In fact, I'd say I'm perfect."

Believing him took a bit of effort, but his cheeks weren't flushed, and his breathing hadn't changed. Aside from him pressing down on his crotch, I hadn't seen any signs of arousal that I needed to worry about.

"Oh, good, because I'm fucking exhausted."

He chuckled. "So am I. And I'm in this bed, all alone—"

"Knock it off, Hamilton. You'll be just fine." I didn't put any heat behind my words.

Michael returned with a warm washcloth. As he gently cleaned me, I rolled onto my back and gave myself up to his ministrations.

When he kissed me, my eyes drifted shut.

That was the last thing I remembered.

Chapter Twenty-Seven

Michael

Watching the Golden Globes was akin to an agony I'd rarely experienced. My life was pretty damn boring. I went to work, I came home, I ate, I watched television, and then I went to bed. Sure, I'd dated a few women, had even enjoyed their company in the bedroom, but I lived a staid life.

Or I had.

Until Caressa'd blown back into it.

Until Cole'd gotten injured.

Until I'd moved in with my best friends.

Now? Every day felt a little nuttier. Each time that I felt like we might be on an even keel and facing smooth sailing, we hit a storm. Sometimes proverbial, sometimes literal.

Today, though, we'd had sunny skies without a cloud on the horizon. The temperature had been unseasonably warm for January, so we'd bundled Cole up and taken him outside for some time in the sun. He'd dozed, I'd read, and Caressa'd fussed with her calendar app.

She was conflicted. Part of her loved staying home and taking care of Cole. The rest of her knew he'd soon no longer need her vigilant care and that her boss was tapping her proverbial toes to get Caressa back. A nasty norovirus was circulating, and people were winding up in the ER.

Personally, I didn't like the idea of Caressa around all those sick people.

With an unrepentant grin, she liked to remind me that was what nurses signed up for.

I held my tongue, but Cole'd casually tossed out she could be doing wellness checks on new mothers.

He'd been turned away from her. He hadn't seen the flash of pain.

I had. And had made a note to talk to him later.

We'd come inside, and Cole'd ordered a pizza. Apparently, this was his ritual on awards nights. Or it had been—before he had to start showing up for events.

Caressa wasn't interested in the red-carpet pre-show until Cole pointed out that Elouise and Kelci would be there. At that, our lover plopped her butt down with a slice and a soda and watched intently.

Elouise stunned in a shimmering white floor-length gown with sequins. The dress showed off an appropriate amount of cleavage—just a subtle hint. I mean, I loved breasts, but I didn't need them in my face.

Kelci tried to stand back as Elouise was interviewed, but Elouise dragged her forward. Kelci's dress was, as Cole informed me, a silk number that accentuated all her curves. The dress was, as Caressa informed me, ombre where the purple bled into the blue which bled into the white. I might not understand all the terms, but her dress matched her blue hair with purple streaks. A wig, Cole confided. Well, more like informed. Apparently, Kelci had alopecia and was bald. She chose to share that news with the cast and crew who were free to share it with anyone else. She wore bold wigs as a fashion statement but, just as often, didn't wear one at all. Tonight, though, Cole said Kelci wanted the focus to be on Elouise—not her bald lesbian wife.

Whatever. Both women looked gorgeous, and as Elouise assured the interviewer that Cole was very much on the mend, she looked directly into the camera.

Cole jolted.

Yeah, he likely hadn't expected that.

He was strong enough to sit between Caressa and myself. His plate with the pizza sat unattended in his lap. For all his wry comments about watching the pregame show, as he liked to call it, the television had him completely riveted.

"Would you like me to reheat your pizza?" The interview with Elouise was over and—

"Cold pizza's fine."

Even as he said the words, Julie appeared.

With Donovan at her side.

Well, that would start tongues wagging. I was quite sure.

She wore a tight emerald-green gown, also with sequins, but this one scarcely covering her thighs. Even in sky-high stilettos, she barely reached Donovan's neck. He towered over her and looked more like a bodyguard than a date.

Julie also spoke in glowing terms about her co-star and how well his recovery was going.

"Why did you pick Elouise to nab your award for you if you win? Why not Julie—" I halted when Cole cut me off with a chop of his hand.

Caressa smirked. "He finally let me shave him the other day, and he recorded a video."

The shave I'd noticed. I hadn't heard about filming

an acceptance speech. Maybe I should have been put out by not knowing this, but I was still juggling work and trying to cook as much as possible. I loved Caressa dearly, but cooking was not her thing.

Cole kept promising to hook her up with a chef he knew. Miguel Fernandez was the renown chef at The Georgian and a personal friend of Cole's.

I didn't ask how.

And Cole felt he could ask Miguel to give Caressa personal lessons. Caressa'd balked. I offered to show her. She hadn't looked particularly pleased at that either.

No skin off my nose. I was happy to continue cooking. I liked feeling that I was contributing to the household. Especially these days when Cole supplied much of the money, Caressa cared for Cole, and I just went to the office every day.

"Okay, how soon into the broadcast before we get your category?"

Cole waved me off as the host stepped to the stage.

I only half listened to the opening bit, instead focusing on my man and just how tightly wound he was. "Caressa, I think Cole needs to relax."

He waved me off.

Caressa clucked her tongue.

They presented the first award…best actress in something…and then the broadcast cut to commercial.

"Maybe I can give him a neck massage." My fingers tingled at the thought.

"I'd appreciate it if you massaged other parts of me." Cole did a little pelvic tilt—as if I somehow might have missed his meaning.

Caressa sipped her soda. "Go ahead."

We both snapped our necks in our haste to look at

her.

She shrugged. "You can, you know…play with him."

I narrowed my eyes.

In her eyes, though, I read permission. Had she talked to the doctor? Was she drawing on some medical knowledge? Maybe she'd read an article?

Whatever, doesn't matter. She says it's safe.

What are you waiting for?

Caressa snagged all our plates—including Cole's, which still had a worrying amount of food—and headed to the kitchen.

"Later," Cole muttered.

"Food or—"

"Fucking food." He met my gaze, those dark-blue orbs mesmerizing me. "The rest of me grows impatient."

And as much as I was willing to dive in, I wanted a bit of foreplay. A chance to get myself in the mood. Not that I needed to be, I could deliver on command, but being a little revved up always added an extra dimension of pleasure. I placed my hand on his pec as I moved in for a kiss.

His eyes drifted shut as he opened for me.

I stroked my other hand down his jaw. Caressa'd shaved him again this morning. He swore he wanted to do it himself, but he wasn't quite there yet.

Caressa pointed out she loved shaving him. Got her all hot and bothered.

He pointed out that it did for him as well but that he couldn't do anything about it.

She grinned.

I chuckled.

Twenty minutes later, he was clean-shaven—and

Caressa and I were making out like horny teens.

Cole had whined. But watched avidly and with enthusiasm.

Now he was all in. He raked his hand through my hair, using his fingernails on my scalp. He clutched my shirt to yank me closer. He guided my hand down to rub his erection.

In the background, some woman was listing the nominees.

Caressa came back into the room.

I glanced over to see her place a tray with three bowls of ice cream on the coffee table. Vanilla, chocolate, and strawberry.

Cole grabbed my cheek and yanked me back into another toe-curling kiss.

Each time I rubbed his erection, he growled.

More applause.

Another announcement.

I didn't give a shit. After undoing the button on Cole's jeans and sliding down the zipper, I helped him shimmy enough so I could free his cock.

Commando.

Cute.

Almost like he'd hoped. Because wearing jeans without briefs was rarely comfortable. Well, for me, at least.

His cock curled up toward his belly, and a drop of precum leaked.

I licked my lips.

Caressa met my questioning gaze and gave me an almost imperceptible nod.

Permission.

Picking the perfect angle proved nearly impossible,

so I slid off the couch and positioned myself between Cole's spread thighs. I went up on my knees so I was eye level with his chest. Then I angled my mouth down and licked his tip.

The tangy precum hit my tongue, and I stiffened further. Yeah, that foreplay thing worked, because I was rock hard in my jeans.

I sucked him farther into my mouth, using my teeth to scrape along his length in that way that always got me off—when I wasn't worried about having my cock bitten by accident.

He bucked.

After pulling up his Henley almost to his nipples, Caressa placed her right hand on Cole's belly to hold him in place. Then she gently feathered her left fingers through his hair in a soothing gesture.

Cole first met her gaze, with such an expression of love that my rhythm faltered, and then he turned those blazing eyes to me.

I read the desire. The affection.

The love.

Redoubling my efforts, I continued to suck him off as best I could—remembering all the little things that made him moan. Mimicking the little things that got me off. Doing whatever it took to bring him to satisfaction.

More applause.

I didn't care.

Caressa whispered soft words of encouragement—whether to him, me, or both of us, I wasn't sure.

Still, I continued to suck him. I wanted to prolong his pleasure, but I also kind of wanted him to come so I could jack myself off. Hell, I might just come in my pants without any manual stimulation.

Gabbi Grey

"I'm coming." Always considerate Cole, giving me ample warning if I wanted to pull off.

I didn't. I took him as deep as I could as he came.

That mightn't have been the best idea since I nearly gagged as his cum hit the back of my throat.

"Cole Hamilton." The announcer's voice rang through the room.

"Holy shit." Caressa pulled back from Cole and bounced on her knees on the couch.

Cole jerked in my mouth, and I damn near bit him.

I let him go with a pop as I gazed up at him.

His focus was riveted on the television.

"Cole is unable to join us this evening, but he sent us a message."

I pivoted in time to see a woman I didn't recognize. Lovely, certainly. An actor, undoubtedly.

The beautiful face I loved so much filled the big screen.

"Thank you to the members of the Hollywood Foreign Press for this tremendous honor." He smiled, a little ruefully. "I would love to be there in person, but circumstances have me staying home for now."

The video had been shot with him sitting in his den, with his bookcase behind him.

"I have loved every minute of my time working on *Vigilante Justice*. The crew are phenomenal, and my castmates are amazing. Especially Julie, who delivers a virtuoso performance every week."

The shot dropped, just for a moment, to show an enraptured Julie with her eyes shimmering. I caught sight of Donovan next to her.

Then the video resumed. "I often tell people I'm the luckiest guy in the world. I have a job I love in the city

I've called home my entire life. I'm surrounded by amazing people, and I'm living the dream I'd always hoped for as a kid but had never believed would happen. I need to thank the amazing doctors, nurses, and paramedics who helped me out a couple of weeks ago— I owe you my life. Thank you for that." His eyes flickered. "Most importantly, I have my two best friends with me. Caressa and Michael, this is dedicated to you."

For just a moment longer, the camera remained on him.

Then the shot went back to the audience as they applauded.

The announcer said something about who was up next, and then a commercial for a sandwich store blared.

Caressa lowered the sound.

"But Elouise—" Cole attempted a feeble protest.

"Won't be on for a minute." She feathered her hand through his hair. "You did it. You finally won."

"It's just the sympathy vote."

"Hey, didn't you tell me the votes were made weeks ago?" I tapped Cole's cock.

He jerked, glaring down at me.

I looked defiantly up at him.

"Don't you have a hard-on to deal with?"

I shrugged. "Maybe getting you off didn't turn me on."

Caressa didn't even try to hide her snicker.

"Fuck her." Cole's eyes smoldered.

I hardened further.

"What about Elouise?" Caressa batted her eyelashes.

Oh, she's game.

"Elouise has Kelci to fuck her. I don't care how you

do it, but I want Michael inside you in the next three minutes."

"Caressa, you know, needs to be ready and…"

My lover was already yanking down her jeans and underwear and positioning a soft flannel blanket under her so her bare ass wasn't on the leather. "If you think that little show didn't get me hot and wet, then you're obviously not paying attention."

Her smell invaded me as she sat beside Cole and opened her legs.

My rock-hard cock begged for relief. "The angle won't work—the sofa's too high."

She turned herself so her head lay in Cole's lap and the rest of her stretched out like a Greek goddess. Her thighs spread in welcome.

Carefully, I rose. I shucked my jeans, underwear, and shirt and lowered myself onto her in record time.

Cole stroked her hair as I gazed deeply into her eyes.

"I love you." Pushing the words past a lump in my throat proved challenging.

"I know."

"Yeah, but…" I swallowed, gazed up at Cole, then looked back down at her. "I really love you. Even without—" I pressed my cock against her pussy.

She bucked. "Yeah, I get it. Now get in me…please."

I didn't make her wait another second. I lined myself up and pressed in. Pushed home. Sank into the joy that she brought me all the time. Our relationship wasn't just about sex—it went so much deeper than that.

But great sex didn't hurt.

And if the day came, fifty years from now, that sex was off the table, I'd be okay with that. But for the next forty-nine years, three-hundred-and-sixty-four days, I intended to get my fill.

"You're thinking too much, Dubois." Cole tapped my temple. "Just fuck her already."

And if I hadn't known him so well, I might have thought this was about being crude. But no, that wasn't it. He'd gotten off, and now he wanted us to.

Experimentally, I moved inside her.

She wrapped her legs around my waist, hooked her heels into my butt, and flexed.

I pushed all the way in.

From there, we just followed the baser instincts. Yin and yang. Giver and receiver. Only, she happened to give as good as she got. And as I drove her higher and higher, she whispered, "I'm coming."

"Thank fuck."

"Elouise Hynes for…"

Cole's hoot of joy cut off the rest of the announcement.

Fortunately, I'd been mid-climax, and nothing was stopping me. I spilled into Caressa as I felt her contracting around me. Then I collapsed—mindful of my weight.

She pulled me closer and enveloped me in powerful arms.

Cole stroked my forehead and ran his fingernails through my hair.

Contentment settled over me as I listened to a speech from a woman I'd never met, telling her wife how much their relationship meant to her.

Realizing I had my mates within my grasp allowed me to sink into glorious oblivion.

Chapter Twenty-Eight

Caressa

Extricating myself proved challenging—most couches weren't designed for fucking on. Or being fucked on. But we managed to untangle ourselves. Much to Michael's dismay, I headed up to the shower in *my* room while he grabbed a quick one in our bedroom.

We could have showered together, but keeping our hands off each other, even after reaching complete satiation, would have been a challenge, and Cole wouldn't have been there.

Currently, he had the remote in his hand and was searching through his recording to watch all of Elouise's speech. Whether he'd rewatched his own while Michael and I showered, I wasn't certain. I noticed he'd also tucked himself back in and done up his jeans. The jeans were a step above the sweats. He claimed he wanted to feel more normal.

Is that even possible? You've been shot.

Yet I didn't voice my ruminations.

Glancing over at the three bowls of melted ice cream, I grinned. "You guys want to drink down the spoils?"

Michael, who had just reappeared, nabbed his strawberry and drank it down in a couple of gulps.

Cole held out his hand for his chocolate and

promptly slurped it up.

I might have sipped mine with a bit more delicacy but enjoyed the vanilla nonetheless. "More?"

Cole offered a sheepish grin. "Might I have a slice of pizza?"

I rolled my eyes. Then took the empty bowls into the kitchen and put them in the dishwasher while I heated a slice.

"Michael?" I called out the word, regretting not having asked earlier because I always hated to raise my voice. Years of listening to Michael's parents shouting on the other side of that paper-thin wall had me reacting to loud voices. That and, at work, people shouted when things were bad.

I didn't want things to be bad.

After a moment, Michael popped his head in. He met my gaze and halted. "What?"

I tried to wave him off.

He persisted, moving right into my space and tipping my head up. "What, Caressa?"

"Just thinking about your parents—"

He snickered, frowning.

"—and how much they used to yell."

"Fight," Michael corrected. "They fought. We're not fighting. We're just lazy people who don't want to walk to another room."

"I don't want to be like them. Please don't ever let me be like them."

He gathered me into his arms. "You could never be like them. You don't have it in you."

"But…what if you or Cole really pisses me off—"

"We'll discuss it like rational adults."

"What if the kids do something horrible and I'm so

scared that I yell?"

"Then Cole will calm you down while I'll explain to the kids that Mommy yelled because she was scared and that she didn't mean to upset them. We'll have a family meeting about whatever set you off." He stroked my hair. "I think these are all things you need to speak to your counselor about, Caressa. Cole and I love you, but we're not professionals. And Hamish is great, but I think you need someone who can focus solely on you. You liked the woman you were seeing at the hospital, right?"

The hospital.

"I froze, Michael. When they wheeled Cole in, I couldn't move."

He kissed my forehead. "No one expected you to. He's your lover. They don't want doctors working on their loved ones for a reason." He gazed down into my eyes. "Are you afraid you'll freeze up again? Even if it's a stranger?"

"I…I don't know."

"Another thing to talk to your counselor about." He pulled me tighter. "You know you can quit, right? That there are less stressful jobs? I mean, I think Cole would prefer to have you home and safe—"

"I don't want that." It tempted me, but I knew, in my heart, that I didn't want to be beholden to Cole that way. My salary might be paltry in comparison to his, but I needed my independence. "Although, maybe I won't take so many extra shifts." I was due to start back in another week. By then Cole could be alone for a few hours. Between visiting friends and Zoey, who had a clear mandate to get him rehabbed as soon as possible without pushing him too hard, he wouldn't spend much time alone. And a bit of time by himself wouldn't be a bad thing. Cole came across as an extrovert, and he was, to a certain extent, but he thrived when he had time to himself when he could recharge. Plus, between my schedule and Michael's, we'd be here a good part of the time anyway.

"You can work enough so you fill your well without overdoing it." He met my gaze. "Are you serious about having kids? That's such an enormous leap—"

"Are you hesitating?"

"No." His eyes flashed gold in the kitchen light. "However we make a family, and whatever the future looks like, I'm in this for the long haul. If we never have kids, that'll be okay. If we have a brood, I'm fine with that as well."

I nearly choked. "No brood, Michael."

"Fair enough."

"Are you making out in there? I'm starving." Cole's voice carried to us.

We snickered.

"Yes, sir." I grinned.

"Oh, don't tempt me."

Michael and I exchanged a look.

His eyebrows shot up, obviously in response to Cole's quip. "The dungeon?"

"Jesus, I haven't had three seconds to think since Christmas Eve. Half the time, I even forget it's down there."

"Maybe when Cole's feeling better, we can get a proper tour." He smiled that wicked grin I loved so much.

"Sir needs his pizza."

"And I need to know you're going to be okay."

"I am, Michael, truly."

Our lips met in a gentle kiss. A sealing of our deal. A promise of more to come.

When we broke apart, I nuked Cole's pizza for another little bit while Michael dished himself some more ice cream.

He shrugged. "I got hungry. We, uh, expended some calories."

"You more than me." I grinned.

"Because of the blow job, or…"

"I just lay back and let you do me—"

He pounced. "I have bruises on my hips from where your heels dug into me. You did not just *lay back*."

I snickered. He grinned. We made our way back to the living room. Cole looked vaguely put out. I handed him the pizza and tried for a smile.

"Julie didn't win."

Ah, so he was pouting. "That's unfortunate. There's always next year, right?"

"I just…I won. How am I supposed to face her?"

"Well, Peter Erickson won in the movie he starred in with you. Does he self-flagellate? Feel badly you didn't win also?"

"Actually—"

I waved him off. "Okay, so you have good friends. The point is you'd never take it away from him, would you? Even if it meant you won?"

"Hell fucking no."

"So I'm quite sure Julie's happy for you. You'll just have to help her up her game for next year."

His mouth twisted, but eventually, a little smile slipped out. "Yeah, okay."

"Great." I sat next to him, mindful of my weight. Yes, Dr. Graham had said we could slowly increase physical activity. Not sure she had a blow job in mind, but Cole was young and healthy. Also, I'd done everything to keep him calm. Well, as calm as one could be while being blown by someone as hot as Michael.

Michael was about to plop down on Cole's other side when Cole held up his hand. Michael stilled.

"I think it's time."

Confusion flitted across Michael's face at Cole's words. "Oh."

"Yeah. You remember where we put them?"

"Of course." He eyed his ice cream. "You realize this is going to melt."

"You might be quick."

Michael mock glared. "Retrieving them will be quick. The aftermath?" He sighed as he put his bowl down. His gaze cut from Cole, to me, and back to Cole. "I'll be right back."

As he took off, I poked Cole in the biceps. "What's all the mystery? He could have finished his ice cream." I was confused. Being on the west coast, the Golden Globes broadcast ended fairly early. We had a couple of hours before we needed to head to bed.

"I…couldn't wait." He grasped my thigh. "I just…now seems like the right time."

I was about to ask for what, but I halted when Michael returned with a turquoise bag. My brooch had come from that store, and I'd assumed that was what had been in the bag. The bag they had brought home Christmas Eve day.

The day I found Cole's dungeon.

Huh.

Michael tried to hand it to Cole. Cole held up his hand. I rescued the empty plate before he dropped it and set it on the coffee table.

Michael pulled the first ring box out of the bag.

Now, I didn't know if the box contained a ring. There might have been earrings or another small brooch or—

He handed the box to Cole.

Cole took it with a nod.

Michael dug out the next box and handed it to me.

With numb fingers, I accepted it.

Finally, he took a third box out. Then he folded the beautiful bag and laid it on the table.

I sat as still as a statue.

Cole cleared his throat. "I, uh, had some big fancy proposal planned. Under the mistletoe by the Christmas tree and—"

"Sorry I spoiled that."

He chuckled at my comment. "Coming home and finding my whip and handcuffs on the table put a kibosh on those plans."

"Don't forget the flogger," I added dryly.

He arched an eyebrow.

"For the sake of being exact." I squirmed. "I shouldn't have—"

"You did the right thing. I'm the one who should've been honest from the start. I just…thought I had time. To…gently introduce you to my world."

"A world we have yet to visit."

He placed a hand over his heart. "I've been a little busy."

Heat crept into my cheeks.

Michael pointed to the boxes. "On the count of three?"

"You both know what's in these boxes." Was I

stalling? Yeah, I probably was.

"Yes, Michael and I went together." Cole tapped his left leg. "Couldn't have done it by myself."

"So he had input." Now I was just whining. Terror still had me seized. *Am I ready for this?*

"Minimal." Michael tried to keep the grin off his face.

Fucking asshole.

He could read me like a book. He'd had almost a month to prepare for this moment.

I hadn't given the little bag another thought once I got the brooch.

"I can go first." Cole flipped open his box.

Naturally, I peered over to get a look.

A silver-colored band sat nestled in a turquoise velvet nest.

I moved in closer.

Cole held it up to me. "Go ahead."

Hesitantly, I put my own box on my lap and took his. I gently removed the ring and squinted to read the inscription.

Three as one. Forever.

My breath caught.

No one would ever see this inscription, but I'd always know it was there.

"Put it on my finger?"

I hesitated. This was such a monumental step, and we'd barely been together a month as lovers.

But we've been together for twenty-seven years as friends.

Somehow, that made sense. This day had never been inevitable…and yet it felt inevitably right. I put the box on my thigh next to mine and slowly slipped the ring onto his finger.

Our gazes held as I reached out for Michael.

Within moments, he grasped my hand and sat on the other side of Cole.

"Now you." Cole pointed to Michael.

Michael let go of my hand long enough to open his box. He presented the ring to Cole.

Cole slipped it on.

Then Michael slipped mine on. To my surprise and delight, it fit.

"This is a forever deal." Cole looked back and forth between Michael and myself as we placed our hands on each other's.

Part of me truly balked at the rapidity of this, but the rest of me reveled because I never wanted to be parted from them, and if this was the way we committed to each other, then I was okay with that.

A pounding at the door had us startling apart.

Michael released our hands and headed out of the room.

Murmuring carried into the living room, and a moment later, he reappeared.

With Detective McGillvary in tow.

The police officer looked distinctly uncomfortable.

My heart seized. "Is there bad news? Is Meggibeth out?"

He held up his hands. "I apologize. I didn't want to come, but your friend was…insistent."

I cocked my head.

Cole muttered, "Donovan."

Tyson cleared his throat. "He's been unable to reach you—for quite some time. He, uh, convinced me something might be wrong."

Michael was the one who burst out laughing. "Seriously? Cole's not entitled to some private celebration time?"

I feathered my hand through Cole's hair. I hadn't even considered that others might want to congratulate him. Or that media might be looking for him. Or the studio might want—

Cole cleared his throat. "I turned off my phone."

I gaped, and Michael guffawed. Hell, I didn't even know such a thing was possible. Cole'd had it on vibrate since coming home from the hospital, but he'd checked it regularly. I assumed so he didn't miss anything about work. I might have been irritated, wanting him to focus on recovery, but it had never occurred to me to simply take his phone and turn it off.

Tyson smiled. A little sheepishly. "I told Donovan that he was overreacting—"

"Oh, you did, did you?" Cole quirked an eyebrow.

Little tendrils of a blush crept into the pale-skinned officer's cheeks.

Good to know. The guy would likely never be able to get away with lying.

As a cop…how did that even work?

"We're about to break out a bottle of nonalcoholic champagne." Cole grinned.

Michael and I exchanged a look. News to us.

Tyson held up his hand. "Really, I appreciate the offer. I'll leave you to it and—"

"I was just about to call Donovan. Surely, you want to be here for that."

The cop's cheeks turned even pinker. "Uh, I'm good and, uh…"

"Caressa, can you hand me the phone?"

I snagged Cole's cell from the coffee table, even as the three of us kept a close watch on the interloper.

He seemed rooted to the spot.

Cole powered on the machine, and it nearly exploded with a pile of notifications, and immediately, it started ringing.

I glanced over to see Donovan's name.

As Cole swiped to accept the call and put it on speaker, I kept a close eye on Tyson.

"Hey—"

"What the actual fuck, asshole? You turn your phone off on one of the most important nights of your life and—"

"Tyson's here, buddy."

That stopped Donovan's tirade cold. Slowly… "And you have me on speakerphone?"

"Yes." Cole grinned wickedly.

Tyson shifted from foot to foot.

Donovan muttered what I was quite certain was another *asshole*.

"Is that Cole?" A female voice rang through. After a moment, she shouted, "Oh my God, this is so amazing."

I winced at the volume she conveyed.

"Hey, Julie."

Michael cut Cole a *told you so* look. No one could miss the genuine enthusiasm. Well, the woman *was* an actress, but I read nothing but genuine joy.

"The trophy's so pretty. Oh, Cole, this is so amazing. You deserve it." She took a breath.

"Sympathy—"

Michael elbowed him.

He winced.

Well, he deserved it. I'd have done it, but I was on the bullet wound side.

"I'm just going to…" Tyson pointed toward the front door.

"Tell Donovan that Tyson's leaving." Cole held Tyson's gaze.

"Uh, sure. Look, Elouise is here…"

More squealing, and then Cole took the phone off speaker.

I still heard an enthusiastic woman's voice, but I rose. "I'll see you out." I linked my arm in Tyson's. "Unless you want to help me find the champagne."

He shook his head as we made our way to the door.

As he put his boots on, I watched with interest. "So you and Donovan…"

"No. No. No. No." He stood up straight and ran his hand through his close-cropped hair. "It's not like that."

Liar, liar, pants on fire.

I kept that thought to myself, but I nearly blurted out a *bullshit*.

Still, I had no idea the dynamics of how a relationship might work. Donovan was a victim. Tyson was the officer investigating the case. That had to cross all kinds of ethical and moral boundaries.

And yet if they were meant to be together, who was I to question it?

After a moment, he pointed to my ring. "I don't remember seeing that."

"You haven't."

"Ah."

"But you probably spotted the three empty ring boxes on the coffee table. Observant police officer and all."

He colored again.

Seriously? How does he do his job?

"I'd appreciate if you didn't spread the word." I looked back toward the living room where I could hear Cole's low voice as he carried on a conversation five years in the making. He so deserved this award. I turned back to Tyson. "At the very least, I think Donovan should hear it from Cole."

"Oh, I'm not…that is I wouldn't…and we won't be…you know…"

Wow, is he ever far gone. Am I like that?

I wasn't certain, but I was pretty sure the goofy grin on my face now betrayed both my amusement at Tyson's discomfort as well as my love and affection for both Cole and Michael.

"Be safe." I opened the front door.

Tyson tipped his head, offered a sheepish grin, and left.

I closed the door, turned, and leaned against it.

Our lives are never going to be the same.

And I couldn't come to regret that.

With a shove, I pushed off the door and headed back to my men.

Chapter Twenty-Nine

Cole

I shouldn't have been nervous the night of the Academy Awards—I wasn't nominated, after all—but I was.

Starring in a movie last summer that had done modestly well at the box office netted me an invitation—that and probably the sympathy thing. I was tapped to present the award for best costume design along with Lizzie Whitehall, a stunning up-and-coming actor just starting to make a name for herself.

Her dress didn't enamor me as I spent the bulk of my time trying to make sure I didn't trip on the train.

In contrast, Caressa's dress was simple—a midnight-black form-fitting silk with embroidered flowers of purple, blue, and gold. She shimmered when she walked.

Michael wore a tux that matched my own.

The organizer hadn't been pleased when I asked for three seats. But after making an offhanded remark that at least they weren't putting my photo in the memorial deck, she gave me the extra ticket.

God, I didn't like to think about all that.

We continued to see Hamish. Well, mostly just me these days.

Caressa'd gone back to work and had the

psychologist at the hospital. My lover had finally agreed to tell her counselor about what happened in Africa and about the pregnancy she'd terminated.

Fucking Franklin, one day out of the blue, took a job in a small Caribbean country. Apparently, he, and a married woman he'd been screwing at the hospital, took off. How long that had been in the works, I'd no idea. One didn't just jet off as a doctor to another country without getting qualifications vetted and stuff.

Right?

I pitied the woman's husband who, Caressa confided, was a really nice guy.

She didn't want to talk about it, and so I let it go. At least the man was out of our lives forever.

Michael keyed in the code to grant us access to Peter Erickson's mansion near Los Angeles.

I hadn't wanted to stay here, but Peter'd insisted—pointing out we'd have more privacy than in a hotel and that we could relax without having to put on a show for other people.

He rarely did Hollywood these days, instead preferring to stay home with Thomas and their two toddlers. Oh, he worked some. But mostly he stayed home and did diaper duty.

Thomas still worked on *VJ*, although he'd cut back from the hours he used to put in. He liked being home with Peter and the kids.

Would that be in my future? We had three more years of the show, and as the star, I needed to put in serious time.

I eyed Caressa as she stepped out of her heels. Not as high as most of the women on the red carpet sported, but still much higher than anything she'd previously worn. I'd told her ballet flats would be fine, but she insisted on dressing up.

She also liberated her hair from some intricate design and let it flow.

God, I loved her hair.

"I'm taking a shower. I want this gunk off my face."

I grinned. "I'll join you."

She held up her hand. "I'm tired, Cole. If you join me in the shower, then Michael will want to join me, and we'll use up all the hot water in Peter's tank."

Huh. I was pretty sure he had hot water on demand, but I got her point.

"Michael and I will clean up as well, and we'll meet you in the bedroom. Unless you want a nightcap—"

Two sets of hands shot into the air.

"You're nuts. Two after-parties were more than enough." Caressa stretched, her dress showing off every curve.

I salivated. "Well, we had to support Elouise."

Michael snorted. "She was so high in the clouds that I don't think anyone but Kelci registered."

"They make a stunning couple." Caressa massaged her foot.

"And way to go, Kelci, for going without a wig tonight." Michael undid the first two buttons of his shirt, revealing just a smattering of chest hair.

I licked my lips.

Eight weeks post surgery and I'd been given a green light. Working with Zoey to rebuild my strength and stamina had proved challenging. I'd thought she worked me hard with the IT band injury—that had been child's play. She regularly took me to task, and come Tuesday, I was back on the set of *VJ*. I hated how long I'd been away, but coming back before my body had properly healed would have only ended in calamity. And perhaps an even longer convalescence.

Caressa leaned up to press a kiss to my cheek. "You did good tonight."

She wasn't just referring to the fact I hadn't tripped over another actor's dress.

"Thanks." I almost said I couldn't have done it without them, but that wasn't strictly true. I could have shown up, presented the award, attended a few parties, and then headed back home. In the end, I possessed the physical capacity to do those things. But I would have lacked the…willpower? The drive to be the best I could tonight. Strutting down the red carpet with Michael on one arm and Caressa on the other had been our coming out of sorts. One reporter had asked, but the rest chose to be circumspect. Still, I'd chosen brutal honesty—I was in a consensual exclusive relationship with two people I loved deeply.

We'd see what studio executives and show producers had to say.

Tomorrow.

For tonight, I had plans.

We parted ways, each heading to a separate shower. Peter's house was so big that we could have each had a couple to ourselves.

I'd contemplated getting a place in LA when my show first took off and the movie roles started coming in. But Peter'd always offered this place. Thomas didn't like it, or Hollywood, so they rarely came down. Peter talked about maybe giving the place up, but he liked having a base of operations for when he was in the States. Me borrowing it, on occasion, meant it didn't fall into a state of disrepair. He had people to take care of it, of course, but he liked knowing friends visited. I was pretty sure Julie'd also stayed, and if Elouise gave up her LA condo, she might as well. Of all of us, she had the most ties to the town. And a very beguiling and compelling reason to stay in Canada.

Shower complete, I dried off and then availed myself of some unscented moisturizer. I believed in taking care of myself—and my skin.

Caressa was forever shirking off such things. *Will she regret that when she's older and has wrinkles?*

I wouldn't. Every laugh line and individual groove would show a life well-lived.

Making my way to the bedroom, I found Michael already on the bed and Caressa shutting off the water.

I met his gaze. "You sure?"

He pointed to the bottle of lube.

Momentarily, I wondered how Peter would feel knowing we were making out in his bed.

He'd likely get a kick out of it.

Caressa breezed into the room, removing the clips from her hair. She'd obviously put it up so it wouldn't get wet, but little tendrils clung to her neck.

I advanced toward her, telegraphing my intention.

She grinned, and when we were flush, she pressed herself against me.

We'd made love numerous times over the past few weeks—but always with me on my back. Nothing that might strain my heart or my leg injury.

Both were healed.

Well, except for the scar on the left side of my chest. A reminder of how fucking lucky I really was.

"Hey." Caressa pressed a kiss to my chest. "You

having second thoughts?"

"About?" I met her gaze. "Oh…none." I offered her a wicked smile.

She grinned. Then she plopped down in a chair facing the bed.

I cocked my head.

"Oh, I want the full view. I'll join you afterward."

Huh. I hadn't given much thought to logistics. Had just assumed she'd be in bed with us. Somehow physically connected.

This way, though, had some eroticism to it. She as the voyeur while Michael and I finally made love.

Michael, as if sensing my trepidation, held open his arms for me.

I crawled onto the bed to join him.

And again, it struck me that we hadn't talked logistics. Just that he and I were finally going to do this. And yeah, he could have ridden me during the last couple of weeks, as Caressa had, but neither one of us had been ready for that.

Caressa understood my progress from a healthcare perspective and could tell Michael and me how much I was improving. Michael, though, held back. I'd catch him staring at my chest with a discomfort neither Caressa nor I could soothe. Now, though, I believed we were past the hesitation.

On to the good stuff.

About fucking time.

Yet I'd also have been willing to wait forever. This had to be on Michael's terms. He'd asked for tonight, a thought that flitted through my mind as he lay flat, watching my every move.

I lay atop him. He opened his thighs to make room

for me.

My cock, which had been a chubbed-up semi, perked up when it brushed Michael's. His, also having shown some interest, hardened as well. I met, and held, his gaze for a long moment. He gave me a little smile. I dove in for a kiss.

Unsure of what to expect, I aimed for languid.

Apparently, I'd misjudged.

He grabbed my cheeks and pulled me close. He opened his mouth and thrust his tongue into mine as soon as I reciprocated. Then, as our tongues tangled and fought for dominance, he ran his hands through my hair and tugged. Hard.

I bucked into him.

Oh, yeah.

Caressa.

She'd discovered my little favorite thing, the thing guaranteed to get my engine revving every time, and obviously shared with Michael.

My cock hardened painfully. Michael grinned against my mouth. Oh, I'd get him back for this.

Caressa might have shared a trick or two about him as well.

Our cocks brushed, and I might have whimpered into the kiss. Michael might have grinned. I pulled back and met his gaze. His eyes sparkled gold, as they so often did. God, I loved him so much.

"Are you going to fuck me, Cole?"

"I think something could be arranged." Slowly, I rasped our cheeks. Not much stubble, as we'd both shaved just before leaving the house earlier today. I nipped at his jaw as I slowly made my way down his body.

A nibble here. A suck on his pulse point. A lick to his collarbone. More kisses until I reached his chest. I met his gaze, received a nod, then I sucked his nipple.

He moaned.

Then I bit. Pretty hard.

He writhed.

Nailed it.

I moved lower still, nibbling at his abs and swirling my tongue in his navel. He grasped the sheets and tugged.

"You can grab his hair again." Caressa provided the commentary airily.

Both Michael and I angled our heads to face her.

Resplendently, she sat in the chair with one leg hiked up over the arm and her labia on full display.

Jesus.

Michael grasped my hair. Then he opened his thighs farther to give me full access. I slid down until my face encountered his very erect, very hard cock. I licked the drop of precum off the tip.

Again, he bucked. "Not this time, Cole."

I gazed up to meet darkened eyes with pupils blown wide.

"You. Inside me. Now."

Part of me wanted to torment and tease. A bigger part of me wanted to give him another blow job—this we'd been given permission to do early on. But the largest part of me wanted to give him whatever he asked for. "I have to prep you."

"I know." His cheeks pinkened a bit. "Or I can do it myself."

"Oh, no." Caressa's eyebrow was arched when we glanced over to her. She grinned. "I want to see Cole do it."

Ah, so not a passive observer. Good to know.

Michael snagged the bottle of lube. I took it with numb fingers.

Surreal.

I'm about to fuck Michael.

His cock was an angry shade of purple as it curled toward his belly. Another drop of precum leaked. My dick stiffened. Moving closer, after a moment, I palmed his heavy balls.

Another drop.

"Sooner rather than later." He attempted mock serious.

Our eyes locked. As much as I wanted to tease and torment, he was right. Those things could come later. After coating my fingers with lube, I met his gaze again. He nodded and spread his thighs farther. I settled between them, then gently ran my fingers around his rim.

He gasped.

"Too cold?"

"No…just…" His cheeks pinkened again. "I might've…uh…"

Ah. "The sensation's always different when it's someone else." I could say this confidently from personal experience. I'd experimented at various times as well, but having someone else touch me always heightened my pleasure.

Slowly, I worked one finger in. I expected tightness—and I got it. But I also expected resistance— yet there wasn't much of that.

He relaxed his body around my finger and let out a sigh. "I can take more than that, Cole."

I arched an eyebrow.

More blushing.

"You've been practicing."

"I might've bought him a couple of toys." Caressa grinned.

At her words, Michael winced.

My grin widened. "That's great."

"I wanted…with you…but…"

Working in a second finger, I began to scissor and open him up. "It's great that you wanted to be with me, but there's nothing wrong with a bit of experimentation to know what to expect."

"You're, uh, big."

I held in the laugh. But it was a near thing. Then I twisted my wrist and hit the spongy spot I was so familiar with. And so in love with.

Michael gasped, his eyes drifting shut as he arched his neck back and dragged his lower lip through his teeth.

"Open your eyes." I injected just the right note of command, and he obeyed immediately. "I want to see you." I used a gentler tone. After a moment, I continued my massage of his prostate.

With his eyes glassy and unfocused, he watched me. His cock bobbed. "I want to come, Cole."

Reluctantly, I withdrew my fingers. He moaned. I snagged the lube and slathered my cock. Nice and easy for our first time.

First time.

There would be more of these. So many more times. And he'd take a turn, of that I was certain. Just…I needed to finally prove I'd recovered from this horrible event.

As I positioned myself over him, Michael touched the scar on my chest.

"Don't," I protested.

He splayed that hand so it covered my heart.

"Let him," Caressa admonished quietly. "We both need this."

I shot her a quick glance.

"Hell, maybe we all do."

She wasn't wrong.

I lined myself up and met Michael's gaze. He nodded. I inched my way in.

To say he was tight might have been accurate, but he also worked to keep himself open. To take me all the way. To let our bodies connect in a way they never had before.

He gave me a nod when I was fully seated. I shifted. He dug his heels into the mattress.

I pulled back and almost out before sliding back in.

A moan escaped his lips. "Fuck me, Cole."

As much as I wanted to, I hesitated. My animalistic instinct to rut—to claim—was strong. But I also wanted him to remember tonight with fondness. I thrust in.

He clawed at my sweat-slicked back. "More, Cole. God, please more."

I didn't know how to not give him everything he asked for. Everything he needed. I increased the pistoning of my hips as I drove him higher and higher. My own release receded into the background as I fought to bring him to a climax.

Without warning, warm liquid hit my belly. He hadn't even needed to jack himself. Just the sensation of me fucking him, and nailing his prostate over and over again, had brought him to an orgasm.

His face contorted in that adorable way it did when he came, and as he spasmed around me, my own climax hit me hard and fast. Within moments, I was coming—

buried deep inside him.

He opened his eyes, after closing them briefly during his peak, and he lifted his hand to graze my cheek. "I love you. I know I say it all the time, and maybe just after sex isn't the best—"

I lowered myself and pressed my lips to his. Silly man, thinking that I might believe anything other than the authenticity of his love. Yes, making love changed our dynamic. But only to strengthen the bond that was already there.

Slowly, I withdrew.

He winced.

I arched an eyebrow.

He grinned sheepishly. "I like you being enthusiastic."

I sobered. "Anal sex can cause damage if you're not—"

His finger against my mouth silenced me. After a moment, I nipped it. Laughter bubbled up from his chest.

"Okay, you two. Cole, roll onto your back."

I did as Caressa bade and enjoyed her ministrations as she tried to clean us up as best she could.

"A shower would be better." Caressa snorted.

Despite not wanting to move, I could acknowledge her sentiment. Michael and I needed all our bits clean in case desire overtook us later.

Again, we used separate showers. Caressa wasn't willing to join us, and I figured Michael and I might get up to some mischief if left to our own devices. Not that I was going to get hard again soon, refractory periods were a thing, but my cock liked the idea of getting near Michael again.

And again. And again. And again.

Like, forever.

When I was clean, dry, and moisturized, I crawled back into bed. Caressa lay in the middle and pointed to her left side.

I slid in.

Moments later, Michael appeared and slid in, cuddling up to her right side.

Part of me wished tonight would be a Cole sandwich, but Caressa'd been left out of the major action.

I could make up for that. I traced my finger down her collarbone and to her breast. After a moment, I tweaked a nipple.

She gasped.

Michael, previously languid, perked up.

"I have something to tell you guys." Caressa looked back and forth between the two of us. "I'm pregnant."

Epilogue

Michael

Poleaxed.
Stunned.
Speechless.

"How…" Cole cleared his throat. He tried several more times to push out more words, but they didn't come.

Caressa laughed. "Uh, the way it normally happens. The sperm fertilizes the egg and—"

"But you have an IUD."

"Had," she corrected. She met his gaze. "When we agreed we wanted a child, I made an appointment with my gynecologist. I mean, somehow, in all the chaos and aftermath of, you know"—she pointed to his chest—"it just felt like the right thing to do."

I could barely remember the last seven weeks, given the chaos of our lives. But she'd had the wherewithal to see a doctor?

Most of all, I wanted to know who the father was. She and Cole had resumed sex just a couple of weeks after the shooting—his doctor feeling that kind of exercise was safe. As long as he remained relatively still. I was happy to keep him calmer while he and Caressa made love. Often, I held him in my arms, his head resting against my chest.

Those moments—that bonding—had sealed us together.

Forever.

And aside from the first week after Cole'd been shot, Caressa and I'd had a fairly active sex life.

Cole claimed he loved to watch.

I suspected participating was more fun, but he got his rocks off in all kinds of scenarios.

The dungeon...

Yeah, we still hadn't gone there. Would we ever?

Cole pressed a hand to Caressa's belly. "You must have just found out. Unless..." He looked over at me.

She shook her head. "I'm just a few weeks along. I went to the doctor for a blood test rather than relying on a pregnancy test." She smiled slyly. "Sometimes it's good to know the right people."

"Is it safe?" I cleared my throat. "I mean, it's so early..."

"There's still a chance of miscarriage." Her eyes darkened. "So we're not telling anyone for at least three months. Not even Donovan."

Cole pressed a hand to his chest.

Yeah, right. He so totally would. They were thick as thieves, those two.

I met Cole's gaze. I saw my own confusion reflected in his eyes. We both wanted to know...and yet we didn't. Because it didn't matter. A healthy baby mattered. Both Cole and I had parents who had been addicts, but no other genetic issues that we knew of. Caressa faced the same situation.

This baby would just be...a baby. Eventually, we'd be able to tell. But that time would be far into the future. For now, Caressa's health had to be a top priority.

"Your breasts are tender?" Cole gently caressed one.

She nodded. "And I have to pee more, and a few other things. But there's no reason why this can't be a healthy and normal pregnancy."

And how much was she thinking about the last time she'd been pregnant? When she'd been forced to choose a different course of action?

I pulled the covers over us, snuggled into her side, and reached my hand out to Cole. He grasped it.

"We're going to make the best family ever." I said the words with surety. Because that was how I felt.

Caressa ran her hand through my scalp and then did the same for Cole—tugging on his hair.

He moaned.

I smiled.

She gave us both kisses on our mouths before settling between the two of us.

Of all the moments in our three-way relationship that I would later remember, this was the most poignant.

As I drifted off to sleep, I lay secure in the knowledge that I loved my two best friends.

And they loved me.

We'd make it, of that I was certain.

A word about the author...

USA Today Bestselling author Gabbi Grey lives in beautiful British Columbia where her fur-baby chin-poo keeps her safe from the nasty neighborhood squirrels. Working for the government by day, she spends her early mornings writing contemporary, gay, sweet, and dark erotic BDSM romances. While she firmly believes in happy endings, she also believes in making her characters suffer before finding their true love. She also writes M/F romances as Gabbi Black and Gabbi Powell.

~*~

Visit Gabbi Grey online at:
www.gabbigrey.com

Thank you for purchasing
this publication of The Wild Rose Press, Inc.

For questions or more information
contact us at
info@thewildrosepress.com.

The Wild Rose Press, Inc.
www.thewildrosepress.com